For the Love

of

Willow Walk

A Novel by

S. K. Hamilton

For the Love of Willow Walk is wholly and completely a
work of fiction. Characters are figments of the writer's
imagination, and any similarity to persons living or
dead is purely coincidental. While some locations
are real, they are used fictionally within this context.

Cover art by S. K. Hamilton
Cover design by Linda Lane

Printed in the United States of America

ISBN: 0-9769989-9-8

DEDICATION

To my husband, Ralph G. Hamilton

Thank you, Honey, for your never-ending support
and for being my ideal reader. Most of all,
thank you for your love and caring. You
gave me the strength to carry on through
the first book and now this sequel.

ACKNOWLEDGEMENTS

Linda Lane and Lin Bayhi of Pen and Sword Publishers, Ltd.

Thank you for editing and polishing my book until it
sparkles and shines. Thank you also for the enthusiasm
you showed while working on it. You both are a
credit to the editing and publishing industry.

Deborah K. Woods, my daughter

Thanks, Honey, for always coming to my aid when I needed
help. Your suggestions made it possible to overcome
the hurdles and the stumbling blocks. I love you.

CHAPTER 1

A siren blared.
Doors flew open.
The stretcher winged down hallways.
First left.
Then right.
The room was so cold.
It was too soon.

"Help me, please!" Kat's lips shaped the words. Her tongue forced them out.

In seconds, muffled sounds roared in her ears. *Disseminated intravascular what? Not in labor? Impossible!* Pain clamped like claws around her abdomen and stabbed into her back.

"Prep her for a C-section stat!" Dr. Morgan's voice cut through the commotion.

No! She tried to speak. The words wouldn't come.
Voices faded.
Lights dimmed.
Nothing.

"What's happening? Why's there so much blood?" Dawson couldn't keep the panic out of his voice.

"Katarina has premature separation of the placenta. That's why she's bleeding." The doctor adjusted the IV and nodded at the nurse. An orderly stepped up and whisked the stretcher out of the room. "Walk with me. I've got to scrub."

"Do you have to do a C-section? She didn't want that."

"I'm sorry. The baby's in as much distress as she is. If we don't deliver him now, we'll lose them both."

Dawson swallowed the lump in his throat and quickened his pace to keep up with the doctor. "How can she hurt so much and not be in labor?"

"That's one of the symptoms of premature placental separation. Her abdominal and back pains don't wax and wane like labor contractions." He inserted a card. The double doors swung open. He pointed to a room on the right. "Go in there and get ready if you want to be there for the delivery. Washing instructions are over the sink. Gowns are on the shelf. Someone will come to get you in a few minutes."

Dawson watched the physician disappear. Left alone to prepare himself for the premature birth of his son, he tried to come to grips with the trauma that threatened to destroy his family.

Kat couldn't move. Every muscle seemed frozen. Disjointed memories floated randomly through her mind as she lingered between life and death. Her husband's gentle fingers brushed a strand of damp hair from her forehead. The lower half of her body was numb. Was it the medication? What was going on?

Something was wrong, terribly wrong.

"Daw! What am I doing here?" The words screamed in her head, but she couldn't make them come out. Her eyes fluttered open.

Dawson was frowning. He tilted his head toward her. "How do you feel?"

She licked her dry lips. "Wh . . . why am I . . . here?" she whispered.

"Do I need to tell you about the birds and the bees?"

"No, silly." She felt like a clown underneath a big white fake smile. Only she couldn't manage the smile.

The light began to fade again. She blinked. Her husband's large warm hand closed over her small one. "I'm scared, Daw."

"Sweetheart, being scared's not a sin. Everything's going to be fine. Dr. Morgan will be here in just a minute."

Being afraid might not be a sin, but the words she wanted to say sure would be. She pushed them away and tried to focus on his face. "That's not the . . . the point."

"Take a deep breath and relax. Remember how you learned to do it in the birthing class. Try to think about Willow Walk when we were kids growing up. Remember the tire swing I hung in the big oak tree in the front yard?"

"Uh-huh." *Why the devil does he want to talk about that swing now? Can't he see I'm dying?*

"And the weeping willow across the lane that we sat under? We giggled when those yellow butterflies tickled our noses and cheeks and landed all over our clothes."

"I remember . . . we . . . had the whole world in our hands and were too young and innocent to realize it." She stared at Dawson's red cheeks and wide gray eyes. He was scared, too, she could tell.

"Yeah, then you would kiss your fingers and blow on them, sending butterfly kisses flying through the air. I pretended to catch them and send them back to you."

She'd never forget those times, but they didn't seem very important right now, not when her life was draining out of her.

Our Father who art in heaven . . . let my precious baby boy get through this alive. Let me hear him break out with a bellow that can be heard in all of Wheeling. And for all those I love and for the love of Willow Walk . . . please let me live, too.

She felt dizzy. The doctor walked up beside her.

"What . . . what's wrong, Dr. Morgan? I don't feel the baby moving."

"You won't feel movement at this point, Katarina. We've given you some medication so you won't feel anything." His black eyes, with no apparent pupils, stared straight at her as he spoke. "You'll be fine Katarina." His voice was strangely flat. *How did he know she'd be fine? How did anyone know?* She looked down toward her swollen abdomen. A drape blocked her view. What was that for?

Dawson leaned close to her face, stroking her hair. "I love you, Honey. It'll be fine. Believe in me like you did when we were kids."

"I'll . . . try." She wanted to tell him she loved him, too, but the room faded away and the images returned.

Granddad Jedediah floated through her mind. *I worry about you, Granddad. I want to see you.* She loved that old man. He was her pillar of strength . . . everyone's pillar of strength—the patriarch of the Kahill family.

His powerful voice from the past echoed in her ears. *Great jumping balls of fire, Dawson! We signed the deed to Willow Walk all proper like and up-front. It's yours, Sonny. Now just give me a namesake—a baby boy to carry on the family name. That's all my Emma and me ever wanted. A good strong, strappin', smart man like you and me.* She could hear his words as clearly as though he were standing at her side.

I'm trying, Granddad, I'm really trying. He's about to enter the world, even if I . . .

The light went out.
Voices drifted into silence.
Dawson's warm hand disappeared.
The cry she longed to hear . . .

CHAPTER TWO

A faint sign of worn wax showed on the tiled floor of the waiting area outside the birthing center at Wheeling Community. Granddad Jedediah Kahill paced back and forth, tapping his cane to the beat of an unheard drummer.

"Nobody gives a hoot up a hollow stump about me and my druthers," he muttered. Seemed like his soles would wear thin and his cane would poke holes all over the floor before anyone remembered to notify him of Kitten's condition.

The fifteen-second conversation he'd had with Dawson just didn't cut it. *Stuck his head in the door and said somethin' about complications and they was rushin' Kat off to surgery. Then said to be patient and he was gone.*

Oh, God, keep my old heart pumpin' through all this misery. He took a deep breath and began to hum the little song his Emma had written for him when they were newlyweds. His darlin' bride had sung it to the tune of "Old Dan Tucker," and he sung it now to that same tune.

> "Oh, Jed Kahill's a fine young man,
> But don' like washin' pots and pans;
> Got hisself married, took a wife,
> Now he's havin' a happy life."

The words faded away. *Now I know how a caged wolf feels. That young whippersnapper of a grandson had the gall to tell me to be patient. Well, it's not workin', Dawson boy. Any more bright ideas?*

"My Kitten's tryin' to birth a baby and these fools stick me out here in this blasted waitin' room, and I'm supposed to have patience? They think I got leprosy or somethin'?"

He stopped grumbling and pacing in front of the double doors that led to the birthing center. He threw his shoulders back and wrestled with the idea of breaking through them. His trusty cane would put the fear into those scallywags in green leggings. He didn't live over ninety years not to know more about birthing babies than a mule knows about being stubborn. *A few more minutes and that's it. I'm goin' in.*

Turning, he retreated to the water fountain, hesitated, then moseyed back to the nearly-empty waiting room. With one thumb stuck in the shoulder strap of his overalls and the other hand on his cane, he poked out his chest and started pacing again. He was sick and tired of being told what to do—or what he *couldn't* do. He had kept his temper at bay for hours and what'd he get for it? No updates. No respect. Those scoundrels didn't even know he was alive. Well, he'd show them soon enough.

The toes of his boots caught his eye. He grinned. A clear image of his dead wife formed in his mind. "Emma Baby," he whispered, "I sure do need you right now. My boots are spit-shined to perfection like you always wanted." He hesitated. "I wish you was with me lookin' at them."

He glanced at the folks sitting in a row by the windows. The man looked bedraggled. He had seven boys sitting there, looking like stair steps. Their suspenders hiked their pants almost up to their armpits, every one of their sockless ankles showing. *Hand-me-downs for sure. Good thing they was all boys. Saved a heap on buyin' duds.*

Seem well-mannered enough, Jedediah thought, until one bonked the other over the head, starting a free-for-all. *Kids! Ain't they somethin'? Gotta love them.*

His chuckle grew into a belly laugh that echoed throughout the room. He didn't give a hoot. They probably thought he was nuts anyway. Turning his back to them, he continued pacing—cane tapping to the beat of his "happy song." What else could he do? Sit around and whine? That wasn't for him.

His mouth twitched back and forth, attempting to scratch the itch in his nose from his mustache. He stopped pacing in front of the double doors. They seemed to stare back at him, daring him to try to get through them. Leaning on his cane, he studied his next move.

Maybe he'd just blast through those dang doors and worry about the consequences later. But what if Kitten didn't want to see him while she was hurting? He wouldn't upset her for anything. *Me, the one who cares more about my family than anybody else in the whole world, and I can't even be there for them when there's trouble.*

Arching a bushy eyebrow, he ambled back to the waiting room and plopped into an overstuffed chair next to the man and his brood. He twisted into a comfortable position. Closing his eyes, he drifted into sleep. The world around him dissolved—and then he saw her.

"Emma, if you was here you'd help me put these . . . these . . . hooligans in their place." She looked at him with those sparkling eyes, clear as spring water. *"Oh, Baby, I miss you. I'd even welcome you chasin' me and my dirty boots off your shiny kitchen floor. One of these days . . ."* Her image faded away like the final strains of a love song.

A sudden pain jerked him awake. His hand flew to his chest. It was the second time this month. Must be nerves again, worrying about Kitten and the young'un this time. *Yep, that's it. Nerves.* The stabbing pain left as fast as it came. He couldn't bother with it now, but if it happened again . . . A few slow breaths calmed him. Nothing else to do but wait.

The young man beside him stared straight ahead. The fellow's flame-colored hair screamed 'fire in the attic.' Freckles polka dotted his face. His eyes twinkled greener than the threads of a leprechaun's suit.

The young man lay back in the chair, arms crossed and his legs stretched out. His strawberry blonde eyebrows met in the middle. Jedediah scratched his snow-white beard, envying the fellow's ability to be so calm at a time like this. *How in tarnation does he have the nerve to look so smug when he's about to have another kid to clothe?* The guy even had the nerve to look comfortable. Jedediah studied him for several seconds.

"You havin' a baby, Mister?" he asked.

"Only me eighth. Aye, a wee lassie this time, we hope. Call her Molly Anna, we will, after her own mother's mother. Got enough lads for a while." The guy eyed him. "Is this your first?"

Jedediah laughed out loud and puffed out his chest. "You betcha it's my first . . . great-grandchild, that is.

The man gave him a hearty slap on the back. "Congratulations!"

"I thank you, Son. What's your name?"

"Name's O'Malley. Clancy O'Malley. Hail from Galway County, Ireland, but I be livin' outside Wheeling these days. What be your title?"

"Jedediah Joseph Kahill." He shifted in his chair. "Good work, young feller." Jedediah cleared his throat and shook his head. "Seven lads and a lassie on the way, huh?" A sly smile crossed his face as they swapped a look. "You've been workin' overtime, O'Malley."

"That's what me wife keeps sayin'." A twinkle in Clancy's green eyes spoke volumes.

Jedediah began to fidget. "If I'd a known it was going to be this long I'd've brought my dang recliner," he said under his breath. He folded his hands and bowed his head. *You know, Father, I'll soon be ninety-one. These rusty old hinges o' mine ain't gonna last forever. I'll thank you to hurry up and bless me with this great-grandbaby. You won't be sorry.* Looking up at the ceiling, he winked. *Amen.*

Tapping his cane on the bottom of his boot, he felt his determination returning. He pushed himself to his feet. Talking with Clancy made him feel like everything would be all right.

But everything was *not* all right.

The serenity of his surroundings worried him. No scurrying. No news from behind those closed doors.

Whatever was happening to his Kitten couldn't be good. He needed to know what was going on.

Now!

CHAPTER THREE

Jedediah picked up his cane and rapped on the double doors leading to the birthing center. No response. He rapped again—this time harder.

The doors parted. He put the tip of his cane down on the floor and started forward when an amazon in white filled the opening in front of him.

He planted his feet firmly apart, his cane in front of him. "By golly, it's high time somebody showed their face around here. I want to know what's goin' on with my Kitten, and I intend to see her since none of you cared enough to tell me a darn thing. Now *where* is she?"

"I beg your pardon."

Her icy stare collided with his hot one.

"Kat . . . uh . . . Katarina Kahill my granddaughter, she's havin' a baby. Now take me to her."

"Sir, you can't come in here. I'm sorry." She crossed her arms.

He leaned forward on his cane. "You're gonna be a whole lot sorrier if you don't get out of my way."

Dark round orbs glared at him over a nose as long as Pinocchio's after his third lie. Linebacker shoulders seemed to widen with each breath that dared him to defy her. *Huh. She could be a professional wrestler on her nights off. Maybe that's how she got that chipped tooth.*

"That's not possible. Your Mrs. Kahill is in surgery. Now please take a seat, and someone will let you know when she's delivered."

"The devil they will. Ain't nobody told me nothin' so far, so I got no reason to believe that's gonna change. Now I need a minute with my Kitten. I'll not be long."

Ms. Linebacker took a threatening step toward him. "Sir, you need to find a seat in the waiting room."

Digging his heels and his cane into the floor, he smiled at her. "You may be in the habit of orderin' everyone else about, but you better not take a notion to tell *me* what to do."

"Either you sit down immediately, or I'll call security to escort you out of the hospital."

"Great balls o' fire, woman, I'll sit. But you get someone to let me know what's goin' on with my Kitten!"

"I already told you someone would keep you informed." They stood toe-to-toe, her eyebrows pinched together and her mouth turned down. Her displeasure dripped from her expression like acid from a leaking battery.

"Darn fool looks like a moose," he muttered, turning toward the waiting room.

"What did you say, sir?"

Sounds like she musta swallowed some of that battery acid. "Darn fool rules you got around here." He hesitated, then gave her a big smile. "May I lie and say how nice it was to have met you?"

The white ox disappeared behind the closing doors. He shuffled back to the waiting room and took a seat, not knowing any more than he had before. The words he wanted to say to Kat played over and over in his mind.

Listen, Kitten, you got fire in you; don't put it out. Be strong. Little Jed needs you more than ever now. This birthin' business ain't easy, but I got faith in you, Kitten. That young whippersnapper's granddad's waitin' to see him. A lump formed in his throat. *Please, God, let them two go on livin'. I know I ain't always done things right, but I'm comin' to you now and beggin' for my Kitten an' little Jed. If ever you listened to a prayer from me, I'm askin' that it be this one. Amen.*

A fleeting thought of Granddad fluttered through Kat's mind. He'd be worrying everybody around him by now, but she couldn't help that. She had to think of her baby's life—and her own.

The pale blonde nurse hovering over her looked like she was made of Dresden china. She spoke in a velvety contralto voice. "It won't be long now."

"Won't be long now? What does that mean?" Her words sounded like they were coming from someone else. *It won't be long till I die? Why is Dr. Morgan standing over in the corner, talking to Dawson like there's some big secret?*

She blinked her eyes, and Dawson stood beside her. He bent forward and brushed his lips to hers so lightly she couldn't be sure he had done it.

"I love you, Daw. You don't have to stay for the surgery. I'm so sleepy I won't even know you're here."

She heard his voice answering her, but she couldn't make out the words. The room seemed to come and go. *Please, dear God, let me live—for my baby, for Dawson, for Granddad, for Willow Walk. Please . . .*

"She's ready, doctor," the nurse said.

Dawson stepped to Kat's head, above the drape that kept him from seeing the incision that would bring his son into the world too soon. Blinking back the tears, he forced his thoughts back to Willow Walk and the days he'd shared butterfly kisses with Kat.

They had been so innocent then. If only they'd stayed innocent children—if only he hadn't fallen in love with her and married her—she wouldn't be lying here now, hovering somewhere between life and death.

A thin wail jerked him back to the present. The doctor held Little Jed up for him to see. He looked so tiny, so blue.

Surely, that wasn't normal.

Surely, he shouldn't be that color.

Something was very wrong . . . .

CHAPTER FOUR

Jed tapped his cane and his foot in alternating beats. Where in tarnation was that blasted nurse anyhow? She'd better show soon, or he'd be pounding on those double doors again. And he wouldn't be near as nice to the old battleaxe next time.

He sat as close to the doors as possible when he wasn't walking around talking to himself. Had to make sure that old crow would see him as soon as she showed her ornery face. He couldn't remember the last time he'd met up with a meaner-spirited woman.

"I'm sorry Clancy O'Malley's not still here." He turned to look at the perfect stranger sitting next to him. The man didn't respond. "I'm sorry Clancy O'Malley's not here," he repeated. Was the guy deaf or what? "I said I'm sorry Clancy O'Malley's not here!" This time he shouted.

The man gave him a blank look. "Who's Clancy O'Malley?"

"A redheaded Irishman with seven boys and a baby girl about to join them." Jedediah raised an eyebrow in delight at the look on the man's face. At least he got some conversation out of him.

"Having one is hard enough. I don't think I want—"

"This your first?" Jed interrupted.

"Yeah, it is. Anyway—"

"Well, let me tell you, fella, when you hold your little one in your arms, you'll want a dozen more." He paused and cocked his head. "I'm surprised you're not in there with your wife. Of Course Clancy couldn't be there because he had them seven boys with him, but it's allowed these days."

The man rolled his eyes. The color in his face seemed to fade away. "I was there at first, but I couldn't handle seeing my wife in all that pain.

20

Nothing in those birthing classes we took prepared me for that. I almost passed out when her water broke. The nurse told me I'd be better off out here. She was right, but the waiting's a killer."

Jedediah gave him an understanding pat on the arm and let his thoughts wander back to the Irishman and his clan. *I'm gonna see if I can find old Clancy one of these days. Find out if Molly Anna has red hair and freckles same as her brothers.* He looked back at the man next to him, who was thumbing through a magazine so fast the fella couldn't be seeing anything on the pages.

His gaze was pulled to the wall clock like it was some kind of eye magnet. Had time stopped? No, the minute hand still rotated. Must be the terrible suspense that made the small hand seem to stand still. Seconds ticked into minute after minute. Jedediah tapped his cane on the floor. The stranger hung his head and paced.

"This confounded wait will send me to an early grave, Mr. . . . . . say, what's your name anyway?"

"Name's Jake. I know what you mean."

"Glad to meet you, Ja . . ."

The double doors swung open. Dawson emerged. He wasn't wearing the smile of a happy new papa. Something wasn't right.

"What's wrong, Sonny? Is it my Kitten? the baby?"

"The baby's holding his own at the moment." He smiled slightly. "A little underweight, and he needs some help breathing right now. He's been through a lot to get here."

"How's Kat?" Jedediah asked.

"Well . . . there've been some complications. But they're keeping a close . . ."

Jedediah pushed himself to his feet. "*What* complications?"

"Kat's blood pressure dropped because she lost so much blood. She went into shock. They're giving her antibiotics for infection. I didn't catch all the medical terms. We'll know more later."

"Know *what*, for blasted sake? You mean it's *that* serious?" He felt the blood drain from his face. "Can I see her? I gotta see my Kitten, Sonny. Help me get in to see her."

"Not just yet. She's in recovery, and they're checking the baby out."

Jedediah led him to a chair. "You doin' okay, Sonny?"

"I'm fine, but it's been rough. Kat's in bad shape." He wiped his eyes with the back of his hand.

"And you say the boy's doin' okay, right?" Jedediah held his breath.

"I heard him cry before they took him away, but his color wasn't good."

Jedediah's heart felt like it was going to stop. He could lose them both—his Kitten and the namesake he'd waited almost a century for.

Oh, God, if you got ears for the prayer of a stubborn old man, please turn them my way now. My Emma's already gone, and I don't go a day without talkin' to her about somethin'. I know that may seem foolish to you, but I miss her so much and talkin' to her helps me feel better . . . even if she can't hear me. Now I could be losin' two more who are much too young to go. Won't you please help them hang on? They got lots of livin' left to do.

He turned to Dawson, who was staring off into space. "Everything will be all right, you hear me, Sonny? Listen to your granddad."

Dawson nodded. Then he dropped his head in his hands and wept.

Jedediah wrapped his arm around his grandson's shoulders and pulled him close. It'd been a long time since he'd held his boy like this.

"She'll make it! Don't doubt our girl, Sonny. Remember, Kitten is as strong as you and your old granddad. She'll fight. She's a Kahill. You'll see."

"Granddad, you don't know how much I love that woman. She's everything to me. I don't even want to think about living without her."

"Is that right? You slay me, boy. You say I don't know? You think you're the only one who loves her? Buck up. Stop feelin' sorry for yourself. You think she'd want to see you like this?" He pulled off his foggy glasses and made a pretense of cleaning them. His voice softened. "I know exactly how you feel, Sonny. I remember so well when my Emma passed away. I wanted to die with her. Willow Walk still calls her name from every nook and cranny in the old house." He looked straight into Dawson's eyes. "But I go on livin' because I know that's what she'd expect me to do."

"I'm sorry, Granddad. Of course you're right. I was just thinking of myself."

Jedediah replaced his glasses low on his nose and looked over them as the double doors opened. Dr. Morgan appeared.

"Mr. Kahill?" The doctor stood straight, an air of confidence surrounding him as he walked over to the two men.

"Yes?" Both men stood and answered at the same time.

"Mrs. Kahill's condition is stable. Her vital signs have improved, but she's still sedated. We're moving her into ICU." He smiled that doctor-type smile that spoke encouragement.

Jedediah leaned on his cane with both hands. His mouth turned down. "Is she out of the woods, Doc?"

"She's *stable* is what I said." He drew the words out. "Rest assured, Mr. Kahill, I would tell you more if I could." He turned to Dawson. "You can go to the neonatal intensive care unit and visit with your son if you'd like. I think that little guy would like to hear a familiar voice."

"Familiar?" Jedediah asked.

"Oh, yes," the doctor said, "babies hear what's going on in the outside world for some time before they're born."

Jedediah shook his head. "Well, I'll be. Now that's one I didn't know. But he heard *my* voice, too. I was with Kitten every day. Does that mean I can see him?" Maybe he was finally gettin' somewhere with these people and their ridiculous rules.

"Now that's up to Mr. Kahill and his wife. If they put you on the list of approved visitors, you'll be coached in the NIC-U rules and be allowed to visit the baby."

"More durn rules. Well, we'll—"

"Thank you, Doctor," Dawson interrupted. "We'll take care of that from our end."

"Yes—er—um—thanks, Doc." Jedediah turned and ambled to the window after the doctor left. He stood for a long moment, looking out. The black night sparkled with tiny city lights below. What was left of the moonlight filtered in through the window.

Dawson walked up beside him. "I'm going to see little Jed, Granddad. He needs to know he's not alone. I'll set it up so you can come and see him too in a little while."

Jedediah watched him disappear through the double doors. Spent with worry, he allowed his mind to drift to the tranquil place where he was born—Willow Walk, with its winding lanes, hills and valleys, white board fences, and later, Emma's gardens. They all lent a park-like air to the countryside. It was his home—his safe haven. If only they were all there now . . . safe.

The home itself rose square and solid. Drawing rooms sat on either side of the entrance hall and grand staircase. One received guests and the other was reserved for the family. A morning room, library, kitchen, formal dining room, and smaller, more intimate eating area for casual meals completed the main floor. Emma had transformed his house into a home. She poured her love into Willow Walk. It was Emma who had insisted on building greenhouses so plants and fresh flowers could adorn every room.

No wonder he had such a hard time going on without her. So many memories of his life there with her filled his senses, even when he slept.

He grinned. She would always own Willow Walk—and him. It was Emma—the love of Willow Walk—that had kept him going these last years.

Aw, my dear, dear, Emma, I'm wishin' you were here to tell me our Kitten and my little namesake will be okay. I told Dawson they would, but I can't quite convince myself. If you can't be here, I wish I was where you are because I know you're not feelin' the ache I'm havin' in my heart.

Oh, Emma Baby, I miss you so much. And right now I think I'm lonelier than I ever been in my whole life.

CHAPTER FIVE

Jedediah hunkered down in the recliner at the foot of Kat's bed. After so many hours in that dadburned waiting room, he wasn't about to complain.

Dawson was catching a catnap in the matching chair next to the bed. He hadn't closed his eyes for the first hour after Kat had been in the room, but he finally agreed to take a short nap because the machines monitoring her vital signs never wavered.

Jedediah's old bones begged for rest. But he knew he couldn't sleep— not till he talked to his Kitten. *Only then will I know for sure she's gonna be alright.*

A large window overlooking the city below glowed with the sunrise. He got up to close the blue and green plaid drapes so the brightness wouldn't disturb his grandson, but he hesitated. *There's been way too much darkness since we got here. A little sunlight might just signify a new beginnin'.*

He looked at the marketplace below, already bustling with vendors from nearby farms. Tables displayed a colorful variety of fruits and vegetables brought by farmers from Wheeling, Tridelphia, Valley Grove, and other nearby towns.

He'd spent many Saturdays at that market when he was a boy, running up and down the aisles while his grandmother picked through the produce to find the best for the next week's meals. *But that was another story.*

Jedediah stepped away from the window and picked up Kat's limp hand. *Granddad's here with you, Kitten. You just rest now and get better so you can take care of that sweet little boy you brought into this world. I saw him, Kitten. He's a bit small and wrinkly, but he'll be a fine strappin' fella before you know it. When we get back to Willow Walk, everything'll be just fine. You wait an' see.*

Dawson stirred and raised the recliner into an upright position. "Sit over here, Granddad, by Kat. You look worn out."

"Just a little, but for a senior gentleman I look pretty dang good. At least that's what Penelope Weatherbush tells me."

Dawson snickered. "Of course—you do. Mrs. Weatherbush should be proud to be seen with you. What would Grandma Emma think about her if she was here?"

"Oh for cryin' out loud, Dawson. My Emma Baby would just say, 'Watch your step, Jed, you can't be too careful these days. Don't you be foolin' around with any of them there hussies. If you feel the need for companionship, you find yourself a proper lady.' That's what she'd say."

They looked at each other in all seriousness, then burst out laughing.

"Yeah. You know that Weatherbush woman's had her eye on you ever since you two met at Kat's boutique opening."

"Not sure you know it, Sonny, but now's as good a time as any to tell you. She's crazy-nuts about me. Came over the other day while you were gone to town. She wants me to come to her house Sunday for wine and a nice home-cooked meal. 'Lamb makes the best gravy,' she said."

"Are you going?" Dawson spoke to Jedediah, but his gaze stayed on Kat.

"I was, but I don't know now. All depends on Kitten."

Dawson watched Kat breathe. What would he do without her? What would Granddad and baby Jedediah do? She was the heart of their hearts. What would Willow Walk do without her?

He leaned on the bedrail, searching her face for some kind of response. She lay there in the soft morning light, paler than he had ever seen her and infinitely more beautiful. Her shiny black hair on the white pillow framed her face like a raven's wings when the sun hit them.

Jedediah stood close to the bed, her hand still in his.

"Kitten? Can you hear me? Listen up now. This is old Granddad spoutin' off. You're gonna make it through this. You have a fine baby boy waitin' for you. We saw him in the nursery. Why, he's screamin' his lungs out and wavin' his fists in the air. He's complainin' even louder than me, and you know that's goin' some. So you buck up now." His voice caught in his throat. Leaning closer, he kissed her cheek and patted the side of her head.

Kat didn't move. She didn't even blink. She lay there with tubes in her nose and IVs in her arms, looking more like a fragile porcelain doll than a living, breathing person.

Dawson stood behind his grandfather, resting his hand on his shoulder and listening to the reassuring beep of the heart monitor.

The door to the room opened. One of Kat's best friends and business partner tiptoed in. "How's she doing, Dawson?" she asked in a whisper.

"She's still with us, Deb. They're keeping her sedated."

"Bonny and I came up last night, but they wouldn't let us in to see her. We aren't family, so they wouldn't tell us anything either."

"Well, it *was* a bad time." An awkward silence hung over the room. "She's stable, the doctor tells us." He didn't want to continue.

Jedediah picked up the conversation. "Your college buddy and her baby are gonna be fine, Deb. Now don't either you or Bonny worry your pretty little heads. Our Kitten has the Kahill will. So tell me, how's the boutique doin'?"

"It's doing well, Granddad. Business is great despite the slow season and lack of tourists this year. We just need Kat to finish the designs she started before she went on maternity leave." Deb lowered her head, sucked in a big gulp of air and burst into tears. Jedediah stood and put his arms around her.

"I'll be okay now, Granddad." She wiped her eyes and walked over to Kat. Placing a kiss on her forehead, she said, "I love you, Sweetie. Bonny said to give you a kiss for her and not to worry about the boutique. We have everything under control. Hurry and come back to us." She smiled and turned to Dawson and Jedediah.

"If—if there's anything at all we can do, please, we're just a phone call away. "

"Just mind the boutique. That will be more than enough. Kat'll be back soon," Dawson said.

"Yep, and tell Bonny she'll be bringin' a little baby boy who looks like me with her. My great-grandson, Jedediah Joseph Kahill." Jedediah winked at Deb as Dawson walked her past him and out into the hall.

"Are you sure she's going to be alright, Dawson? Don't hold back on me."

"She's a fighter, Deb. The doctors are encouraging. She's on IVs and a strong dose of antibiotics, so the crisis should pass soon. I'll let you both know in the morning how things are."

"Thanks Dawson. We, Bonny and I . . . Well—we..."

"It's okay, Deb. I understand. Try not to worry."

* * * * *

Deb nodded. "Keep us posted." She walked toward the elevator. *God, please take care of Kat and her baby. Please, that's all I ask.*

Glancing at her watch, she hurried to her car. Fashions by Kat opened in twenty minutes and Bonny would already be there. Good, dependable Bonny. What would she and Kat do without her? It was the same now as it had been when they were in college. What she and Kat forgot to do, Bonny always remembered.

She'd never seen anything like it. Kat's designs had soared to the top. Even the Big Apple was clamoring for a downtown boutique like Wheeling had, only ten times bigger.

Even though it had been some time since Katarina Kahill's work had taken first place for Wolf International Fashions at a worldwide competition, the chic styles of Fashions by Kat were still in demand. Orders arrived daily from wealthy New York clients.

They should be rejoicing, but they couldn't. Not with Kat fighting for her life.

CHAPTER SIX

Hot tears streamed down Deb's face as she drove to the boutique. She couldn't remember the last time a day had dawned with such gloom. Her thoughts were even gloomier.

Whatever happened to my dreams—my hopes and plans for the future? I want a husband, children, a family. Four years out of college and still no Knight in Shining Armor comes galloping up to my front door. But who cares? I have everything I want and need—don't I? A one-third interest with Kat and Bonny in the boutique, plans for future expansion, and a perfectly handsome friend in Bill Perry.

Bill Perry. A smile played at the corners of her mouth as images of her senior prom waltzed through her memory. King and queen of the prom, they had whirled around the dance floor in perfect step.

He could have been the Knight in my life. We had a great thing going that night. Floating across the floor in his arms had been a dream. Why didn't the dream become a reality?

It had been her special night, beginning with the romantic dinner at her favorite Italian restaurant. But the most wonderful memory of all was sitting next to Bill in his green Chevy and tasting the sweet warmth of his kisses. They'd talked about their dreams and a future together. Nothing could have been more perfect—until graduation. Then she enrolled in Pennsylvania State and Bill went to Duke.

They didn't see each other again until after college, when both returned to Wheeling but not to each other. At least they kept in touch from time to time. They just hadn't reconnected the way she wanted to.

If only we'd gone to the same university, we might still be together, happily married like Dawson and Kat. If Kat doesn't make it . . .

"Kat's got to make it," she scolded herself aloud. "Get positive! We're successful beyond our wildest dreams, and our future looks even brighter. I couldn't ask for two greater friends than Kat and Bonny. I'm not quite twenty-eight, and that hardly makes me an old maid. Besides, Bill is back—and single!"

The words her mamma used to say popped into her mind. *Sing your own song of happiness. Don't whine about what you don't like. Change it.* It was time for a change.

When she arrived at the boutique, it looked dark inside. She glanced at her watch. *Bonny's never late. I wonder if she's sick. Surely she would've called me if she wasn't able to come in.* She pulled into the alley and drove to the rear of the shop to enter through the back door into the lunchroom. Bonny's new Buick was parked in its regular spot. *I wonder why the open light isn't on. She must've forgotten . . . but that's not like Bonny.* She maneuvered her Dodge into her own space, turned the ignition off, stepped out of her car—then stopped. Why was the back door standing wide open? And why weren't the lunchroom lights on?

The hair on the back of her neck prickled. She got back in the car and grabbed her cell phone. Best way to find out was to ask. Bonny didn't answer She tried again. Still no answer. *That's odd. Maybe she forgot her phone or the battery's dead. Should I dial 9-1-1? Not yet. There's bound to be a logical explanation. I'll make sure she's okay. Don't want the police to think I'm a hysterical female.*

She shoved the phone into her pocket and stepped back out of the car. Her heart pounded like the bass drum in a marching band as she crept up to the lunchroom door. She peeked inside. One tiny light shone from the open refrigerator beside the door. Her roaming hand found the light switch and flipped it on.

She gasped. Milk, butter, and strawberry jam from the refrigerator lay on the floor. Broken eggs dripped their contents from the counter into the sink. Anchored to the spot, she said in a voice barely above a whisper, "B-Bonny?" She tried to call out louder, but the lump in her throat wouldn't let the sound pass. Her first inclination was to run to her car—but not without Bonny. She had to find her. *What if whoever did this is still here?*

Swallowing hard, she braced herself and walked toward the swinging door that led to the showroom. She froze, then took a step forward. *I've got to chance it. Every second may count for Bonny.*

Tiptoeing back to the lunchroom, she grabbed a butcher knife from the block on the counter and sidestepped the eggshells and broken dishes on the floor. Armed with her weapon, she walked back to the door and pushed it open. Her heart no longer pounded. It thundered.

She wanted to believe Bonny was with Sky, that he had swung by and picked her up to help him with a sick dog or injured cat. But she knew better. Bonny would never leave the boutique unopened during business hours, and that handsome Cherokee veterinarian was quite capable of taking care of any critter emergency on his own. They had something going between them, but neither would have put togetherness ahead of their responsibilities.

"Bonny? Bonny?"

Her unbelieving eyes couldn't quite grasp the scene in front of her. Racks had been tipped over, their elegant contents lying crumpled on the floor.

Her breakfast rose in her throat. She swallowed hard.

"Bonny? Are you in there?"

Nothing.

"Bonny!"

Still nothing.

Am I alone? If someone were here, he would've pounced on me by now. I'll check the office.

The door swung closed behind her, tapping her backside. A blood-curdling scream escaped her open mouth as she vaulted into the air. Turning, she thrust her body into a Karate stance. She'd never be a black belt, but the lessons she'd learned in the self-defense class Bonny had talked her into taking had kicked in without any conscious thought on her part. Then she realized she had almost Karate-chopped a door—the assailant who had slapped her derriere.

"Bonny? Bonny!" She called again, hoping and praying to hear Bonny's voice.

Nothing.

With purposeful steps, she walked toward the office. The door was closed. *I know this was open when I left last night.*

It made no sense that Bonny would be in there, especially with the door shut. She would have answered by now . . . if she could.

Bracing herself for whatever awaited her, she opened the door and stepped inside. An envelope was propped up against the monitor on the desk. A shiver shimmied up her spine as she read its contents.

I've no time to plead and pine,
I've no time to wheedle,
Kiss me quick and then I'm gone,
Pop goes the weasel.

She looked around the empty office. Where was Bonny? Fear washed over her like a flash flood. *I've got to get out of here and call the police. Has Bonny been kidnapped?* She stifled her desire to run as she checked the dressing rooms. They were empty. She took a ragged breath and fled into the lunchroom. Where was Snow White? Was she gone too?

"Here, kitty, kitty."

She loved that little feline, and so did Kat and Bonny. Snow White was one of the family.

"Come here, kitty. Hurry." Snow White peeked her head out from the back of the refrigerator, her hiding place since she had moved in. Deb scooped her up, tucked her under her arm, and ran to the car. Maybe she should have locked the lunchroom door, or at least closed it. *Not much left to damage, so what does it matter?*

"Hands, stop shaking," she muttered as she reached into her pocket and pulled out her phone. Her trembling fingers would hardly stay on the keys long enough for her to dial.

"Nine-one-one. What's your emergency?" a voice answered after three rings.

"Please send someone to Fashions by Kat. It's been vandalized, and my friend is missing. It's awful. I'm so afraid for Bonny. There was a note. Please hurry."

The dispatcher confirmed the address. "Someone's on the way. Now please leave the premises. Wait down the block, and give them a chance to secure the area."

"Yes, thank you. I'll go right now."

She turned the key in the ignition.

What was that?

She rolled the window down just a little. There it was again. Somebody was pounding on something. The dumpster maybe? The noise seemed to come from down the alley.

"Is that you, Bonny?" she called through the partially open window.

Was she crazy? It could just as easily have been the intruder.

"I'm over here!" came the shaky response.

"Stay where you are. I'm coming right now. Just keep talking to me."

Looking over her shoulder, she saw a squad car and then another pull in behind her vehicle.

"Over here!" she called out. "Help me, please!"

She ran toward the form she could now see. *What if Bonny's hurt? Or what if she's dying? I could lose my two best friends on the same day.*

Stay calm, Deb, a stern inner voice admonished. *You haven't lost anybody . . . yet.*

CHAPTER SEVEN

Stay calm? Who am I kidding?

At least she knew Bonny was alive. In a moment she'd know a lot more.

Footsteps pounded the pavement behind her, coming closer and closer. Her heart leapt to her throat and threatened to choke her.

An instant later, a policewoman sprinted up beside her. Just ahead, Bonny lay on the pavement next to the dumpster, one hand shielding her eyes and the other holding a large rock. They knelt beside her.

"I thought you were told to vacate the premises," the officer said to Deb as she appraised Bonny's condition.

"Leaving my friend behind wasn't an option."

Bonny pushed herself up into a sitting position. Deb wrapped a protective arm around her shoulder.

"You got away with it this time," the officer persisted, "but next time it could cost you your life."

Deb ignored the scolding. "Who did this to you, Sweetie?"

"I . . . I don't know. I couldn't see his face."

"It was a man?" the officer asked.

"I assumed so, but I can't say for sure."

The policewoman stood up. "I'm calling for an ambulance."

"Please don't," Bonny begged. "I'm just a little shaky. I'll be okay in a few minutes."

"Maybe so, but we want to be sure."

"I can take her to the emergency room myself," Deb offered.

The officer raised an eyebrow. "This time we're doing it *our* way. I'm going to see that's how it happens."

"Can I ride with her?" Deb asked. Bonny clung to her hand.

The officer gave them a serious look, then smiled. "Why don't you follow the ambulance? That way your car will be there, and you can take your friend home if she's released."

"I can drive myself," Bonny insisted. "Really. I don't want to leave my car here."

"No way!" Deb and the officer said simultaneously.

"Your car's fine right here," Deb continued. "I know how much you worry about that new Buick getting dinged, but you're in no condition to drive. Believe me, it's safer where it is."

Bonny leaned against Deb, closed her eyes, and began to tremble. Big tears rolled down her cheeks.

"You want to tell me what happened, Honey?" Deb stroked her hair.

"I was standing by the cash register, getting ready to open," she said between sobs. "Someone came up behind me and slapped something wet over my face. It felt like a rag, and it smelled a little sweet. I also remember a sweetish taste in my mouth. He whispered something in my ear, but I can't remember what it was. The next thing I remember—I woke up here. But I don't know how I got here."

"You're okay now. Just try to relax." Deb tried to sound reassuring. You can talk to the police later."

"We'll send an officer to the hospital with you," the policewoman said. A siren wailed in the distance. "You can tell him about it after they check you out."

"Deb, is that you?"

She turned at the sound of a familiar voice. "Bill! I didn't know you were on duty today."

"Why didn't you call me on my cell phone?"

"I . . . I just dialed nine-one-one. The only thing I could think about was getting help for Bonny."

"You did the right thing," he assured her.

Bonny tried to stand. The policewoman stopped her. "No, ma'am. You stay still. The EMTs will be right here. Let them help you up onto a stretcher. Detective Perry will follow you to the hospital and take your statement."

"Deb, why don't you ride with me?" Bill said. "I'll bring you back for your car later." He reached out for her hand and led her to an unmarked vehicle.

"I heard on the scanner that you were told to leave the scene, Deb. You shouldn't have gone looking for Bonny," he said almost as soon as they were on their way. "You could've put yourself in a very dangerous situation."

"That thought crossed my mind. I just couldn't bear the thought of leaving her behind."

"You were lucky this time. But please don't do it again."

"I'm counting on there not being an 'again.'"

She tried not to feel chastised—the tone of his voice was only kind—but she couldn't help remembering the time when he'd said almost the same thing when she'd done something really stupid during their senior year in high school.

The five-minute ride to Wheeling Community was over almost before it began. The stay at the hospital was another matter. Deb waited in the corner of the emergency room cubicle while the doctor examined Bonny, an orderly wheeled her off for x-rays, and a vampire from the lab drew what seemed like endless vials of blood.

Bill was pleasant, but all business. No personal talk, not even any idle chatter to help pass the long minutes that stretched into longer hours. By the time the doctor came in with the results of the examination and tests, Bonny was lucid and almost her old self.

"You're a lucky lady," the doctor said. "No broken bones, no lacerations, no internal injuries. Did your assailant hit you anyplace?"

"Not that I recall."

"How did you get into the alley? Didn't you say you were accosted in the building?"

"Yes. Now that I think about it, I believe I woke up inside. My head felt so woozy. All I could think about was getting some fresh air."

The doctor nodded. "That makes sense. Somebody gave you a good dose of chloroform."

"Chloroform?" Bill was taking notes.

"What do you mean 'chloroform?'" Deb frowned.

"It has a very strong odor, and I noticed it when I first examined you. Your description of the sweet taste in your mouth when the rag was pressed over your nose pretty much confirmed it."

Bonny smiled a faint smile. "I'm glad nothing more happened. I could be dead or even . . . oh, I can't think about it."

The doctor patted her shoulder. "Count your blessings, lucky lady. The use of chloroform as an anesthetic was discontinued decades ago. Our present generation of anesthetics is much safer for the liver, heart, and kidneys. You didn't get a very big dose."

"Was I . . . was I . . ." Bonny couldn't seem to finish her question.

"No, you were not raped. We're faxing a report to your family doctor. You need to make a follow-up appointment with him as soon as possible."

A huge sigh of relief escaped Bonny's lips. Her eyes filled with tears. "I want to go home."

"You're coming home with me, Bonny Woods, and I'll not take any back talk," Deb announced. "You've had enough trauma today to last a lifetime. I don't want you to be alone for a while."

Bill had waited in the background until the doctor left. "I'll take you ladies back to your car, Deb, and come by your place later. If you're up to it, Bonny, I need to get a statement while this incident is fresh in your mind."

"Works for me as long as Bonny's feeling okay."

Bonny nodded.

"I'm going back to the boutique and see what they've come up with. I'm working in forensics now, so I need to explore the scene a bit."

"I see you've found a way to use both your interest in science and in law enforcement," Deb said.

"Yep. It's the perfect marriage."

Did you have to say marriage? I want so much to be with you, Bill Perry. Why can't you see that?

"Are you ready, ladies?"

I'm glad he can't read my mind, Deb thought as she and Bonny followed him to the car. Her gaze traveled from the back of his head to his heels and back again. She felt the color rise to her cheeks at the very idea that he could know what she was thinking.

"See you at the apartment, Deb, Bonny," Bill said as he helped Bonny into the passenger seat of Deb's Dodge. He walked around to the driver's side and looked in the open window at Deb.

She smiled. She hated what had happened to her friend, but she was glad that Bill would see her later.

"I'm glad you're on the case," she said.

He patted her shoulder and winked. "Me, too. Later, Deb."

"My address is—"

"I know where you live."

They stopped by Bonny's place on the way to pick up several changes of clothes and some personal items. An hour later, Bonny curled up on the couch and sipped a small snifter of brandy. She'd nixed the offer of a cup of tea. Deb watched the stress lines in her forehead relax.

Snow White jumped up and snuggled into the crook of Bonny's free arm.

"You're looking better," Deb said.

"The warm shower helped." She took another sip.

"How are you going to feel about going back to the boutique? We'll need to reopen by next week, I'm sure."

"I'm . . . uh . . . I think I'm fine with it . . . as long as I don't have to go in alone."

"Have you given any thought to what you'd say if Sky asked you to go to the reservation with him? I mean . . . you would feel free to tell me right? We could find somebody to help run the boutique. You wouldn't stay on our account, would you?"

"If I stay, it'll be for myself, Deb, don't worry. In fact, Sky has asked me to go to North Carolina with him. He wants to open a veterinary clinic there and have me as his assistant. I love working with animals, but I love the boutique, too. I know I wouldn't be happy in North Carolina. I'm a dyed-in-the-wool West Virginia girl. Unless something unforeseen changes my mind, I'll never leave."

"You're not in love with Sky?"

"Maybe, maybe not. Regardless, not enough, I guess, to follow him. Besides, he hasn't proposed marriage. And shacking up isn't my game. It's all or nothing for me."

"Okay, sweetie. I just want you to be happy."

"Thanks, Deb. Who knows? Maybe someday day I'll meet the right guy, and I'll know he's the one for me. It just hasn't happened yet."

Wow! She's exactly where I am—waiting for her Knight in Shining Armor. I'd go to North Carolina or anywhere else with the man I loved. And nothing would stop me. Her thoughts turned to Bill. She pushed them away. It hurt too much to fantasize and then have her hopes dashed . . . again.

"That's the way. Don't sell yourself short," she said.

"I won't. And you mustn't either. I saw the way you looked at Bill. And I saw the way he watched you when you weren't looking."

"He was watching me?" Her heart skipped a beat.

"Oh, yeah. But don't tell him I said so."

Deb laughed. "I'm not telling him anything." She turned serious. "Did you take your medicine?"

"It's a sedative, Deb. I don't think I should mix my relaxers." She swirled the brandy in the snifter. "Besides, Bill's coming. I need to be clear-headed when I talk to him. Was there any damage to the shop?"

"The lunchroom's a mess. I saw several overturned clothes racks, but I didn't look close."

"Why would anybody do this to us? Our competitors are in New York, not Wheeling. We contribute to the community. We donate our last season's clothes to organizations that provide clothing to women who've come out of abusive relationships and are trying to find jobs and get their lives back together."

"I know, Bonny. It doesn't make any sense at all. But it happened. This last blow is going to be hard on Kat and Dawson, especially after all the complications she's had with this baby. I don't even want to tell them."

"Maybe we shouldn't say anything until we get the place cleaned up. Do you think the gowns can be salvaged? How about the daywear?"

"I don't know. But I do think we should let Dawson in on what's happened. He's Kat's strength and protector—just like when they were kids. He'll know when's the right time to tell her."

"That makes sense," Bonny agreed. "We'll dig in and start cleaning up tomorrow . . . if the investigation's finished." She sighed. "I'd love to visit Kat, but not the way I look right now. She'd know for sure something's wrong."

"Kat's pretty perceptive that way."

"Something keeps bothering me. It's like just below the surface, but I can't bring it up."

"What's that?"

"Whoever shoved that rag over my nose whispered something in my ear—something about a game, I think. Then I swear I heard somebody whistling 'Pop Goes the Weasel.' How weird is that?"

"'Pop Goes the Weasel?'" She remembered the note.

"Yeah. Strange, huh? Do you know if the intruder got the money I'd just put in the cash register?"

"I'm not sure. My concern was for you, not for the money. Maybe Bill can tell us when he gets here."

"Do you think he'd pick up my car for me?"

"I bet he would. Where are your keys, Sweetie?"

"In my purse, which is . . . where's my purse, Deb? Did you bring it?"

"No. I didn't even think about it."

"Oh, no! If that intruder has my purse, he has my address. He knows where I live."

"Let's not borrow trouble. We'll ask Bill about it when he comes." She flipped on the television and set the channel on HGTV. "I know you like home decorating. Watch this for a few minutes while I pop something in the oven for supper." *And there shouldn't be any disturbing news to upset you on this channel.* "Bill should be here anytime."

She poked around the kitchen for anything quick to fix, but she couldn't focus. Her mind kept wandering back to the boutique and the cash register. *I think the money was still there. In fact, I'm sure it was. What's going on?*

All of a sudden she knew—this was not a robbery.

Something else, something far more sinister, was behind the break-in at Fashions by Kat.

CHAPTER EIGHT

Deb paced back and forth in front of the sofa. Bonnie had given up and gone to bed at nine.

Where's Bill? He should have been here hours ago. Picking up her cell phone from the coffee table, she flipped it open and then closed. *He's probably sleeping and forgot to call us.* For the umpteenth time, she looked at the clock. *Almost midnight. No point in waiting any longer.*

Slipping into her room, she put on her gown and robe and returned to the couch with a book in her hand. *If I read, maybe I'll get sleepy. Maybe I'll forget that he didn't show up like he said he would.*

A soft knock on the door startled her.

"Yes?" she said in a low voice.

"It's me. Bill."

She removed the chain, flipped the deadbolt, and opened the door. "I thought you weren't coming."

"I'm sorry to be so late. It's been a crazy day. We had three more cases that required forensics, and most of my crew's out with the flu."

They stood inches apart. His warmth beckoned her, and the years melted away. In one smooth movement, he wrapped his arms around her and pulled her close. She snuggled her head against his broad chest. The spicy aroma of his aftershave made her lightheaded. Or was it his closeness? Her hands felt the muscles in his back tense. *Is he feeling what I'm feeling?* She lifted her head and stared into his eyes. *I'd forgotten how tall you are, Bill Perry.* She wanted more. She wanted to stay there forever.

"You look . . . beautiful." His gaze locked on hers. "You know how much I've always loved your blue eyes."

Her breath caught in her throat as his finger traced the delicate lace that edged the top of her robe but stopped short of following it any further than her pounding heart.

She pulled her gaze away from the intensity of his and glanced down at her pale green silk gown and matching robe that had come from Kat's spring collection two years ago. She had fallen in love with its modestly feminine yet alluring style. *Thank goodness I didn't grab my flannel pj's and chenille robe.* "If you'd come a little earlier, I'd still be wearing makeup." *Why did I say that?*

His grin broadened into a full-fledged smile. "If you recall from our high-school days, I always preferred 'natural' to war paint."

"I'm so glad you came, Bill. I'm afraid the intruder might be after me, too." His strong arms sheltered her from the trauma of the day.

Keeping one arm around her, he placed his forefinger under her chin and raised her head until their eyes met. The tenderness in his smile nearly brought tears to her eyes.

"I want to be here for you." His arms tightened around her. He took her hand and led her to the couch. "I just couldn't find the right time to tell you that until now."

They sat down. She wanted to say something, but she didn't want to break the spell. *Are you really going to be my Knight?* She was afraid to hope.

"I understand you're frightened, Deb, but I promise not to let anything bad happen to you. Do you trust me?"

"Of course I do, but I'm so . . ."

"Okay, sweet lady, just let me take care of you. We'll find out what this is all about. Your face is much too pretty to be streaked by tears when there's no need."

His soft words and tender drying of her tears made her feel better. As their gazes met again, his hand caressed her cheek. She took it and kissed his palm. *Bill, we still have that connection.* Her breath caught in her throat. *I feel it in your touch, and I see it in your eyes.* She didn't speak the words. She didn't have to. He knew what their looks meant.

He took her small hands in his big ones. "I don't want you to worry any more about all of this, you hear? If our perpetrator had meant to harm anyone, he could have hurt Bonny. He didn't. Think you can remember that?"

"Yes, Bill, but—"

"No buts. I mean it. All you have to do is call me . . . anytime. Program my number into your cell phone."

"Okay."

"Now, I've brought the money from the register with me. The drawer was open, and the money was in plain sight. But the intruder didn't take it. Oh, and we found Bonny's purse."

"She'll be thrilled about that. She wondered where it was."

"Funny thing, though, the contents were strewn on the floor beside it. The money's still in the wallet, so maybe our perp was looking for something else."

"Like what?"

"I don't know, but I think we can conclude that robbery wasn't the motive. Has Bonny said anything that might shed some light on other possibilities?"

"Not much. She did mention again about the person whispering in her ear. Something about a game, she seemed to recall. And she swears she heard somebody whistling 'Pop Goes the Weasel.' And oh, I forgot to give you this." She reached into her pocket and handed him a piece of paper. "This note was left on the desk in the office." The message doesn't make any sense, but it seems to tie in to the whistling Bonny heard.

Bill read the strange message aloud:

"I've no time to plead and pine,

I've no time to wheedle,

Kiss me quick and then I'm gone,

Pop goes the weasel."

"What do you think that means?" She tried to keep her voice calm.

"Don't know. Why didn't you show this to me earlier?"

"I was so worried about Bonny that I didn't think about it. I found it in my pants pocket when I was getting ready for bed."

"Let me take it to the lab. We still may be able to lift a print from it—besides yours, that is. We didn't find anything in the boutique so far." He stared at the note. "This is really strange, but it seems there's a twisted method to somebody's demented madness. Don't worry. We'll figure it out."

He stood to leave and drew her to her feet. She didn't want him to go. Her hands were still locked in his.

"Bill . . . thank you so much for—"

"Hey, what are high school sweethearts for?" He looked at her like he had invented love.

Lost in limbo between the past and the present, she held her breath. *What's happening here? Why do I feel like my life has changed forever? I don't understand . . .*

"Try to get some sleep. I'll come by about ten in the morning to talk to Bonny. You think she'll be up by then?"

"She's an early riser."

"Lock the door behind me."

"I will."

He bent and grazed her lips with his. They were so soft, so sweet, so tempting. She nestled against him. His teasing kisses sent shivers all the way to her toes. Tears of joy filled her eyes and trickled down her cheek. He drew back and wiped them away.

"What's this all about?"

His gaze searched hers. Was he looking for an answer? Did he know that, after all this time, everything she wanted was right there in her arms at that moment?

"I . . . was remembering the last time you held me and kissed me this way."

"I've never forgotten it . . . or you."

The huskiness in his voice brought more tears to her eyes. He kissed them away then found her lips. She tasted their saltiness. He raised his head, cupped her face in his hands and whispered. "I think now we'll both remember *this* one."

The searing kiss left her wanting more. "And I'll dream about the next one."

A teasing twinkle sparked in his eyes. "I don't think you'll have to wait too long."

"I hope not." She opened the door. "Good night, Bill."

"Good night, sweet lady."

She closed the door behind him, flipped the deadbolt, and put the chain on.

The fragrance of his aftershave lingered. She took a deep breath and let it out. A shadow of the shiver that had run all the way from her lips to her toes made its way along the same path. Her longing for a husband and children seemed more of a possibility now than it had since that night of the high school prom.

Are we together again, Bill Perry, or are you just being nice to an old flame? I want you so much, but I'm afraid to hope. Almost as afraid as I am of the intruder who's out to get us.

CHAPTER NINE

Kat woke before dawn. Afraid to move, she tried to get her bearings. The rhythmic ping, ping of the monitoring device disturbed her, and then she remembered.

My baby!

"Daw." She tried not to sound frantic. "Dawson!" She couldn't suppress her fear anymore. "Where's my baby? Is he alright? Please tell me he's alright. Daw, where are you?"

"I'm right here, Kat." He was suddenly at her side. "I'm so glad you're finally awake. How are you feeling?" He brushed her hair back from her face.

"It doesn't matter how I'm feeling. All that matters is our baby. Where is he, Daw? Why isn't he in the room with us? He's not okay, is he? Is he alive?" The pitch of her voice rose with each question. In the dim light her eyes shimmered with unshed tears.

"He's in the nursery. And he's going to be just fine."

"*Going* to be just fine? What does *that* mean? He's okay, isn't he?"

"Yes, Kat, he's okay."

The low light didn't hide Dawson's frown or his disheveled sandy hair. A cowlick stood up on the crown, an untidy lock fell on his forehead, and that darling dimple she loved so much didn't dance. She tried to raise her head. It swayed unpleasantly, and the room suddenly became a merry-go-round.

She watched him force a smile. "Daw, tell me about our baby." Her lips pursed and formed unspoken words. Her mouth was dry as a desert, and her eyes brimmed with tears. She patted her tender, empty belly. "They took him from me. He wasn't ready, but they took him anyway. Why did they do that, Daw? What happened? Please . . ." She licked her parched lips. "Take me to him, Daw. Let me see for myself."

"Take my word for it. He's okay, Honey. Little Jedediah had a rough time just like you did. You both gave us all a scare."

She turned toward Jedediah. "Granddad, have you seen him?"

"You bet your boots I've seen him. He's the spittin' image of me. How you feelin', Kitten?"

"I—I'm not sure yet. A little groggy, and a little hurting." She turned her head to Dawson. "I want to see our baby, Daw. Would you ask the nurse—please?"

"Why don't you wait until you're a little stronger, Sweetheart? You've had quite a time of it. You need to rest as much as possible."

Rest? Wait a little longer? Until I'm stronger? I don't think so. What's wrong? What are you keeping from me?

"Please. I want to see my baby—now." Dawson and Jedediah exchanged glances. "What's going on, Daw? Granddad? What are you not telling me?"

Dawson's eyes darted to Jedediah, then to the floor. "The baby is undergoing some tests. There's a mild respiratory problem. Nothing to worry about. The doctors are confident that he'll be just fine, and—" She turned her head away from Dawson.

"Nothing's *mild* when it comes to respiratory problems. I know because my baby sister . . ." She brushed away the scalding tears with her fingers. "Be honest with me—please." She turned back to look into his tearful eyes.

"We don't know any more than we just told you. Dr. Morgan brought in a neonatalogist, one of the best in the state. He'll explain the whole thing as soon as the tests are completed. In the meantime, have faith."

"Yeah, right. You tell me to have faith when my baby might be dying?"

"Land sakes, girl! Get hold of yourself. Our baby ain't dyin'. He's just . . . tryin' to adjust to this world. And he will. You know what they say, *fear makes the wolf bigger than he is.* So stop fearin', Kitten."

She turned her head toward the window and closed her eyes. Her mind drifted into another place, another time, to something her Mama Suzanne had told her. The words, their meaning not quite comprehensible to a young child, now haunted her. Now, in a mist of memories, she was six years old again, sitting on the edge of her mama's bed, her bare feet dangling from the side.

"I thought I was going to have a baby sister, Mama. Where is she?"

"Sweetheart, I'm so sorry. Sister Sherry couldn't stay with us. She had respiratory problems and..."

"Reps—a—pory? I can't say it, Mama."

All of a sudden, it all came tumbling back. Her eyes flew open.

"No, not my baby sister! I wanted to see her. I wanted to hold her and take care of her. Why can't I see her, Mama!

Mama Suzanne's eyes filled with tears. "She's gone, Kat. She died. She came too soon, and she couldn't breathe. But she was beautiful. She looked just like you."

Kat's sobs shook her whole body. "No! I have to see my baby. I have to know he's alive."

"Kat!" Dawson grabbed her hand. "What's wrong? You're as pale as the pillowcase."

"I—I have to see our baby. Please, Dawson, I won't sleep or eat until I've seen him and touched him and told him how much I love him and how much I want him to stay with us." She forced herself into a sitting position and tried to lower the guardrail.

"Lie down, Kat!" Dawson said.

Granddad was on his feet. "Yes, Kitten, you gotta lie down now."

"No!" she yelled. "I've got to see my baby. If you won't help me, I'll do it on my own."

A large nurse bustled into the room, an aide on either side of her. "What's going on in here, Mrs. Kahill? The monitor's gone crazy."

"I've got to see my baby!" She gripped the rails on both sides of the bed to keep herself upright.

"Lie down, Mrs. Kahill," the nurse urged. "You can see your son in a little while."

"Please," she begged between sobs. "I must see him. My baby sister died of respiratory failure. I have to know the same thing hasn't happened to my son. Please . . ."

"I'll tell you what," the nurse offered. "If you'll lie down and let your heart and that monitor get back to normal, I'll personally take you to the nursery in half an hour. What do you say to that?"

Kat sank against the pillows. "That's all I ask . . . just a few moments with him. Thank you."

Her eyes drifted shut. The rat-a-tat pings of the monitor gradually slowed to a steady rhythm.

She must have napped, for it seemed only an instant before the nurse returned with the wheelchair. Soon the entire entourage—Kat, Dawson, and Granddad—paraded down the hallway to the NIC-U.

The baby opened his eyes and turned his head toward his mother the instant she began speaking. His gaze locked on hers and never wavered.

"He's not as small as I expected," she said in a low tone.

"Five-and-a-half pounds is a good weight for a preemie," the nurse said. "He's doing well now."

"Why's he still on oxygen?" She looked at the nasal cannula.

"He's only getting a little now. His breathing is much improved. Would you like to hold him?"

She glanced down at the IVs running into both her arms. "You mean I can?"

"Of course. Mr. Kahill, do you want to do the honors?"

Dawson lifted the tiny infant and placed him in her arms. He felt so fragile, so light.

"See how much he looks like me?" Granddad beamed.

"If you're talking about his lack of hair, the resemblance is very strong." Dawson was grinning.

"Watch what you say, Sonny!" the old man huffed. "I just may write you out of my will and leave everythin' to my namesake here."

Baby Jedediah turned his head to look at each one in turn.

"He knows our voices, doesn't he?" The awe in Kat's voice couldn't be missed. She looked up at the nurse. "Will I be able to breast-feed him?"

"Why not try and see," the nurse suggested.

"I think I need to go out for . . . uh . . . a drink of water," Granddad said.

Dawson chuckled.

The old man gave him a sour look. "This ain't no place for me. That's a mommy thing. I'll be helpin' the boy when it comes to learnin' about Willow Walk." He strutted out of the room.

Kat tried to entice the baby to grasp a nipple, but he didn't seem interested. He just kept looking at her. She began to feel dizzy.

"Take him, Daw. I need to lie down."

Dawson put the baby in his tiny bed, and they headed back to the room.

"Don't you worry about the baby not eating," the nurse reassured her as she helped her into bed and lowered her into a reclining position. "Somebody'll be here tomorrow to teach the two of you how to do it. He'll get the hang of it, you can be sure of that."

Kat nodded and closed her eyes. She could sleep now. *My baby's alright. He's even better than alright. He knows his mama.*

* * * * *

Dawson steered the van into the long driveway that led to Willow Walk. Each turn of the gently swerving road burst with autumn colors. The weeping willow's light limbs bent with the wind's full passion, and Kat absorbed the fresh clean air flowing in the window.

She turned her head and looked at the baby carrier that securely held little Jedediah in the middle seat.

Someday, my dear son, you'll love Willow Walk just as Mommy and Daddy and Great-granddad do. Someday, it will be yours. Tears of joy filled her eyes.

"What're we gonna nickname the baby, Kitten? We can't go around callin' him Jedediah. Both of us will come a runnin'." Granddad, sitting right next to his namesake, grinned, proud as Dawson but twice as boastful.

Kat laughed. "We could call him Joseph, or Joe, or maybe Josey?"

"*Josey?* I don't think so." Granddad frowned. "That's for a *girl*. The kids at school'd never let him live that name down. *Joey* might work though.

"Seems there was a movie where the main character was called Josey. Was it a Clint Eastwood film?" Dawson glanced at Jedediah in the rearview mirror. The old man glared back at him. "But I like Joey. Good idea, Granddad."

Kat glowed inside. Love and contentment—and most of all thankfulness that her baby's respiratory problems hadn't been as serious as her little sister's—filled her heart. At that moment, she had to be the happiest woman in the world.

"Really, Dawson and Granddad, have you ever seen a baby as handsome as this one?" She gave them both a smug smile. "Just leave it to me."

"Hey, don't count *me* out," Dawson said.

"Humph!" Jedediah spouted. "Did you ever see a picture of *me* when I stormed into this world? Some evenin' I'll get out the old photos and you'll see just how handsome a baby can be . . . and you'll see just how much our baby looks like his old granddad. When we get inside, you'll let me hold him, won't you, Kat? Don't know how many days I—well, you know what I mean."

"Of course, but you're going to be around for a long time yet, Granddad. You've got a namesake to raise now."

She saw the pride in his face as he looked down at her baby son. For the first time in a very long time, they were bringing a new Kahill home to Willow Walk.

* * * * *

They walked through the front door into a bevy of bright balloons clinging to the ceiling, colorful strings hanging down like branches of the weeping willows along the lane.

"What's *this*?" Jedediah frowned.

"Welcome home!" Bonny and Deb stepped into the large foyer from the guest drawing room.

"We can't wait to see that baby!" Bonny squealed. "Here, let me take him." She reached for the bundle in Kat's arms.

"Here, here!" The old man stomped his cane on the marble floor and pushed the long strings from the balloons away from his face. "We'll have none of this!" Our Joey's too little to be passed around like a bag of potatoes."

Kat handed the baby to Bonny. "It'll be alright, Granddad. They're almost family, and you know it."

"Huh! My words don't mean nothin' here no more. Don't know why I even bother stayin' around." He shuffled past the large staircase and headed toward the kitchen. Dawson followed him.

"Come in and sit down." Kat led them into the family drawing room.

Bonny nuzzled baby Joey. Deb gazed out the window.

"Fall colors are exquisite, aren't they?" Kat asked.

Deb's head bobbed up and down.

"Who's minding the boutique?"

"We closed for lunch, but we put a sign in the window. Said we'd be back at one o'clock," Bonny replied.

Kat glanced at her watch. "You've got a few minutes."

"We were so busy this morning we figured we'd earned an hour's escape." Bonny didn't take her eyes off the baby. "He smells so sweet. I can't wait till I have kids."

"They gave him a bath just before we left the hospital." She turned her head and sniffed. "Speaking of odors, I'm picking up the scent of something . . . spicy?"

"I came by on the way to work and put some green chile chicken in the slow cooker. Thought you might be hungry this evening, and all you have to do is make some instant rice. Deb brought a salad, so you're set for the evening."

"Whatever would I do without my two best friends? I appreciate your help so much. My strength isn't coming back as fast as I hoped it would." She nodded toward Deb, who still stared out the window. "What's with her?"

"Ask her."

"All right, Deb, fess up." Kat grinned. "What's going on in that lovely head of yours? Did Bill Perry ask you to marry him and you can't figure out what to say?"

Deb turned toward her, big tears spilling down her cheeks. Kat's grin faded.

"I wish that was it." She sniffed. "Bill's gone."

"What!"

"He's gone, Kat. Took a job in LA. He said this opportunity came up, and he had to take it. Something about the experience he'd gain in forensics would be invaluable when he comes back. At least that's what he told me when he came by last night."

"But I thought—"

"I thought so, too. We connected—just like we did before. Everything was so good. He said all the things I wanted to hear. I thought . . . He let me think . . . And then this. Maybe he has a woman in LA. He worked there for a year before he came back to Wheeling. Some reason besides *experience* must be drawing him back there." Sobs punctuated her words. "What am I going to do? I don't think I can live without him." She wiped her eyes. "I don't even *want* to live without him. Right now, I just want to die."

CHAPTER TEN
Four years later

"Joey Kahill! Where are you? Great balls o' fire, boy! You come here this minute or you get the switch." Jedediah could hear Joey snickering from behind the sofa in the drawing room. *I love that boy. He knows I would never lay a hand on him.* "You hear me, boy? You get out here right now." Joey scrambled out, laughing and jumping up and down. Granddad grabbed him and gave him a good tickling while the boy laughed, wiggled, and giggled.

"You hungry, Mr. Joey?"

"Yeah, I'm *really* hungry. I could eat a b'ar."

"Me too. I could eat two b'ars," Jedediah said.

"I could eat *three* b'ars," Joey yelled as he ran to the table.

Two big men and one little one waited impatiently for Kat to serve the evening meal.

"That boy's the spittin' image of me. He needs a little sister, Kitten. Don't you think we need a little dear Emma runnin' around here?" Jedediah rubbed his chin and winked at Dawson. "See what you can do about that, you hear, Sonny?" Jedediah glanced sideways at Kat, who was engrossed in pouring coffee, and then he turned to Dawson, shook his finger and burst into laughter.

"Whatcha talkin' 'bout, Granddad? What's a 'dear Emmy?'" Joey scratched his head.

"Talkin' about your great-grandmother, boy," Jedediah said. "Pretty soon I'll be showin' you pictures of her."

"When, Granddad?"

"Soon."

"But when? I wanna see 'em."

"Maybe when the cows come home."

"We got cows? They comin' home tonight?"

"Yep, sure are."

"Then can we see the pi'chers?"

"What pictures?"

"Oh, Granddad, you know what pi'chers."

"Joey, that's enough."

"But Mama, the cows are. . ."

"No more of this talk, I said."

"Oh, shucks. I wanna see Great-grandma when the cows—"

"Joey!" Kat rolled her eyes at Jedediah. "See what you've taught him? 'Shucks' is not something a little boy should be saying."

"Aw c'mon, Kitten. Nothin' wrong with 'shucks.' There's a whole lot worse words the boy could be sayin'."

"And I'd better not hear any of them come out of his mouth."

Jedediah nodded at his great-grandson and changed the subject. "What about that baby girl I asked for?"

"Sure, Granddad." Dawson glanced at Kat. "We'll . . . talk about it."

Dawson winked at his wife as she placed fried chicken and buttered lima beans on the table. He gave her a pat on the backside as she walked to the stove. She turned to meet his stare.

"You're a scoundrel, Daw." She frowned and grinned at the same time, then filled a gravy bowl with the best gravy ever to grace a table, so he and Granddad always said.

He watched her bend and straighten as she moved about, setting the supper table. She was even more desirable now than when they first married. He grinned when he thought about another baby. But then again, he'd almost lost her when Joey was born. They would talk about it later.

"Say grace, Granddad, and let's eat before everything gets cold." Kat sat down. They joined hands and bowed their heads.

"Can we eat now?" Joey asked, eyeing the fried chicken as soon as Granddad said "amen."

"Go right ahead, Son." His father put two wings and a small spoon of lima beans on the wide-eyed boy's plate.

Dawson tried to follow the conversation, but the ongoing construction of a ski lodge on the south end of the property distracted him.

He'd worked long and hard on the plans, the permits, the details of the large project, and finally it had become a reality. It would be a legacy for his son—and any other children they might have—in addition to Willow Walk, of course. More than that; he wanted Joey to have an interest in some profitable endeavor for his younger years—and for later years, to keep his hands and mind active.

"You okay, Daw?" Kat was giving him a strange look.

"Yeah, why?"

"You're so quiet. That's not like you."

"Sorry, I was thinking about the lodge. It's almost finished now." He gnawed on a chicken leg. "The boutique doing okay?" When nothing was left but the bone, he laid it down and licked his fingers.

"Fine. Better than fine, actually. I need to devote more time to my designs though. I was invited to two runway shows for the spring season, and Bonny took a few new creations to both. But I have to go myself next fall with a full new line if I want to keep my edge. It's just so hard to leave Joey and go to work. Every time I walk out the door without him, I keep remembering that I almost lost him."

"I'm not lost, Mama. I'm right here." He waved both arms, a partially eaten chicken wing in each hand.

They all laughed.

Granddad patted his head. "You're not kiddin', boy. You are definitely all here."

Dawson grew quiet again. The conversation about the boutique reminded him that the break-in had never been solved. There had been no fingerprints and no real clues. Bill Perry had had nothing to go on. Due to the lack of evidence, the case had been shelved, but Bill had returned to Wheeling and was still working on it in his spare time. He was a good friend.

Because robbery was obviously not the motive, he worried. Did someone have it in for Kat? If so, why? She was kind to everyone. Yet the number of times the girls answered phone calls with no one saying anything on the other end of the line seemed unlikely to be just wrong numbers. He couldn't shake the feeling that the perpetrator was still out there, still watching.

He shoved the upsetting thoughts from his mind and glanced at Jedediah, who was pouring gravy all over his mashed potatoes. How in the world could he put away so much food and not gain weight. *I should be so lucky.*

"Granddad, have I ever thanked you for the opportunity you gave me?"

"Opportunity? For what, Sonny?"

"Financing me so I could get my degree in architectural design?"

"Weren't no doubt you'd come through with flyin' colors. Your father wasted his brain chasin' skirts instead of studyin', so I expelled him myself—beat Duke to it." He stopped, looked up at the ceiling, and sniffed. "That boy hurt Emma and me so much. But he's gone now, and we know why he was like he was—at least one of the reasons. Never mind. You make me proud, Sonny." He scraped the rest of the lima beans from the bowl onto his plate.

"Better get this guy more limas, Kat." Dawson said.

"I want more limas, too, Kat." Joey picked up one bean at a time with his fork and popped it into his mouth.

"Joey! Don't call your mama 'Kat.'"

"But *you* call her Kat." Joey puckered up his lips and frowned.

"She's not *my* mama, and you heard what I said." Dawson took a deep breath and wondered what in the world their precocious boy would be saying next.

"Speakin' of a great-granddaughter reminds me—" Jedediah began.

"That was ten minutes ago," Kat interrupted. "It's a closed topic."

"We'll see about that," Granddad huffed. "But talkin' about baby girls reminds me of that Irishman I met in the hospital when Kat was birthin' Joey. You remember, Sonny, Clancy O'Malley? I told you about him. I think I found him. Been doin' some checkin' on that dangfangled computer thing in your office, Kitten. Thanks to my brilliant, inquisitive mind, I remembered he told me he lived just a few miles away. Got his phone number and address."

Dawson glanced at Kat as she lifted her eyebrow and peeked at Granddad under her lashes.

"You must have taken a liking to Clancy, Granddad." Dawson filled his and Joey's plate with mashed potatoes then passed them to Jedediah. "Why haven't you contacted him sooner?"

"Called him a couple times a while back, but got no answer. Don't rightly know if he's still there." Jedediah poured the last of the gravy over his potatoes. "Yep, it's not every day you meet a good family man havin' a baby same time you are. I'm gonna try again to get hold of him, invite the family for a Sunday meal. Maybe the young'uns will get a chance to meet and play." Jedediah laughed. "Or fight, whichever comes first. You game for that, Kitten?"

Kat wrinkled her nose at him. "That's a great idea. I remember you told me about a lady who had a baby the same time I did. By all means, invite them over. I can't wait to meet the family."

"It's settled then. I'll try callin' again." Jedediah pushed his chair back and rose from the table. "I'm helpin' with the dishes tonight, and I don't want no ifs, ands, or buts about it."

Kat laughed. "Have at it, Granddad."

Dawson watched them carry dirty dishes to the sink, Joey right behind them with his plate so clean it looked like it could be put away instead of washed. Rather than stay for the chatter that always accompanied the dishwashing, he slipped off to the den to work on an advertising spiel for Willow Walk Ski Lodge. He wanted to bombard the public with notices of the grand opening in November, not long away.

Gazing at a blank screen on his computer, he let his thoughts meander back to the time Jedediah sat him down for a lengthy talk. "Duke University awaits you, Sonny," he had said. "How lucky they'll be when you show up. I have one order: you graduate with high honors and show up everyone you can. Duke *is* your choice, isn't it, Sonny?"

Duke had been his choice. But even if it hadn't, he would have gone there to please Granddad. That old man's financial support and interest in his life couldn't have been greater if he'd been his father rather than his grandfather. Now it was his turn to show Jedediah that his confidence hadn't been in vain. It was up to him to make the lodge work, to make Granddad proud of him. Too bad Grandma Emma hadn't lived to see it. She'd have been just as supportive.

Must keep the Willow Walk name on top of the barrel. How many times had he heard Granddad say that?

He nodded and opened up his graphic design program. The spectacular drawings for the lodge had been completed. Now he just had to work up the ads and buy TV time.

Seating in the lodge's great room surrounded a centered open fireplace. A stone wall housed another fireplace on the far outside wall, and the remaining walls were made of logs. Open pine rafters suppported a twenty-four foot cathedral ceiling. Guest rooms opened to a wrap-around second floor walkway that circled the great room.

Granddad had had a hand in the planning and regularly patted himself on the back for the idea and design of the front desk. The old man himself had carved a beautiful leaf design on the edge of the counter and engraved his name on one of the shelves behind the desk, no doubt thinking nobody would be the wiser.

He couldn't imagine life without that old man. Jedediah spent most of his days monopolizing little Joey's time. Although the boy was getting spoiled, neither he nor Kat complained. *Granddad's happy and Joey's healthy. That's what matters.*

Still, he worried. At ninety-five, Jedediah's pace had slowed and his eyes had sunk a little deeper. His gait, less steady than even last year, still remained determined. He swore he knew his limitations, but Dawson knew better. They wouldn't have him with them for many more seasons.

Bonny and Deb sat in the lunchroom with Kat before the boutique opened at nine.

"What's the plan now?" Bonny asked.

Kat hedged. "I'm not sure yet."

Deb frowned. "Good grief, Kat, before the fire you promised we'd be in New York and California, and maybe even Paris with new shops. That's been what—almost five years ago? Don't you think it's past time to start expanding? Joey's old enough now, and with Granddad taking care of him most of the time, you should think about spreading your wings. The shop looks great, but it's just the beginning."

"I've not abandoned the plans for expansion, only suspended them temporarily."

"*Temporarily?* We're *way* beyond temporary."

Kat poured herself more coffee. "You're right. But I worry about Grand-dad. I don't think he's being capable of caring for Joey full-time. He's in his mid-nineties now and not as spry as he used to be."

"Dawson's right on the property, checking in all the time. The contractor and laborers are doing most of the work at the lodge. Dawson's at the house when things don't require his attention." Bonny reached for the coffee pot.

"I know. I've been working at home, and I'll be the first to admit the designs have suffered—at least in quantity—because I'm distracted there. Joey interrupts me at least half-a-dozen times an hour. It's time I move my office back to the boutique."

"Yes!" the girls said in unison.

"And start planning for expansion," Deb added.

Kat suppressed a smile. Deb was not going to stop pecking away at their expansion plans until they were realized. *That's okay. I need the nudge.* For the first time since Joey's birth, she felt her future firmly in her grasp. They would begin with New York.

She threw up her hands in surrender. "Will tomorrow be soon enough?"

"All right! It's about time. Why don't you bring Joey with you?" Bonny asked. "We don't get to see him very often, and he's such a doll. Looks just like Granddad."

"Don't let Granddad hear you say that. His hat's already too small for his head." Kat laughed. "I *don't* want to take Joey away from him unless it becomes a safety issue. It would kill him not to be able to care for the little boy he always wanted to carry on the Kahill name. Besides, the idea of coming back here to work is to get away from Joey's interruptions that slow me down."

"That's your call, but we need to run with the expansion ball before you lose your edge completely, Kat." Deb said.

"Okay, okay, I hear you. To tell you the truth, I'm getting excited." *I can be a good mom and a good designer, too. It'll just take some organization. I know I've neglected the boutique, but Joey came first. He still comes first. But I can do both and not let either one suffer. I know I can.* Her resolve seemed to flip on a switch. New design ideas floated through her head. She grabbed a piece of paper and began sketching.

"Not to worry," she said, her pen moving in fluid lines as an exquisite gown took shape. "I'm sure Granddad can take care of Joey until I come up with a better plan. At least, I *think* I'm sure."

CHAPTER ELEVEN

On Sunday morning, Jedediah ambled to the kitchen to make coffee while everyone else still slept. He'd call Clancy as soon as he'd had his first eye-opening cup.

Drip—drip—drip. The new coffee pot tried his patience beyond his endurance.

Dang that thing. Takes half the mornin' to do its job and the smell's a drivin' me crazy. As soon as the last drop dripped, Jedediah grabbed the pot and filled a mug, then tiptoed to the porch swing.

"Yes, Emma Baby, I was careful not to slosh coffee on your spotless floor. You think I want that fierce broom of yours comin' after me?"

He imagined her retort. "See that you don't, Jed, you old fool." He knew Emma would be grinning despite the stern look on her face. If only he could touch her like he used to and see that little hand slap at him when he patted her backside. *You don' know how much I miss you, Baby.* After the last swallow, he headed to the kitchen to call Clancy and get a refill. The first cup was for waking up and the second was for savoring.

Four rings—five rings—six rings. Jedediah was about to hang up when finally he heard, "Clancy O'Malley here. Who might ye be?"

"Well, hello, my boy. This is Jedediah Kahill. Remember? Wheeling Community Hospital. We had babies together awhile back."

"Ah, 'tis me heart's delight ta hear yer voice, Jedediah. What a grand surprise. How be ye?"

"I'm doin' fine for an old man, but I called to see how you've been. Did you have that lassie you wanted?" He sputtered as a sip of coffee burned his tongue.

"Did at that. She's the light of me life. But, Jed, I'm a man with supper for only one now. Me Anna passed on almost four years ago. Never got over an infection she picked up when Molly Anna was born. Her water was leakin' fer days, and she didn't tell anybody. Guess she thought it didn't matter, but it did. Cost me sweet woman her life."

Jedediah gasped. The agony of his Emma's passing raked his heart like steel claws. And then almost losing his Kitten . . . Clancy was a whole lot younger—and at an age when he ought not to be worrying about being widowed. Setting his coffee down on the table, he wiped his moist eyes with the back of his hand.

"As I live and breathe, that's an awful thing. Are you gettin' along okay, Son?"

"'Tis me nature to get along. I sure do miss her, but I'll not be blowin' on dead embers. So how's yer laddie?"

"A strappin' big young'un. He's a carbon copy of me. Listen, Clance, me and the family want you and yours to come for Sunday dinner next week. And don't say no if you know what's good for you."

"Ye won't get no protestin' from me. Give me directions and we'll be there. What time are ye wantin' us?"

"How's eleven o'clock soundin' to you?"

"Eleven it be then. Now may yer day be tetched with a bit o' Irish luck. Goodbye, me friend. See ya soon."

Jedediah stared at nothing in particular. Just the thought of that young mother who wouldn't get to raise her young'uns chilled him to the bone.

"Granddad, can I have some coffee now?"

Jedediah's head turned at the sound of Joey's voice.

"Granddad, I said I want my coffee now." Joey sat down and banged his fist on the table.

"You may not."

"Why not?"

"'Because you're too little."

"Oh! 'Member that li'l Molly girl you tol' me 'bout? I'm bigger den her I bet."

"If she was here, she couldn't have coffee either."

"Why?"

"It'll stunt your growth, boy. Hers, too. I told you that before. You can have orange juice."

"I don't want orange juice. I want coffee."

"Not now. When you grow up."

When the cows come home?" Joey gave him a big smile and shot toward the door. "Race you to the porch, Granddad."

"You little scalawag," Jed called after him. "I'll get you. And when I do, you're in a heap of trouble."

That boy's growin' up way too fast. He sighed and flopped down on the old porch swing that hung from whitewashed rafters. It had been painted more often than he could remember. Every spring Emma had handed him a bucket and a brush. It'd been every color but pink.

"Joey? Joey, boy!" Jedediah watched as Joey sat on the porch, playing with his toy horses. "Now don't you be puttin' your dirty hands in your mouth. Don't want you to get down with some terrible disease."

Joey looked up at him with defiant gray eyes. He grinned, stood up, and threw the horse down.

"By golly, boy, you got your old great-granddad's temper. Got his eyes, too. Gray as a winter sky and just as mysterious." *How I love that child.* "That's a good feller. Little Molly Anna will be here one of these days, and I bet she'll light up Willow Walk with Irish green eyes and torchin' red hair like her papa's."

"You mean she's got red hair like Batman's boots?" Joey plopped down and went back to playing.

Jedediah chuckled. That boy was somethin' else.

The week buzzed by. Sunday morning, coffee cup in hand, Jedediah sat on the swing, his ear cocked toward Willow Drive. *Yup, must be Clancy haulin' up the road.* The vehicle sounded like a country clog dance on a Saturday night. Jedediah jumped up, ambled to the porch steps, and cupped his hand around his mouth.

"About time you got here, Clance, old boy. I only been waitin' for nigh on to four years."

Clancy leaned his head out the old truck and hollered back. "Mornin' t' ya, Jeddy." He parked, lifted Molly Anna out of the truck, and headed for the porch.

"By golly, it's been a long while, Clancy, since we seen each other. You've aged a might." Jedediah cast his eyes on the little red-headed girl in front of him. "Joey. Joey, boy. Look who I got here. Meet Molly Anna O'Malley. She was born the same day as you." Jedediah took Molly's hand and led her to the swing where Joey sat, watching them. The two children stared at each other. Neither spoke.

"Would you look at that, Jed?" Clancy hooked his thumbs in the back pockets of his jeans, stuck his chest out, and rocked back and forth on his heels. "Me Molly's never at a loss for words, but yer boy's tied up her tongue. Ye think we might have kindred spirits here?"

"Same for Joey boy, so you may be right, Clancy. Seems to me they're sayin' a heap to each other without speakin' a word. Come on, let's sit down and catch up." He motioned him to the table and chairs at the other end of the porch. "But first, I'm gonna get us a cool one. You do want your Irish whiskey, don't you?" Jedediah hollered back to Clancy as he disappeared through the kitchen door.

"Me throat's waitin' for that torchlight procession goin' down. Make 'er a short one, Jeddy. Gotta drive home. And take yer time. I'll keep me eyes on the wee ones."

Jedediah paid no attention to Clancy's request for a short one. He returned with a hearty shot of whiskey for both of them. Kat and Dawson followed Jedediah back onto the porch. He introduced them to Clancy.

"Dinner will be ready soon, you two," Kat said. She looked around. "Are we missing somebody? I seem to recall that Granddad said something about seven red-headed sons. I set the table for thirteen."

"I was meanin' to ask you that very thing," Jedediah said, "only I got sidetracked fixin' somethin' to quench our thirst."

"'Twas another sad day fer me when I had t' pack me boys off to me moder and far in Ireland. Fer a year I kept us all together. Then me work slowed down. Food and shoes for eight growin' wee ones strains the budget t' breakin', I tell ye. Me funds dwindled, and me moder came fer a visit. Took me lads home with her. Broke me heart, but 'twas for their own good. They got a fine home now. Me far sends a ticket fer me and the lassie t' come once or twice a year fer a visit, but it's not enough. Me lads are growin' up without a far as well as without a moder. 'Tis a terrible shame."

Kat reached out and patted his shoulder. "I'm so sorry. I wish we'd known. Maybe we could've helped some way."

"That's very kind o' ye, Missus. But we couldn't have imposed."

"It wouldn't have been an imposition," Kat assured him.

Jedediah waved his cane. *That a girl, Kat. You let him know the Kahills help their neighbors. Ah, my Kitten's a fine lady, a lot like my Emma.* "We'll be ready to eat, Kitten, whenever it's ready to be eaten." He turned to Clancy. "It's dandy havin' you here, Son. Don't know why we waited so danged long to get together."

"Yer right, Jeddy. We should've done it sooner." Clancy gave him a look of woefulness. "It's been a wee mite difficult fer the lassie and me. Being moder and far both to Molly Anna, 'tis—well, never ye mind. Me dear wife died soon after Molly Anna was born, like I already told ye. Never even got to hold her wee one. Little lassie needs a moder as well as a far. Been doin' me best t' fill the bill. Aye, may the dragons spit fire on ol' Clancy if me story ain't a sad one. Never ye mind, though. I didn't come 'ere t' cry on yer shoulder."

"I'm right sorry for your loss, but I got confidence you'll raise that green-eyed gal to be a good woman—and her brothers to be fine young men. And I seen some good-lookin gals out there just waitin' for a red headed, freckled face, stubborn bull of a feller like you."

"I'll drink t' that, Jeddy, but what woman in her right mind would give two blinks of an eye in me direction when she sees the baggage I got clingin' to me britches?" Clancy and Jedediah clinked glasses, eyes twinkling and mouths grinning. "Here's t' ye, me friend. May ye have long life and good health—not that ye ain't had these already." They both howled and then tossed the Irish whiskey down.

"Clance, what've you been doin' for work these days?"

"Just a little carpentry here and there. That's why me lads are gone. Just a *little* here and there won't feed so many hungry mouths. Got Molly Anna in a nursery school now, but she hates it. And I hate it 'cause me lassie hates it. But not much else to do when a little bit o' work comes along."

"Hmm . . . maybe something will work out for you right here. Your needin' a job, and Dawson's needin' help. Sounds like a good thing for everybody."

"Why don't you and Molly Anna spend the night?" Kat said after serving apple pie with homemade ice cream to top off the meal. "We've got plenty of room, and that'll give you and Dawson some time to go over our needs at the lodge and see if you might be a good fit."

She watched the children while the men talked. Finding a pair of pajamas that Joey had outgrown, she gave them warm baths and tucked them in. Two bedtime stories settled them down, and both were sleeping when she turned out the light. The men were still talking business when she returned to the drawing room, so she slipped back upstairs and went to bed. Tomorrow would be a busy day.

Jedediah watched the old truck disappear down Willow Drive. He rubbed his chest. The pain in his heart for Clancy O'Malley gripped him like a vice. The boy'd be returning in a couple of days to start work, but his life had sure taken a sad path.

Maybe he could help. The ache in his chest eased at the very thought. Of course he didn't know many women Clancy's age, but he could ask around. Ought to be somebody in Wheeling who'd appreciate a good family man.

CHAPTER TWELVE

"Dadblamed indigestion," Jedediah muttered. Would this day never end? Here it was two o'clock, and he didn't feel any better than he had when he woke up this morning. "Somethin' I ate last night sure didn't sit right."

Something else wasn't sitting right. Everyone fussed over him. "Don't do this, Granddad." "You shouldn't do that, Granddad." "You must . . . blah, blah, blah." They meant well, but they were beginning to get on his nerves.

No wonder m' stomach's complainin' Don't do the digestion no good when somebody's always on your case. Who in tarnation do these whippersnappers think I am anyway? I'm gettin' older, but I still got my right mind, and it works danged good if I say so myself.

Dawson drove down the road from the lodge to Willow Walk for the third time in three hours. He knew Kat worried about Granddad's ability to keep up with a healthy, adventurous four-year-old, but the constant back-and-forth trips put a strain on his own work. Her words replayed in his mind . . .

I'm worried, Daw. Joey's a scamp. He can get into more trouble in five minutes than even I can get him out of. Granddad's not as spry as he was, and at his age anything can happen. He could have a heart attack or stroke and be gone in seconds. I know you don't want to think about that—neither do I. But Joey's safety's at stake here. If I'm going to keep working at the boutique, we need to do something about this, and we need to do it soon.

64

He agreed with her reasoning—but none of that changed his schedule. Something had to give.

The lodge would open the first of December. It had passed the final inspection, and the furniture had arrived three days ago.

It was looking like something out of a magazine, thanks to Kat's expertise in choosing colors, textures, and fabrics. The rough log exterior and interior fit perfectly into the setting outside. Gigantic picture windows treated visitors to panoramic views of the mountains and countryside. Inside, splashes of color complimented the rustic woods. Already the fading autumn leaves slept under the season's first blanket of snow that beckoned skiers from all over.

Long ski runs turned the massive windows into big screen TVs, allowing viewers to enjoy the warmth of the fireplaces while watching graceful skiers glide down the slopes. Neutral-colored oversized couches surrounded the large central fireplace. Smaller ones in a slightly darker tone provided a cozy conversation area around the fireplace in the stone wall.

Kat had chosen a heavy tapestry fabric in shades of rust, gold, and blue for the accent pillows and valences. She and Dawson decided on burly pine for tables, chairs, and shelving that displayed local sculpture and pottery. Artwork in mediums of oil, acrylic, and pastels graced the walls. Suspended from the overhead beams, huge chandeliers of antique brass with frosted glass chimneys provided subdued lighting. Small lamps of the same metal and black wrought iron sat on the pine tables for the reading pleasure of their guests. On one wall, Dawson's elaborately carved bookcase housed an extensive library. The artistic blending of rustic charm and luxurious amenities created the exact effect they wanted.

They had advertised extensively and were booked with a full house for the grand opening. Reservations well into the winter season were coming in every day.

Kat and Dawson, bundled in warm clothes, peered up at the hand-carved sign that hung over the entrance of the lodge. Created from the same pine as the exterior walls, it depicted a delicate willow tree. From its drooping branches, the lodge's name welcomed visitors.

She pronounced each word with emphasis. "Willow . . . Walk . . . Ski . . . Lodge. It's exquisite, Daw. You've outdone yourself this time."

Dawson crossed his arms and frowned. "Hey! Wait just one minute. What about your sign for the boutique that I slaved over—twice? Isn't that the most magnificent one?" She saw his sideways glance and knew he was trying to keep from laughing.

"Yes, of course it is . . . or was. Oh, Daw, you know how much I loved that first sign you made with such care. If it hadn't burned in the fire, I would still have it. But your second one is just as beautiful—and almost identical to the first."

She snuggled her arm around Dawson's waist and tried not to think of that horrifying night when the boutique burned. The images kept coming—the intense heat of the fire, the crackle of burning boards, the death of the arsonist—Dawson's mentally ill wife who had seemed determined to destroy all of them. Her threats to take Willow Walk away from Dawson in their divorce proceedings had died with her. However, she had almost succeeded in destroying Kat's dream when she torched the boutique.

That was long past. Kat looked at Dawson and felt his closeness. Valorie Kahill *hadn't* taken away her dream. Nor had she undermined Dawson's dream of opening the lodge. He looked down at her and cupped her chin in his hand. The image of the burning boutique vanished with his kiss.

"Funny how life gives and takes," he whispered.

"Yes, Daw. We've been given so much. A second chance for both of us." *Our marriage is a second chance for happiness. My surviving Joey's birth. The rebuilt boutique. Our new markets. The lodge that would provide a summer get-away for visitors after the skiing season ended.* "Now we have to be able to give something to others."

It was the perfect opening for Dawson. "You're right, Kat. We need to give back, and that should start with family." She looked up at him. "I've been thinking about inviting Polly Dee and her son—my half-brother, Cable Darrell, to come up from Mexico to help manage the lodge. And her husband, Darrell, if he wants to come. What do you think?"

"Oh, Dawson, what a perfect idea! I do hope they accept your invitation."

"Me, too. I've interviewed dozens of applicants for key jobs, but they just aren't what I want. We need experience, and Polly knows how to run an inn. She's done it for years."

Kat tugged at his arm. "Let's go home and call them right now."

She stood at his elbow while he talked to Polly Dee, then Cable Darrell, and Darrell. Finally, he hung up the phone.

"Do they want to come? Are they excited about it? What does Cable Darrell think of it?"

"Why don't you make us some hot chocolate? Then I'll tell you what everybody said. By the way, they don't have the money to make the trip.

The economic downturn has hit them hard. We're footing the bill for their trip . . . if that's okay with you."

She laughed. "More than okay. I can't wait. Daw, I have to fix up some living quarters in the lodge for them. I'll pick up the materials I need on my lunch hour tomorrow. Let's see, new linens, fresh flowers, fruit, and comfortable chairs. They must have one of the kitchenette suites."

"Kat. Kat! Slow down, I thought they could live in the guest house."

"It's so small, Daw."

"It worked fine for me when Granddad suggested I live out there to escape Valorie's wrath. It's bigger than the kitchenette suite."

"There's only one of you. There're three of them."

"Two. Darrell's staying behind to keep the inn open."

"It's still small."

"It has two bedrooms, two bathrooms, a living room, eat-in kitchen. Isn't that enough for two people?"

We can spare the room at the lodge, and they'll be close to work."

"Yes, but we can't spare two rooms," Dawson said.

"*Two* rooms? I don't understand."

"I've been meaning to tell you . . . Clancy and Molly Anna are coming this weekend. You know we talked about hiring Clancy to do the maintenance and relief desk work. Also, the man's an excellent carpenter. Of course, I said yes. I didn't think you would mind."

"Not at all, but I wish you had told me a little sooner. You always do this—make plans without my knowledge."

"Well, someone has to make them. You're forever busy with Joey or the boutique or . . . Anyway, Clancy's rent is due on the first of the month, so it's perfect timing. I think Granddad can watch over both those children while Clancy works, don't you?"

Kat frowned. "As long as I hire a housekeeper to look after all three of them, unbeknownst to Granddad, of course. I've already interviewed several women and picked one out. Carla will be starting tomorrow."

"And you complain about my not sharing my plans with you? When did you plan to tell me about this?"

"I was going to tell you tonight. You know I worry about Joey's safety. This way I can have peace of mind while I work."

"Thanks for letting me know."

"I wasn't trying to keep it from you, Daw. You're busy, I'm busy, and we sometimes seem to be going our own separate ways. It'll work out."

Dawson stared at the hot chocolate in his cup and then out the window. She usually knew what he was thinking, but this time she couldn't read him.

"What's on your mind, Sweetheart?" Kat jotted down several items to pick up for the guest house.

"I wish they'd find whoever broke into the boutique. I worry every time you leave the house and don't relax until you drive in the driveway. I think the police have all but forgotten about it. The last I heard, they believed it was someone trying to cause trouble for *you*, Kat. Do you have any clue who it might be? Someone from your college days maybe?"

"They've never closed the case, Daw. For the life of me, I can't—oh, wait a minute. In college there was this guy who . . . I forgot about him. No, that can't be it. Too long ago."

"*Who*, Kat?"

"Randy Van Henkle. We called him Rip. He was one fireball of a quarterback. He kept hitting on me until I finally told him to leave me alone. 'You'll be sorry,' he said. And something about he'd see me at the football game that night. But I didn't go to the game because I had several designs to finish for a class project the next morning. Oh—I don't have time to think about that right now. Too much to do."

"The police need leads, Kat. You'd better let Bill Perry know about this Van Henkle fellow."

"Maybe tomorrow . . . if I have time. I don't think we need to worry. If anybody had a serious grudge, I think he would've come back already. After all, I'm there full-time, and that's a well-known fact around town. Right now I have three rooms on the east side of the lodge to finish and two hungry men to feed." She tromped off to the kitchen to fix supper.

"I should know better than to argue with you," Dawson called after her. He sat down at the window in the den. *Is Granddad up to keeping two preschoolers—even with somebody else in the house? And what's this about some guy in college and a football game?*

He needed quiet, needed to resist the turbulent feelings that charged through his mind. Why hadn't Kat remembered this guy before? Something wasn't right.

CHAPTER THIRTEEN

With Carla's help, Kat had put the guest house in order and stocked its pantry, cupboards, and refrigerator. Polly and Cable Darrell would arrive at the end of the week. How Granddad would accept them Dawson didn't even want to guess.

Clancy and Molly Anna had moved into the small suite of rooms at the back of the lodge that were designed to house an onsite manager—which met with the old man's enthusiastic approval. Granddad had been much less enthusiastic about the arrival of Kat's new housekeeper.

Dawson reviewed the assignment sheet. He'd act as manager, which had freed up the quarters for the O'Malleys. Polly Dee's housekeeping crew would keep the lodge spotless. Desk clerk duties and reservations went to Cable Darrell with Clancy as backup. Bringing Clancy onboard to handle maintenance had already prooved to be a good decision.

Jedediah looked after Molly Anna and Joey. He had guffawed at Kat's teasing suggestion that the two four-year-olds would be taking care of him. Of course no one mentioned that Carla was keeping an unobtrusive eye on all three of them.

Jedediah stood at the kitchen window. A young man with a familiar gait sauntered up the walk from the guest house. He stepped out onto the back porch. "Great balls-o'-fire, boy, you're a carbon copy of your pa."

"That's not saying much," the young man replied. "Call me Cabe, will you, Granddad?" Cable squinted his eyes. "You are my grandfather, right? Mom finally told me that Darrell wasn't my real dad."

"I am that." Jedediah's bushy brows went up as he looked at the face that bore a haunting resemblance to his dead son's. "And I suppose I can call you . . . uh . . . Cabe. But you just remember one thing, boy . . . Cabe. Your daddy was a sick man for a lot of years, and none of us knew it. There'll be no bad-mouthin' of Cable Kahill on Willow Walk land, you hear? And you best be right proud of that name your carryin'."

Cabe shrugged. "Whatever you say, *Granddad*."

Something about the boy's demeanor bothered him. Was it his walk? The way he cocked his head? His attitude? He couldn't quite pinpoint the reason for his uneasiness. But his "sixth sense" had never let him down, and he doubted it would this time. He'd be paying close attention to everything the boy did for a while. Those red flags that were popping up in his head just wouldn't go away.

Dense trees lined either side of the road that meandered downward from the ski lodge to Willow Walk. Their leafless limbs allowed a clear view of mountains across the deep cut of the valley.

Jedediah strolled onto the porch and contemplated the brewing storm. Slate-colored clouds rolled across the darkening sky, propelled by bitter gusts that seemed to blow right through him. Somewhere in the distance, a calf bellowed for its mother. The sound echoed in the air that was suddenly still.

The storm took on a life of its own. Gray clouds deepened to black, obscuring hilltops and sky. Jedediah closed the massive double oak doors to the entrance hall, crossed the threshold, and entered the drawing room, where Joey and Molly Anna sat on the floor, playing with blocks. Molly Anna giggled when the blocks tumbled down. Joey frowned, puckered his lips, and smacked at the blocks with his hand.

The large fireplace warmed the room, but a strange chill hung in the air. The children began to fuss at each other, whining and throwing their toys around.

"Play nice! Don't throw your toys at Molly Anna, boy. You'll hurt her."

Joey lay the block down on the floor, lowered his eyes and peeked under his lashes. "I'm sawy, Molly. I fergot you was a girl."

"Okay, Joey. Wanna play blocks some more?"

"Uh-huh."

The ruckus brought Carla in from the kitchen. "Are you two giving Granddad a hard way to go?"

Both children shook their heads. "We won' do that, Miz Carla," Joey said.

70

"No," Molly Anna agreed.

"Hmmmm," Carla gave them both a stern look and then a smile.

The children had taken to her right away. Granddad wasn't so sure. But she knew how to cook, and her chocolate chip cookies were the best he'd had since Emma baked her last batch. *Guess I can put up with her as long as she stays out of my way and doesn't tell me how to raise my boy.*

The ringing phone was just the distraction he needed.

"Granddad? Is everything okay? Looks like there's a storm brewing."

"Everythin's fine on the home front."

"Are the kids behaving?"

"Don't you fret none. The kids're playin' real nice." *Well, sort of anyway.* He rolled his eyes upward.

"I'll be heading home soon. The last reservation has already checked in. Got a full house. We're all running around like we know what we're doing. You sure everything's okay?"

"We're fine as wine, Sonny. Now don't worry. Do what you gotta do."

"Right. Be home in an hour or less." Dawson sounded stressed, but then he'd sounded that way for weeks. "I'm going to give Kat a call and ask her to stay put."

Fifteen minutes later, the storm slung its fury at the old clapboard sides of Willow Walk. The relentless wind sought out all the crannies around the windows and forced its way in to push against the heavy drapes.

Jedediah shuffled to the window. *Didn't hear nothin' like this on the forecast. Nice of the weather guys to leave the blizzard part out.* Pulling the drapes aside, he took a quick peek, then closed them. *This is a dandy. Nothin' like what the news said. Them weather people better get off their haunches and get back to school. Even I can say more than 'The weather forecast for tonight is . . . dark.'* Grinning, he silently mimicked the weather forecaster.

He peeked through the curtains again. This storm was building up to be a humdinger for sure. He'd seen a passel of storms in his life, but this one—well, there was something foreboding about it.

"Carla," he called out, "you better be thinkin' about makin' a pot of soup. Dawson'll be home soon, and it's a night for soup."

"I started some minestrone an hour ago, Mr. Kahill."

Dang that woman. I'm s'posed to be in charge here, and she's always one step ahead of me."

He checked the windows in the drawing room. They were shut tight. But before he could get to the French doors, they blew open. A cold blast nearly knocked him off his feet. The ceramic vase on the end table teetered and crashed to the floor. He shook his head.

"Emma Baby, I'm so sorry. I know that was one of your favorites. I'm just glad it wasn't my fault. I'll look for another one just like it. Will that be all right?"

"Who you talkin' to, Granddad? I don' see nobody," Joey said.

"I don' see nobody eider," Molly Anna echoed.

Jedediah frowned at them. "Jus' never you mind. I'm the only one that needs to know. Now you kids don't move till I pick up this mess."

"Look at *my* house," Joey bragged. "It's bigger dan yers."

"I don' care. I'm gonna' get mine bigger," Molly Anna said.

Oh, to be a child again. Jedediah swept up the shattered remains of Emma's treasured vase. Dawson would be home soon. The lodge wasn't that far away. *Wonder if Kat'll stay at the boutique?* Surely, she had too much sense to go out in this. *Might be a good idea to call Dawson and see if he's left the lodge yet.* He picked up the phone. No dial tone. *Lines must be down.*

Now what? Couldn't even dial nine-one-one. Of course, no need to do that.

Great balls o' fire, stop this old fogey from thinkin' negative. Ain't never been afraid of nothin' in my life. But this storm—this storm's different. I don't like it.

CHAPTER FOURTEEN

Dawson looked out the huge window at the thick snow-swirl. Intensifying by the minute, the storm would deposit a solid snow base for their skiers. *I hope Kat changes her mind and stays at the boutique.*

Their guests sat around the fireplace, drinking cocktails, laughing and chatting, apparently unconcerned about the brewing storm. After all, snow was what they had come for. He rubbed his chin. Mother Nature was cooperating far beyond the call of duty.

"Dawson?" Clancy held the phone receiver over his head. "No dial tone, laddy. Methinks it's dead."

"Try the cell phone."

Clancy shook his head. Signals at the lodge were whimsical on good days. He'd doubted the phone would have any signal in this storm.

Weather forecasters had predicted the early storm would dump up to a foot of snow. What he was watching outside threatened to exceed the annual average of thirty-six inches in a matter of hours. He walked over to the desk. "Do we have any more guests due to arrive this evening?"

Clancy studied the reservation book. "Naw. Not till tomorrow afternoon."

Dawson cast a dubious glance out the window. "That may not happen."

"Soon as the phones're workin', I can call an' suggest they wait a day fer safety's sake. Maybe offer an extra day at the end o' their stay if we got the room or a coupon for a free day on their next visit."

"Great idea. Good PR, too. You're thinking, Clancy."

He liked that Irishman. The man was honest, and he was a good father. If anyone knew how to raise a child, it was Clancy O'Malley. Molly Anna displayed the manners of a proper young lady and was just as charming and flirty. She knew how to pout and show a bit of anger when she didn't get her way. But she also obeyed her father. When Clancy spoke, she listened.

"Maybe ye better not go out," Clancy said. "The weather's a wee rough out there. Yer welcome to stay with the lassie an' me—although I'm thinkin' she may be at yer place tonight since she's there with Joey and Jeddy now."

"Yeah, maybe. Turn up the radio. Let's see if we can get some news on the storm."

"Here's the latest advisory from the National Weather Service," the newscaster began. "The storm has intensified into a full-fledged blizzard. The police are asking everyone to stay in their homes. Streets and highways are unsafe for traveling, and many are closed. Mountain roads have also been closed. Stay tuned for the next advisory in . . ."

Clancy turned the volume down

"I guess that answers that," Dawson said. "But I've got to try to get back to Willow Walk. Can't leave Granddad alone with the kids."

"Isn't that lass Kat hired workin' today?"

"She is, but you know Granddad. He'll fight her on everything just for the sake of argument. She's wonderful with the kids and the house, and she's cooks almost as well as Kat. I can't let his cantankerousness drive her away."

Clancy nodded. "I understand, but I'm not feelin' good aboot yer leavin' until this storm calms down."

"I need to. I just hope Kat isn't trying to come home." He slipped into his jacket and ski hat and pulled his scarf tight around his neck.

Clancy shook his head. "Ye shouldn't be goin', but I might as well be whistling jigs to a milestone. Ye be careful out there, Dawson."

"Don't worry, Clancy. The worst of the storm is a while off yet. My four-wheel-drive should make it okay. See you later. Stay warm and keep the guests happy."

Dawson opened the door. A powerful gust pushed him backwards. Leaning into it, he stepped outside. His almost-knee-high boots disappeared in the snow. The wind sliced through his ski jacket and turned his bones into icicles. He fought his way to his new Chevy pickup. *Whoa, I don't know if I can make it to Willow Walk.*

He brushed the snow off the windows and headlights, turned the key in the ignition, slipped the gear into four-wheel-drive, and started toward home. The wipers labored to keep the driving snow from building up on the windshield as he inched his way downward. Just a little further . . .

The worst section of the road was coming up. "Dead Man's Curve," the locals called it, but now the worn-out cliché took on new meaning. If he could get past this section, he'd make the rest of the short drive with no problem. Wind whipped a wall of snow across the hood as he neared the old homestead. The jarring blast blinded him. He knew he was on the curve . . .

Too close to the edge . . . Steer to the left! To the left, to the . . .

The big truck spun and came to an abrupt stop. Where was he? How close was the drop-off? The truck teetered as something below the back wheels gave way. His heart pounded like a tom tom. He took a breath and reconnected with the small voice in his head.

"Don't panic. Not now. Be still. Be calm." *Yeah, right!*

If he could open the door easily without rocking the pickup, he could jump out. What if the movement was just enough to plunge the truck down the mountain—with him in it? Surely the density of the trees would stop it before it reached the bottom. *Comforting thought!* He wiped the cold sweat from his forehead with the back of his gloved hand.

What if another vehicle comes around the curve? Stop stalling and do something. Make a decision, man. Open the door.

His hand gripped the handle. The latch clicked. He pushed down in slow motion. The back of the truck sank deeper. Its headlights pointed upward.

Would he ever see Kat and Granddad and little Joey again? They needed him. Willow Walk needed him. His granddad's words from year's ago came softly at first, then louder until it boomed in his ears. *Never forget, Sonny, Willow Walk is your heritage. Willow Walk is your heritage. Willow Walk is . . .*

He nudged the door open. The front wheels of the truck left the ground as the vehicle rocked backward. He unlocked the seatbelt and jumped. The arm of his coat caught in the retracting belt. Jerking it loose, he dropped toward the ground. His foot slipped between the step bar and the truck chassis. His head smacked a rock beneath the snow.

"Ahhh . . . !"

His head felt woozy. He tried to raise his upper body so he could free his leg. The vice-like pain stopped him. Again, he tried to position his body to free himself. His leg below the knee felt like somebody'd slammed it with a ball bat. He bit his lip to keep from crying out.

My leg's broken. It won't move. Think, man. Get it together. Your life depends on it. Willow Walk's just down the hill.

Who am I kidding? I'm stuck here. It might as well be a thousand miles away.

CHAPTER FIFTEEN

The howling wind's eerie song continued to whistle through the cracks around the old four-paned windows. Snow and sleet pelted the house like a thousand BBs shot from a giant air rifle. Jedediah shuddered. *Dawson said he was leaving the lodge some time ago. What if . . . Don't think negative, old man.*

Dressed in warm sweaters and oblivious to the raging storm, Joey and Molly Anna busied themselves with their coloring books. A large box of crayons lay scattered on the floor.

"I want the red one." Molly glared at Joey, who was scribbling with the red crayon.

"Use the blue one."

"I don't *want* the blue one!" She sniffed.

"Okay. Here. Don't cry." Joey handed her the red crayon, picked out the yellow one, and began coloring again.

Hmmm, kindred spirits, these two. Kind of reminds me of Dawson and Kitten as young'uns.

Leaning on his cane, he tapped his way to the large window in the drawing room. Green velvet drapes edged with cream-colored fringe hung from the top of the tall window. The room had always been his favorite—and Emma's. Mahogany and Teak woods covered the walls. Ornate, hand-carved inlaid panels, placed symmetrically around the room, added a formality. Crowded bookshelves reaching to the ceiling housed a collection of rare books. He peered out the window. *Reminds me of pictures of the North Pole. Don't think I ever seen Wheeling lookin' like this.*

"Dang it. Where in blazes is Dawson?"

"Granddaddy! 'Memba what you tol' me? I'm gonna warsh your mouth out with soap if you say that naughty word again," Joey said.

He cleared his throat. "You're right, boy. I'm sorry."

Hiding a grin, he approached the massive brick fireplace, poked the fire, and added another log. Flames crackled and popped on their way up the chimney. Sitting on one of the matching leather wing chairs that flanked the fireplace, he watched the flames form images that came and went in an instant.

You know, Emma Baby, I wish you was here with me, sittin' on my lap like old times. I'm gettin' mighty tired. Don't wanna leave the young folks, but I'm thinkin' I may be joinin' you before long.

He picked up the book he was reading from the end table beside him. In the middle of the third chapter, his head nodded. His glasses slipped down on his nose.

A loud crash close by startled him awake. Molly Anna screamed, jumped up, and ran toward him. She bounded onto his lap and cuddled against him. He held her close for a moment. "Don't you fret none, Molly. Let Granddad see what's goin' on." He lifted her off his lap and pushed himself up.

Joey marched over to Molly and put his arm around her shoulder. "Don' you worry, Molly, Granddad and me'll take care of you."

Molly Anna's lips quivered. Then she gave Joey a beguiling grin and lowered her eyes.

"You kids stay right here. Don't follow me," Jedediah ordered.

The massive antique grandfather clock in one corner of the hall ticked away like there was no storm outside. Fresh flowers from Willow Walk's greenhouse filled the Sheffield silver vase that sat on the console table. Above it hung a copy of Monet's *Mother and Son* that Emma had purchased long ago. Rays from the front porch light filtered through the etched windows on either side of the double mahogany door, creating dancing specks of brightness that littered the Italian floor tiles. Emma's pride and joy—a hall tree with an umbrella stand—stood close to the door. Everything appeared intact. *Must've been somethin' that hit the door from outside.*

It would be foolhardy to venture out in the weather just to see what it was. Hercules couldn't budge those doors against the wind-driven snow, so what made him think he could? Joey came tearing into the hall. "I wanna see. I wanna see, Granddad," he hollered.

"Didn't I tell you whippersnappers to stay where you were? Now dad-blast it, get back in there, boy. Don't need no disobeyin' young'un nippin' at my heels."

"Oh, dang it, I will, but I don't wanna." Joey shrugged his shoulders and marched back where he came from.

Jedediah shook his head. "What'd you say, boy? Do I need to get that bar of soap?" Joey didn't answer. Maybe he didn't hear. *Yeah right. That boy' is gettin' so much like me it's plum scary.*

Molly Anna stood with her feet apart, hand on her hips, pointing a finger at Joey. "How many times do Granddaddy have to tell ya? You ain't—I mean—aren't s'posed to say 'dang.' You want your nose to grow long like Pokeoo's?"

"It's not Pokeoo's, Molly Anna. It's Pin-o-co." Joey shook his head.

"You kids'll drive me crazy yet." Joey and Molly Anna exchanged glances and snickered. "Now both of you get back to your colorin'. And it's not funny,"

"You've got a call, Mr. Kahill." Carla came in from the kitchen, a cell phone in her hand. Jed looked at it and shook his head.

"I ain't never talked on one of them dad-blamed things, and I ain't about to start tonight."

"I think you might want to make an exception just this once. It's Clancy. He wants to talk to you."

"Clancy," he shouted into the device. "When's that boy of mine comin' home? Supper's waitin'." She put the phone in his hand.

"Jeddy," Clancy said, "away with yerself. Dawson left a time ago."

"What d' you mean—*a time ago*? What time ago?"

"Forty-five minutes at least. He's not arrived yet?"

"Somethin' must of happened. Call 9-1-1 for me, would you, Clance? I don't know how to use these blasted cell things."

"Aye," Clancy said. "Neither chick nor child should be outdoors this day. 'Tis astray in the head, I say."

"Yeah. Okay, Clancy. Let me know if you hear anything." Jedediah hung up. He didn't move.

"What's wrong, Granddaddy?" Molly Anna tugged on his pant leg. "Your face is a funny color."

The pain in his chest traveled down his arm. "I'm just a mite tired, young'uns. Just a mite tired. Nothin' to get your pretty little heads in a dither about."

"My head ain't pretty, Granddadd. I'm a boy and boys' heads ain't pretty."

He didn't feel up to correcting the boy—or even laughing. He'd get after him later.

CHAPTER SIXTEEN

The wind calmed. Gusts of snow no longer pelted the house like a sand-blaster. Jedediah peeked out the window. The gently falling flakes painted a postcard-worthy picture in the beam of the outside light. It would have been a serene scene if he didn't know his grandson was lost somewhere in it. He paced pack and forth. His mind fogged at the thought of anything happening to Dawson.

"Carla!"

The woman hurried into the drawing room. "Yes, Mr. Kahill."

"Will you dial the sheriff for me? Those new-fangled cell phones and my old fingers just don't work together. And would you mind takin' the young'uns t' the kitchen for a bite of supper? I don't want them to hear me."

"I'll be glad to, Mr. Kahill. Alright, kids, who wants cookies and chocolate milk—as soon as they eat their soup?"

"Me! Me!" they said in unison, giggling and taking Carla's hands.

"But I only wan' a li'l soup," Joey added.

"Me, too," Molly Anna echoed.

Glad she's here today. Good for somethin' other than cookin' and cleanin', I guess. Jedediah's trembling hand managed to hold the cell phone to his ear. One ring. Two rings. He shifted from one foot to the other.

"Jedediah Kahill here," he sputtered when someone finally answered. "I'm wonderin' when the roads'll be cleared so we can get some help up here at Willow Walk."

"Plows have cleared the main road to your place and beyond. We won't get to the one to the lodge until tomorrow, I'm afraid, Mr. Kahill," a sweet voice replied.

"Well, Missy, my grandson left the lodge almost an hour ago, and it's less than a five minute drive. He hasn't arrived at Willow Walk yet. We need someone up here to find him—*now*."

"We'll get someone there as soon as we can, Mr. Kahill. We have a lot of folks needing help tonight."

"I'll thank you to hurry. I'm afraid somethin' terrible's happened."

"Yes, sir, as soon as possible."

Loud thuds on the heavy entry door pulled Jedediah from the tangle of his thoughts.

Joey ran in from the kitchen and tugged on his pant leg. "Granddaddy, hurry up. Maybe it's Mama." He grabbed the old man's hand and coaxed him to the entrance.

"I don't think so, boy. Mama has a key." Jedediah turned the dead bolt and pulled open the door. The wind had lost its fury, but the cold still rushed into the hall. Along with it came a snow-covered Clancy, Dawson draped across his shoulders like a newborn calf.

Dawson's gray face appeared lifeless. His limp arms hung down on one side, his legs on the other. Jedediah gasped. He wanted his grandson to be home, but not like this.

"Great balls of fire, Sonny. Here, let me help." Jedediah reached toward his grandson, but Clancy was already heading to the drawing room. "Bless Pete, man, if this ain't some development. What happened?"

"I'll be needin' some blankets, Jeddy. We need t' warm 'im up real quick."

Dawson mumbled something unrecognizable as Clancy laid him on the davenport.

"Carla, we need some blankets!" he hollered. Blinking back the tears, he turned to Clancy. "How'd you find him?"

"After talkin' t' ya, Jeddy, I knew something was amiss. I called Polly to mind the desk and headed on down here at a snail's pace, hopin' ta find a sign of Dawson. Didn't take long to locate his truck on Dead Man's Curve. Another few inches and it'd be over the mountain. As 'tis, it's teeterin' on two wheels, and the back bumper's lodged against a tree stump. Dawson was sprawled in the snow, not fittin' to mind mice at a crossroad, his leg caught in that runnin' board pipe. Close t' unconsciousness, he was."

Dawson groaned. "Get my—my truck."

"Soon as we can, m' boy." Clancy glanced at Dawson, then back at Jedediah. "Aye, his leg be broken and no tellin' what else. Ye better be callin' nine-one-one, Jeddy."

"Is my daddy gonna live?"

Jedediah turned to look at Joey's pale face and wide eyes that stared in horror at his father's shivering form. "Carla, come get this boy!"

She scurried into the room with an armful of quilts and blankets. "Let's go, Joey. Your daddy's going to be just fine." Molly Anna followed her like a shadow.

"I wanna stay with my daddy. I'm scared."

Jedediah patted Joey's head. "You and Molly Anna run back in the kitchen for them cookies and chocolate milk. Clancy and me, we're gonna help Daddy. He'll be fine, just like Carla said. Don't you worry none."

Molly Anna peeked out from behind Carla's skirt. "Uncle—Daw—I'll get a band-aid for you." She sniffed.

"You go on now, Molly. Those cookies are waitin'." Jedediah held the phone out to Clancy. "Will you dial it for me, Clance?" He tapped his cane on the floor while he waited for an answer. "I'm hopin' you folks are a mite more efficient than the sheriff that never got here," he sputtered when a voice picked up. "My grandson'd be dead if it weren't fer a friend who found him in the snow with a broken leg and who knows what else. So hurry up and get here. Our boy needs to get to the hospital, and quick." He repeated the location and hung up.

"Granddad, the—the truck . . . Gotta see what happened to—to my truck. Where's Kat?"

"Not now, Sonny. There'll be time enough for the truck when we get you fixed up—and Kat's got more sense than to take a chance on these roads. You ought to know that."

Clancy interrupted. "I'm thinkin' I should be bringin' ye a stiff brandy now. And one fer Dawson, too."

"I'm thinkin' you're right, Clance, but not for Dawson. And would you mind callin' Kat on this fandangled thing and let her know about his bein' hurt? She might be able to get to the hospital from the boutique easier than she could get home. Sonny needs her."

Dawson slept the drugged sleep of those who had been anesthetized. He had awakened enough in recovery for them to bring him to his room, but he was a long way from being able to carry on a conversation.

Jedediah sat beside his bed and watched him breathe. Both bones in his lower leg were broken. They would heal with time, but the damaged muscles and ligaments were another matter.

Alone with his thoughts, Jedediah closed his eyes. *I thank you, Father, that our boy's livin' an' breathin'. It's a miracle, seein' as what he went through out there in all that cold, his leg broke and him lyin' in the snow. But I do need your help to make Sonny understand his life may not be quite same because his leg could be givin' him some trouble from now on. And one more thing, Father, please be lookin' after Kitten. Clancy never got hold of her, and I'm hopin' nothin's wrong. Don't rightly think I can handle another tragedy. My old ticker don't seem to wanna work as good as it used to.*

CHAPTER SEVENTEEN

Another thirty minutes and I should be through here. Kat looked out at the worsening storm. Her all-wheel-drive minivan should make it to Willow Walk as long as the roads were open.

She'd been alone since noon. The impending storm had kept all but the bravest of shoppers at home, so Bonny and Deb had taken a well-deserved afternoon off. Deb had a date with Bill, her second one this week. Maybe they'd have a wedding soon. She smiled.

Bonny was going to check out the ski lodge. She hadn't seen it since it opened. Kat cast another look out the window. Well, *maybe* she'd check out the ski lodge. Or maybe she'd be staying the night there if she went up before the storm had escalated into a blizzard.

Turning from the window, she walked to the sitting area and from this vantage point scanned the boutique. Sweaters in beautiful jewel tones sat in neat piles on the shelves. Numerous racks held gowns, daywear, and casual separates, all categorized by size and color. Photographs of local models wearing this year's line graced the walls in an artful display.

The girls certainly knew what they were doing when they put this layout together. The accessories they brought in enhanced her lines. Scarves of various sizes and shapes, unique jewelry pieces, and an extraordinary assortment of handbags and exquisite hosiery often went out the door with happy shoppers who had found just the outfit they were looking for. She thanked the girls silently for their expertise and for friendships so special. The soft sound of water coming from the decorative fountain against the wall fixed her mind on another time and place.

For a brief period, she had imagined herself in love with Lincoln Wolf, owner of Wolf International Fashions. While she was working for him, her exquisite designs had been featured over those of all the other designers at the company. Why couldn't she have seen then what she knew now? Dawson tried to tell her that she didn't need Lincoln Wolf—that her designs would stand on their own—but she had worn blinders. Her infatuation, however, had come to an abrupt end when she learned there was also a *Mrs.* Lincoln Wolf.

Pulling herself out of her reverie, she crossed the kitchen to the back door and opened it. A rush of snow slapped her in the face. The drive home might not be quite as easy as she had thought, even in an all-wheel-drive vehicle. She glanced in the direction of Willow Walk. Heavy black clouds churned across the sky. If she were smart, she would spend the night at the boutique, or at least stay until the storm lifted. She pushed the door shut and brushed the snow off her face and blouse. The blow-up beds in the storage room off the kitchen were surprisingly comfortable. It would be the perfect time to catch up on some much needed spring designs.

Deep in thought about her new line, she started back toward her office. *Where's that draft coming from? I know I shut the door.* She ran her hands up and down her crossed arms and stopped. Someone was behind her. Whirling around, she stood face to face with the past. Her heart skipped a beat, then felt like it was suspended in her chest. For an instant, she thought it was going to explode.

"Randy Van Henkle! What are you doing here?"

He gave her a quick up-and-down look. "Hello, Katarina. You haven't changed a bit. You're as beautiful as ever." His raspy voice sent an icy chill down her spine. She couldn't move. Her mind screamed "run!" but her feet didn't obey. Where would she go?

Forcing back her fear of his greater size and strength, she felt her azure eyes light with sudden fire. "Get out of here! I told you years ago never to come near me again. Nothing has changed, *Rip*. I want to you leave this boutique . . . right now." She spit the words at him.

Her anger seemed to amuse him. A smirk crossed his face and he chuckled. "I'm not going anywhere, Katarina. We have some unfinished business about a game. We'll see who wins *this* time."

"Game? Ah, the one you threw for the sake of a few dollars? I still remember the lead article on the sport's page. 'Penn State quarterback Rip Van Henkle throws college football game.' I was stunned, couldn't believe it. But what has that got to do with me?"

"You, dear Katarina, were the *reason* I got caught. Tell me you don't remember what you did." His tone dared her to deny his charge.

"I don't know what you're talking about." She inched her way toward the telephone on the hallway wall.

"That night after the game, Coach Johnson called me aside and told me he knew I'd thrown the game. He said you had telephoned him and told him. You not only cost me my college career, but any chance I had at making it as a pro."

She felt his anger rise with each word. *How can I defuse this? The man is mad.* "Coach told you a bold-faced lie. I knew nothing about it. I remember your being expelled, but I didn't know why until I read it in the paper. I didn't turn you in, Randy. It *wasn't* me." Hot fear rose from her neck and beat about her face in waves.

"You knew, all right. I swore then I'd get even with you. I didn't know Bonny was in the dress shop the last time I was here. I assumed it was you."

"Why you no good . . ." Kat screamed. "You could have killed her."

His laughter echoed down the empty hallway. "I've spent years nurturing my plan to get even. Tonight I will carry it out." His laughter faded. "I didn't want to hurt Bonny. She's okay, isn't she? Everything about that morning is a fog. I barely remembered being here. But I know I'm here now. And I'm with you, not Bonny."

Had throwing the game so long ago warped his thinking this much? Had he been drunk? Was he drunk now?

The maniacal laughter began again. She started for the door. He stopped her with a restraining arm. She glared at him. He slammed his mouth down on hers.

She jerked her head to the right. "Let go of me!"

He grabbed her chin and pulled it back so that she faced him. Still laughing, he kissed her again.

He's crazy, a raving lunatic. But how do I get away from him? He pinned her hard against the wall. She took a breath and then another. Tears welled up in her eyes. "Rip, listen to me. Don't look back. What is done is done. Move on now. Please believe that it wasn't me who turned you in. I'd never hurt you or anyone that way."

He searched her eyes. Releasing her, he stepped backward toward the kitchen. She thought he was going to leave.

"Yeah, right. But you *did* hurt me, even if it wasn't you who told the coach I threw the game. I wasn't good enough for you. You put me in a small corner of your life and every now and then you turned around and smiled at me, but I wanted so much more. I hated you for that." His face contorted. She saw he had no intentions of leaving.

"But it had nothing to do with you. I wasn't looking for a relationship, Rip. I needed to focus on getting my degree. I was about to build my career, and my clothing designs came first with me. Had I been ready for a relationship, I would have dated you," she fibbed.

"That's an outright lie, and you know it." He drew in a sharp breath. "I wanted to be more than a football hero with all the senseless chicks clamoring after me. I wanted to be *your* hero. But you rejected me. I don't take well to rejection. I vowed you'd be sorry."

"Come on, Rip. You're far too intelligent to react like this. A good-looking guy like you can have almost any girl he wants."

"I didn't want *any* girl. I wanted *you*. I still want you." The softness of his voice belied the wildness in his eyes.

"I'm married now, so you can't have me. Not unless you force me, and I don't think you want to do that." *I hope the strength in my voice hides the fear in my heart.*

He came closer and pulled her toward him. Her gaze locked on his. She forced her best smile. "Rip, why don't you direct all that anger to something constructive? I know you can rise above it if you try. You proved your ability to beat the odds time and time again on the playing field."

He opened his mouth but didn't speak. His grip on her arms loosened, and he let her go. *Run, Kat, run! What's wrong here . . . I'm not going?* His soft moans told her he was crying. Now it was her turn to take his hand. He tried to pull it away, but she held on tight. He shook his head. She wouldn't let go.

"What am I doing, Katarina? I mean you no harm. Not then and not now. I love you too much to hurt you. I've always loved you. Yes, I vandalized your shop, and I came close to hurting Bonny. I want to pay for the damage I did to the boutique. Can you ever forgive me?" His demeanor changed drastically. "I need help, help you can't give me. Maybe . . ." He ceased talking as suddenly as he began and looked at her as though there was some question he needed to have answered.

She stared back at him, tear marks streaking her cheeks. "I know a good doctor, Rip, and a place you could go for counseling. Would you like me to get you the number?" She couldn't put her finger on why, but she had never wanted to help anyone more than she did Randy Van Henkle.

"I don't know. Maybe. Maybe not." He was as wide-eyed as a deer in a headlight.

"This isn't football, Rip. You don't get to pick sides, and you don't get to throw the game."

He walked toward the kitchen, then pivoted to face her. "Do you love your husband, Katarina?"

"Yes, Rip, I do. I love him very much. We have a little boy, and I'm very happy. I wish the same for you." She smiled a gentle smile, this time a genuine smile.

He nodded, his voice as soft as hers. "Here's my number." He handed her a business card. "Call me with the doctor's name and number, please. And I . . . I'm sorry, so very sorry."

Blinking, he turned and walked to the door, stepping lightly as a cat, despite his bulk. He turned to face her. "I didn't want to hurt you . . . I only wanted to love you."

He studied her again. This time she didn't feel afraid. She didn't know what word or look released it, but pity engulfed her. For the first time, she felt compassion for this man.

Should she tell Bill and Dawson and the girls? Would they understand her wanting to help the man who almost destroyed her boutique? No, to both questions.

Bill would want to bring him in for questioning, and no telling what Dawson would want. The girls would never understand. She didn't understand herself. But if Randy really wanted help, she'd give him the numbers he needed.

He opened the door. The storm had let up, and only a light snow was falling. He held her gaze one last time, then disappeared into the night. For a long moment, she stared into the emptiness where he had stood.

Shaking away the conflicting emotions of the last half hour, she grabbed her coat and purse and hurried toward her car. Her cell phone rang just as she got in.

"Kitten, it's Granddad. I been tryin' to reach you, girl, but you're not answerin' your cell phone. It's after midnight."

"Sorry, I . . . didn't hear it. What is it? What' s wrong? I can tell from your voice . . . is it Joey?"

"Joey's fine. But there's been a li'l accident. Dawson was hurt while drivin' home from the lodge. Come to the hospital, but don't break your neck gettin' here. He's gonna be fine."

"Tell me what happened. Are you sure he's okay?"

"Take my word for it. He's out of the woods now. I'll fill you in when you get here. Now you drive safe on them slick roads, you hear?"

"Yes, but . . ."

A dial tone hummed in her ear.

CHAPTER EIGHTEEN

Kat rushed into Dawson's room. Granddad leaned on his cane, his shoulders bent, staring out the window.

Her hand flew to her throat. "Where's Dawson?"

Jedediah turned toward her. Tears streamed down his cheeks. "They took him away, Kitten."

"Took him *where*?"

"There's a problem. Somethin' about the bone marrow gettin' in the blood and . . . and . . ."

"*Where is Dawson*, Granddad? *Where's* my husband?" For the first time in her life, she wanted to shake the old man.

"They was doin' them blood tests, an . . . somethin' ain't right."

She wanted to scream. Instead, she took a deep breath, let it out slowly, and took him by the arm. "Come and sit down, Granddad. Tell me what happened." She plopped down in the other chair.

"Aw, Kitten, I don't rightly know what happened. Those nurses, they come in at all hours and take blood and do all sorts of things. Well, they come flyin' in here about fifteen minutes ago and whisked Sonny outta here like there's no tomorrow. Said he was bleedin' somewhere and they's takin' him to ICU so they can watch him better. They sure was in a rush."

She tried to digest the information. Nothing was making any sense. "Who's his doctor, Granddad?"

"I don't remember his name, Kitten."

"Maybe I can help you." A large man in blue scrubs stood in the doorway. "I'm Dr. Jared Cassidy."

"I'm Katarina Kahill. Are you taking care of my husband?"

"Yeah, he's the one that's been checkin' on our boy," Granddad said in a stage whisper.

The physician came in and shook her hand. He sat down on the wide storage unit built in below the window.

"I just learned about my husband's accident and surgery. Can you fill me in on what's going on?"

"It seems he was driving home from the ski lodge when he lost control of his truck on a curve. When it skidded to a stop, he tried to jump out. His coat sleeve got tangled in the seat belt, and he dropped straight down. His leg slipped between the step bar and the truck body. He laid in the snow for quite a while before somebody from the lodge found him. He has a nasty break, considerable soft tissue damage, frostbite, and hypothermia."

"Oh, no." Tears spilled down Kat's cheeks.

"That's not quite all," Dr. Cassidy continued. "It wasn't a clean break, but we were able to put him back together. We put a steel rod in and repaired most of the muscle and ligament damage. With physical therapy and a lot of work on his part, he should be able to do almost anything he did before. However, we have another problem. The bone marrow that escaped from the break entered the blood stream and is causing bleeding in his lungs."

"*What!*"

"We've got him on IVs and oxygen, which should correct the situation. At least that's our hope."

"Your *hope*? You mean you're not sure?"

"There are no guarantees, Mrs. Kahill. I wish I could tell you that your husband will be fine—and I do think he will—but I can't say that for certain. He's young and he's strong. That's in his favor."

"Can I see him?"

"Come with me." He turned to Jedediah. "You, too, Mr. Kahill."

They followed the physician from the surgical wing to the intensive care unit.

"You say my grandson's gonna be okay, Doctor?" Jedediah asked as they walked.

"As far as we can tell at this point, yes. A lot depends on him. It's going to take work and determination for him to walk again."

"Don't sound like you're very sure of yourself, Doc."

"As I told Mrs. Kahill, we don't make guarantees. But I see no physical reason why he shouldn't be fine—once we get him past this immediate crisis."

"Huh." Jedediah frowned and turned to Kat. "Doctors make no guarantees? He might walk again or he might not? I'm not feelin' very good about this, Kitten."

Kat laid her hand on Jedediah's shoulder, "Granddad, they're doing all they can do. Now it's up to Dawson. You know how strong-willed he is."

"Yeah, I know. I think it's time I did some more prayin'. An' I take back what I said before. The feelin' in my bones is that we're *not* out of the woods on this one . . . maybe not for a while yet."

Visions of the young boy who pedaled his bike miles across the border from Mexico to Texas to get away from his father and a young Polly Dee, then bought a bus ticket to get home to West Virginia, filtered through his mind. He was a stubborn one, that Dawson. If he set his mind to something, his determination would make it happen. But if he didn't . . . *I won't think about that.*

The road from the highway to Willow Walk lifted the despair that had hung over Kat since Dawson's accident. She hoped coming home would have the same effect on him. Something needed to soothe the foul mood he seemed to have adopted.

Dawson sat stiffly on the middle seat of her van, his injured leg stretched out on the seat in front of him. She looked in the rearview mirror. He was staring at the toe-to-hip cast that limited his mobility to only those places he could go in a wheelchair or on crutches. No time that she had cast a glance at him had he been taking in the view through the bare willows and over the sweep of snow-covered fields. *This should be a day filled with laughter, Daw. We should be celebrating. You're alive. You're going home. I've got to do something to bring joy back into your eyes.* Her mind churned. *I know! The lodge.*

"Daw, let's drive by the lodge before going into the house. Clancy's really outdone himself this—"

"No!" he snapped. "Take me home."

His tone, icy as the winter wind that blew down from the mountain, ended her hopes of a happy homecoming. The celebration that Granddad and the children had planned wouldn't be well received.

She opened the front door and hesitated on the threshold before she wheeled him into the entrance hall where the family waited.

He turned his head toward the driveway. "Where the hell is my truck?"

Joey and Molly Anna scurried behind Granddad. Kat and Jedediah exchanged shocked glances. The Daw she'd known and adored all her life didn't curse. He'd been testy in the hospital, but she hoped all that would go away as soon as he came home to Willow Walk.

"Whoa, Sonny." Jedediah frowned. "Your truck's in the garage. You've been in the hospital for a couple of weeks, in case you forgot. We told you about your truck. Them medications must be playin' tricks with your mind—in more ways than one."

"I don't give a damn what you told me. I don't give a hoot about anything else. What good am I if I never walk again? Who's gonna take care of Kat and Joey and Willow Walk and the ski lodge? Who the hell will take care of —" Joey and Molly Anna peeked out from behind Granddad, their hands covering their mouths.

"There's no need for you to be spittin' the likes of those words to anyone around here. The only one sayin' you'll never walk again is *you*. I think that broken leg has affected your brain. And since when do you cuss, especially in front of the children?" Jedediah walked over to stand in front of Dawson. He softened his voice. "I think I know how you feel, boy, but you can't let this accident stop you from what you set out to do. The lodge's been your dream since you been in college. You gotta beat this, Sonny. You're a Kahill."

"Yeah, just like your son . . . my father . . . the infamous Cable Kahill. Now there's a real *prize* for you . . . and *he* was a Kahill through and through. So quit throwing the damn family name in my face. I'm a chip off the old block, as the saying goes, so get used to it." He ran his hand through his hair, giving it a shaggy, unkempt look that made his expression appear even more fierce.

Kat cast a warning glance at Jedediah. She hoped her eyes conveyed her thoughts. *I understand where you're going with this, Granddad, but let's give him a little breathing space.* What had happened to their lovable, levelheaded Dawson? Who was this belligerent stranger who was glaring at them from his wheelchair? Maybe the drugs and the painkillers had something to do with his bad attitude. *You can make all the excuses you want, my dear husband, but you will walk again. The doctor may not guarantee that, but I will. We will get our lives back. You wait and see.*

She touched his shoulder. He shrugged her hand away. "If you don't mind, Dawson, the kids want to see you. That is, if you can watch your language."

"Don't preach to me, Kat. I got the message. Let it go at that."

"Daddy! Daddy!" Joey hollered. He ran toward Dawson. "You gonna stay home now?" Before she could stop him, Joey jumped in his father's lap and wrapped his arms around his neck.

"Ow!" Dawson pushed Joey away. The boy fell to the floor.

"Come here, Son." Kat held her arms open and Joey ran to her with big horse tears in his eyes. "What's wrong with you, Dawson? Your son loves you. He wants to welcome you home. Fine welcome you gave *him*."

"Don't make a big thing of it, Kat. Remember the rod holding my leg together? He could have knocked it out of place, jumping on me like that."

"Through that thick cast you're wearing? I doubt it. Besides, the rod's screwed into place. The doctors said your leg would be as good as new, but they didn't say anything about your head. I guess they figured you'd work on that part yourself. So do it, Daw. You're not as fragile as you're making yourself out to be." She turned to Jedediah and was about to say something when she heard him whispering.

"Dear Father, do whatever you gotta do to make Dawson see what he's doin' to himself and all of us." He bowed his head. "Make him know he can walk if he wants to. Give him back his—his gumption. If I didn't know better I'd think he was glued to that blasted wheelchair. What I can't do, you can, Father, and he needs you bad. Meantime, help us all to have patience and understandin'."

"Amen," Kat whispered.

Jedediah reached out for Joey's hand and led both children toward the drawing room. "It ain't the screw in your *leg* that's loose, Sonny," he muttered as he passed Dawson.

Dawson shot him a look Kat had never seen before. Hostility would have been more acceptable. Bending close to his ear, she put her arms around him and whispered, "Don't deaden your heart to match the lifelessness I see in your eyes, Daw. Don't shut me out." She stepped back and let him wheel his chair into the drawing room reserved for guests. *Think about that, Daw. We've still got our whole lives ahead of us.* She went in to join the others.

"There's something more treacherous on the wind than that blizzard that just passed," Granddad said. "I can't make out what it is, but it's worryin' me a heap."

CHAPTER NINETEEN

Kat opened the drapes and looked out the bedroom window. A fresh carpet of white covered the winter ground. Tree limbs drooped with icicle tears that glistened like prisms in the rays of the rising sun. The frosty morning urged her to stay home, snuggled under a quilt in front of the fire

Frosty. That was the right word. It described perfectly the first night she'd spent in bed with her husband since his accident. She hadn't expected anything romantic, but neither had she expected that he would spurn her every attempt at conversation, comfort, touch.

She stopped by the bed on her way out of the room. "Can I help you get up, Daw? What would you like for breakfast? I want to fix you something before I leave."

"No thanks." He didn't look at her. "Close the drapes."

She didn't do it. "I'll call you later, Darling. Don't forget the physical therapist will be here at ten. I love you." She kissed his unresponsive lips.

Slipping out of the room, she checked on Joey, who was still sleeping, then greeted Carla in the kitchen. "Check on Dawson around eight, will you? The physical therapist will be here this morning, and he needs to clean up and eat." Carla nodded. "He's not in a very good mood these days, so please don't take his . . . testiness personally."

"Don't worry, Mrs. Kahill, I can handle anything he dishes hand out."

Kat sighed. "You're one better than me because I'm not doing that very well. I don't know the man who slept in my bed last night." She bundled up in a heavy jacket and gloves and headed for the boutique.

Bonny already had the coffee percolating when she arrived. Pouring herself a cup, she sank down at the table and helped herself to a Danish from the bakery box one of the girls had picked up on the way to work. She admitted to herself that she was thoroughly out of sorts—sad, mixed up, angry, so lonesome that she hurt.

The shrill ring of the phone broke her train of thought.

"Fashions by Kat. May I help you?"

"Katarina Kahill?"

"Yes."

"This is Rebecca Wolf. I don't know whether you remember me."

"Yes, of course I do. How are you, Rebecca?"

"I'm well, thank you. You've been on my mind for awhile. How are you doing, Katarina?"

"Fine. It's . . . uh . . . good to hear from you, Rebecca. How long has it been now?"

"Oh, my dear, much too long, I assure you."

"What are you doing now?"

"After Lincoln's funeral I pulled myself together and reorganized Wolf International. But the daily grind is proving a little too much for me . . . uh . . . alone. I'm sure you remember Lillian Rae, Lincoln's lead designer before he hired you. She's working with me now—as a model. It's a long story."

"I remember Lillian." Lincoln's mistress had attempted suicide after he left her in hopes of convincing Kat to take her place. She breathed deep. "How can I help you, Rebecca?"

"I . . . need to talk with you about something important—a dilemma if you will—but not over the phone. I wonder if we could meet somewhere and have lunch."

"Are you still in New York?"

"Yes, but I'm driving down your way in a few weeks. I have a meeting with some buyers in Charleston. I'll be staying over a night or two. We could meet then."

Kat frowned. Rebecca's call had taken her to a past she preferred to leave behind. "Call me when your time is more definite, and we'll have lunch. Come to the boutique if you wish. You remember the directions—or should I e-mail them to you?"

"Oh, yes. How could I ever forget?" Her quick answer brought another flood of best-forgotten memories. "I'll let you know when I can make time to drive from Charleston to Wheeling."

"Fine. I look forward to it. Goodbye, Rebecca."

"See you soon, Katarina."

Kat hung up the phone. Oh, yes, she remembered Rebecca Wolf. The first time they met, Rebecca had come from New York to Fashions by Kat—after hours. The woman's haggard appearance, from prescription drugs, she now knew, had been evident even under her wide-brimmed hat and artfully applied make-up. She'd selected a gown, had it fitted, given Kat a mailing address, and disappeared as mysteriously as she'd come. The possibility of seeing the woman again didn't bother her; the memories the visit would dredge up did. *What possible reason could Rebecca Wolf have for wanting to meet with me now? I guess I'll know soon enough—maybe too soon.*

Winter snows melted, and spring flowers peeked out of the ground in search of the sun. Trees wore new buds. Grassy fields exchanged dull winter coats for bright green ones. Robins showed off their beautiful rusty vests. Her new spring designs had come in, and the girls were busy stocking shelves and racks in anticipation of a wave of new customers. *Spring always makes me feel fresh and new. If only Dawson would get a new attitude, everything would be great. Granddad's right. He's a determined cuss. Trouble is, he's determined to be a paraplegic.*

Deb stepped into the office. "What's on your mind, Kat?"

"Same old, same old as the saying goes. It's Dawson. No matter what I do, he turns away from me. Joey wants to play with him, but he tells the child he's tired. He's even lost interest in the lodge. I don't know what we'd do if Clancy weren't here. That man's been a lifesaver."

"Bonny would agree with that. She and Clancy are becoming an item, you know." Deb grinned. "I never would've put those two together, but they're as compatible as French fries and catsup."

"Dawson and I used to be that way."

"Kat, I'm sorry. I didn't mean to make you feel bad."

"It's okay. I feel bad whether you say anything or not. Dawson used to have a dream. That lodge was years in the making, and now he doesn't even go there. He doesn't ask if it's making a profit, if we have reservations . . . nothing. I don't know how to get through to him, and it's tearing me up inside. We used to be so happy together, and now . . . now he's not a husband or a father. He's turned inside himself, and it's taking a terrible toll on all of us. He isn't even nice to Granddad. I never thought I'd see that happen. He almost reminds me of his father."

"He feels useless, Kat. He's found a safe spot—a comfort zone—where he can say 'I can't.' He doesn't have to be afraid of failing because he doesn't try. But he'll get better . . . you'll see. How's his therapy coming?"

"Therapy!" Her tone rose a full octave. He's been at it for weeks, but it's more of that *nothing*. He tells his therapist he's tired, or he feels too weak, or he has a headache—anything to get out of the session. The man can't make him do the exercises. Dawson doesn't *want* to get better. If he keeps that attitude, he'll never walk again. And he'll never be my husband again, not in any meaningful sense."

Deb walked over and gave her a hug. "Come on, Kat. One of you living in the doldrums is enough for the whole Kahill family. Besides, you have too many good things happening in your life to frustrate yourself with sulking. Now get to work on those sketches, my friend." A kiss on the cheek, a squeeze of Kat's shoulder, and Deb went back to the salon.

Rebecca Wolf waltzed into the boutique with the grace of a Strauss tune. Her fashionable white linen hat—its crown adorned with a tiny bouquet of silk flowers in shades of yellow and gold tied with a black organza ribbon above the brim—sat at a jaunty angle. It shaded her big bright green eyes, but not the cascades of butterscotch waves tumbling around her face and shoulders. She wore her gold silk shantung suit jacket unbuttoned to show a delicate black lace bodice. The tiny slubs in the silk caught shimmers of light as she moved. *Amazing*, Kat thought, *a little older maybe, but the woman is still stunning.*

"Rebecca, how good to see you again." She fixed a warm smile on her face and greeted her with a quick embrace.

"Yes, Katarina, it's been a long time. You look, well, just as I remember you." Rebecca removed her white kid gloves, glided to the settee, and sat down. She crossed her legs and smoothed a wrinkle from her skirt. Her eyes scanned the boutique in one swift movement of her head. "The new shop is even lovelier than the first one. I heard about the fire and the sad news of Dawson's wife."

I'm not going to open the door to the past by discussing Valorie with you. "You said you had a dilemma. Let's go into my office, and you can fill me in on your situation and how you think I can help you." Her gaze met Bonny's. "Will you please bring us some iced tea?"

Rebecca crossed her hands in her lap and moved her head slowly to gaze around the room. Kat was suddenly glad that she had decorated her office instead of making it a simple workspace as she had in the first shop.

"I see your sense of style doesn't stop with clothing design. Your office is bold, yet tasteful, with just the right hint of femininity. Burgundy leather chairs; dupioni drapes in shades of burgundy, beige, and soft blue; and that magnificent painting behind you."

Kat turned to view the jewel toned painting of Willow Walk. "This is my home." Other walls held framed drawings of her award-winning gowns.

Bonny entered, carrying a tray laden with a crystal pitcher of iced tea and two matching goblets.

"Thank you, Bonny." Kat smiled at her friend. "Rebecca, do you remember Bonny Woods, one of my partners?"

"Yes, I do. How are you, dear?" Without waiting for a response, she continued, "I'll be frank with you, Katarina." She blinked hard and stared at Kat. "No flowery come-ons. I want you to come to work for me."

"What?" She glanced up at Bonny, who was about to close the door. Her partner made a face behind Rebecca's back. Kat had to bite her tongue to keep from laughing.

"I know how you saved Wolf International years ago when Lincoln was in charge," Rebecca went on without missing a beat. "That pompous man thought he was God, but he had at least enough sense to know that his hand alone couldn't save the company." She paused and smiled. "That's when he hired you. Smart move. If I'd had the least bit of control, it might have happened sooner. But—well, you know the story."

Kat opened her mouth to speak, but Rebecca's cell phone rang, and she excused herself to take the call. Kat rose, walked to the window, and stared at her own reflection in the glass pane. *I think I know where this is heading, and I'm not sure I want to go there. On the other hand . . . does Dawson really need me? He hardly knows I exist. Maybe he'd snap out of his lethargy if I took a position outside of Wheeling for a while. What about Granddad and Joey? The expansion plans? Do I mention Dawson's accident? No, not now. Let me see what she has to offer. So much to consider.* She heard Rebecca end her call and walked back to her seat.

"I'm startled at your offer. Why me, and just what is it that you're proposing in the way of a position with Wolf?"

Rebecca took a sip of tea and scrutinized her. "Wolf International is in a bind. Lincoln had a keen eye for women in lots of ways. He found the most beautiful models to drape in our designs, and sometimes he . . ."

Her caustic smirk sent a chill through Kat.

"He employed the best designers, several of whom had designs on him. But the man was not the financial guru he thought he was. In fact, he left Wolf hanging on the edge of a fiscal cliff. The company needs a rope, a lifeline to pull itself back to the top of the mountain. I'm hoping you'll be that lifeline. If we can win the International Design Show this coming January, Wolf International will be back in the limelight. You have the talent. You have the experience. Your determination has been proven, and you've already pulled it off once." She took another sip and put the glass back on the tray. "I need you, Katarina. The future of Wolf depends on you."

She needed time to comprehend all she'd just heard. "Rebecca, would you like to continue this over lunch. I know a great little French bistro not far from here. We can talk there."

"That's a fabulous idea. I'm famished."

Over bowls of French onion soup the conversation continued. "The year you worked with Lincoln, you met Lillian Rae. She'd been a top designer for years. But she shared more than her artistic designs. I'm sure you're aware she also shared my husband's bed. He dumped her when you came along and put Wolf International back in the running." Raising an eyebrow, Rebecca hesitated. "You wouldn't have a problem working with her, would you?"

Kat met her steady gaze. *We had this discussion long ago. I assured you then there was no relationship between me and your husband. I'll not go there with you again.* "I've no problem with it. Neither her personal life nor Lincoln's has any bearing on this situation."

"I'm glad to hear that, Katarina. Lillian's designs have been exceptional ever since she came back to work for me. Right now, however, she's my top model—and a stunning one if I do say so. She's more valuable to me in that capacity, particularly if you agree to join my team. I'll just conclude by saying I need you desperately."

"There are a lot of good designers out there."

"Yes, but not many whose designs are as . . . elegantly whimsical as yours. Yes, that describes your style perfectly—elegant whimsy. You underestimate yourself, Katarina. You obviously don't know that you could write your own ticket at almost any design house in the world."

"I . . . uh . . . think that's a gross exaggeration, Rebecca."

"No, my dear, it isn't. But be that as it may, I believe you are the *only* one who can establish us as the leading couturier once again."

Kat wanted to answer right then, but Dawson's voice from the past rang in her ears. 'Be sure you know all the fine print before you commit to the contract.' *Cool it, Kat. Listen, show her you're interested, but don't make a commitment you may not want to keep.*

"The show will be in Paris in January," Rebecca continued. "You will be in charge of everything, including employees assigned to the show—with the exception of Lillian. I would like the two of you to work together.

Your salary from the last time would need adjusting—upward, of course. What do you think, Katarina?"

Kat ran her fingers through her hair. "The reason I'm so hesitant to say yes right now is because Dawson had an accident several months ago. He can't walk. My son is just four, and I've only recently returned to work full time. Deb and Bonny and I are in the midst of expansion plans and . . . tempting as your offer is, at this moment I can't give you a definite answer."

"I'm so sorry about your husband, Katarina. I do hope he'll recover soon. It must be awful for both of you." She hesitated. "We have time. We don't need to be in Paris until the end of September. You let me know as soon as you can."

Kat raised an eyebrow. "Be in Paris by the end of September for a January show? Why?"

"I'm moving my entire operation to Paris for six months, maybe longer. We'll see how it goes."

"I can't make a long-term commitment to work in Paris. My family's here. My home's here."

Rebecca gave her a long look. "I understand that. Perhaps we could . . . uh . . . work together contractually rather than your coming on as an employee. We'll need non-disclosure and non-competition clauses. My attorney could draw something up that works for both of us."

"Let me talk to my husband, Rebecca. He deserves to have a say in this. Also, I'd need to fly back to see my little boy. I can't leave him for almost half a year."

Rebecca nodded.

How can I pass this up? Dumb question. Three reasons: Dawson, Joey, and Granddad.

Spring slipped into summer with little change. Dawson remained in his wheelchair, no closer to walking than the day he came home from the hospital. His attitude, however, slid downhill like an avalanche. His perpetual frown painted a portrait of negativity.

Kat wanted to find a place where she could take shelter, a place where she could sort out her thoughts. She curled up on the porch swing and looked out over the valley.

Dawson had refused to discuss Rebecca's offer, just like he refused to discuss everything else. He didn't even look at her when she told her about the opportunity and how it could benefit them in the long run. She'd reached out to touch his hand, to find some connection between them. As always now, he pulled away. Did he find her somehow repulsive? They had no intimacy, no sharing, no communication. It was almost as though they were strangers rather than a man and woman who had pledged to love each other—for better or worse—for a lifetime.

I know the gravity of the situation for Rebecca and Wolf International. But what about my situation? Stop whining, Kat. Dawson's done enough of that for both of us for a lifetime. But he doesn't whine anymore. In fact, he says nothing. If I leave, will he think I'm abandoning him? Or will it be a wake-up call? Could it be the nudge he needs to see what he's doing to all of us? And what of Joey? Carla and Granddad could care for him, but with me gone, he'll have neither parent. Still, this could be the catalyst that would bring my family back together. I have to take that chance.

Confused tears crept from her heart and slid down her cheeks. She would miss Dawson and Joey and Granddad more than she had ever missed anybody, but it wouldn't be that long. And she could come back for some long weekends. The rest of the time she wouldn't have to look at Dawson in the wheelchair and know that he was slowly destroying them all because he had *chosen* to.

She went inside and dialed Rebecca's number. "If the offer's still open, I'll be delighted to do the show. However, I won't promise to work for Wolf after the show."

"Thank you, Katarina." She heard the relief in the woman's voice. "I'll have my attorney draw up an agreement and have it to you within the week."

Kat could almost see Rebecca's eyes fill with tears. She knew how much Wolf International meant to her. She had lost it once to her conniving husband; she didn't want to lose it again.

What am I doing? Can I produce a winning show again with my designs? I've laid my reputation on the line for a woman I barely know. Stop it, Kat. Second thoughts are for losers. I'm not a loser. Fashion has been my life since I had paper dolls as a little girl. This is just the grown-up version. Designing elegant clothing is what I've wanted to do all my life. How many get a second chance to win a major show? And I am going to win it.

Her mind was made up. Now all she had to do was convince her heart.

CHAPTER TWENTY

The night gathered up the day and tucked it away. Kat slipped into her warm velour robe, turned the bedspread and blanket down, and fluffed the pillows.

This would be another in a long string of lonely nights. Dawson never came to bed until he thought she was asleep. He never touched her or acknowledged her presence in the bed. It didn't have to be that way. But that's the way it was. *No more tears in front of you, Dawson Kahill, and no more trying to arouse you. As the saying goes, it takes two to tango, but only one of us is showing up on the dance floor.*

On the other side of the door, Dawson brooded in the master suite's sitting room. This same scene had replayed every night for months. She had to tell him her decision—tonight. But first she would go downstairs to say goodnight to Jedediah.

He sat on the porch swing, staring into the night and tapping his cane on the floorboards. She had to smile. "Don't mess with this here cane," he would say, "unless you want to get bonked on the head or swatted on the rear." Then he would break out in peals of laughter. Oh yes, that cane was more than a walking stick. It was his equalizer in times of adversity.

"Good evening, Granddad. You look mighty comfortable."

"No need not to be, Kitten. How you doin'? More to the point, how's our boy doin'?"

"He's still glued to that wheelchair, if that's what you mean."

"Mercy sakes, Kitten, I don't know what more to do. I don't think it's possible to wear out your welcome with the prayin', but if it is, I've done it."

"Oh, Granddad, he's so pitiful. I don't know him anymore."

He frowned at her, then wrapped his arm around her shoulder. "Don't ever give up on your man. Remember he's a Kahill. He'll come around. Ya still love 'im, don'cha?"

"Of course I love him; I just don't like him. I want the man I married to come back. That's all I ask for, Granddad." She laid her head on his shoulder and wept. The tears emptied her heart, spilled over her cheeks, and came to rest on Granddad's shoulder.

Finally, when there were no tears left, she wiped her eyes with the back of her robe sleeve and sat up. "Do you remember Rebecca Wolf, Lincoln Wolf's wife?"

"Sure do. He drugged her and committed her to a cotton-pickin' mental hospital. Then that good-for-nothin' rascal shoved papers under her nose and made her sign them. There went everything she owned: Winslow House, Wolf International Fashions, and you name it. Oh yes, he did leave her a toothbrush and underwear. Mighty big of him, wouldn't you say?"

She managed a grin at his desparaging description of Lincoln Wolf's treachery. "Right. But she got it all back when Lincoln died." Kat shifted positions on the swing. "I saw her a while back. She wants me to do some work for Wolf International." Kat pursed her lips. "It means working in Paris for a while. I agreed to go, Granddad."

"Well, girly, I reckon you didn't need any help makin' up your mind."

"It will be hard to leave all of you, but I won't be gone too long—four or five months at the most. And I'll come home for some long weekends. Joey has a great time with Molly Anna, and Dawson won't even know I'm gone."

She shook her head and sighed.

Granddad leaned one hand on his cane. "If you want my opinion, Kitten, I'm not so sure it's the right thing to do. Too many people here depend on you." He ran his hand through his beard and wiggled his nose to stop the hair from tickling him. "Then again, maybe that's a good reason to get away from here. Could be the perfect solution to a very perplexing problem."

This time happy tears surfaced. "Thanks, Granddad, I knew I could count on you. I'll fly home for quick visits whenever I can."

"It's about time Dawson stood up and took notice. Maybe your bein' gone will bring the boy around. I imagine when he hears about yer leavin', Willow Walk's roof will go sailing across the countryside like a tornado hit it."

"I doubt that. He doesn't seem to notice that I'm even here."

Jedediah's frown deepened at her sad words. "When are you leaving, Kitten?"

"The shows in January. Rebecca wants me there no later than the end of September, sooner if possible. I need to create a whole new line of designs, and we need to agree on them, as well as on fabrics, staging, and a host of other details. I thought I'd leave as soon as everything's in order here and at the boutique. I know Deb and Bonny can handle things at the shop, and I have my winter and spring designs finished already. Clancy, Polly, and Cabe have done well at the lodge since it opened, and since Darrell closed up the inn in Mexico and joined them, they seem able to handle anything that comes up. My biggest concern is here. Can you and Carla handle both the children?"

"You think I'm too old to take care of my own?" His offended expression almost pulled another smile out of her. "As for Carla, she's proved herself a good cook and housekeeper, and she don't interfere none when it comes to Joey and Molly Anna. We . . . uh . . . came to terms, you might say."

She was afraid to ask what that meant. "I'll need to hire someone to look after Dawson. He's—"

"Just hold them horses a minute, Kitten. Might be that Dawson'll get better if there's nobody here to help him."

Questions scampered through her mind, but the answers were slower in coming. She stared at the old man. "I hadn't thought of that, but you're right. It would force him to do for himself. No one to bathe him or bring meals to his room might make him do something more than sit. No one to do the little things we know he can do for himself, but he won't. It'll be tough here for a while because he won't be happy."

"Kitten, he ain't happy now, and we all suffer for it. Sometimes fixes are painful, but if they work, the pain was a good thing."

"Oh Granddad, it's so nice to be able to share everything with you. It should be Dawson I'm talking to about this, but . . . "I'm going to tell him now." She kissed his cheek. "Thanks for being here for me."

"What are you talkin' about, Kitten? I'm always here for you. You couldn't get rid of this old geezer if you tried."

"I know that, and you can be sure I'm not trying." She laughed and stood up. "Good night, my favorite Granddad."

"Good grief, girly, I'm your *only* granddad." He laughed and blew her a kiss.

She hurried inside so he wouldn't see the tears in her eyes. His kiss reminded her of the butterfly kisses she and Dawson had exchanged as children.

Standing in the doorway, she watched Dawson. He sat in the same spot, still staring out the window. *I guess there's no time like the present to tell him my plans. He'll either blow a gasket or he won't give a darn.* She couldn't predict his moods anymore.

She felt a twinge of dread. Dawson hadn't responded when she told him of Rebecca's offer. How would he react when he learned she'd accepted it?

"Hey, Daw," she said, strolling into the room. "Would you like a back rub? I'm pretty good with them, you know." She winked and tried to keep her tone light and humorous.

He gave her a coldly polite smile. "I don't want anything you or anyone else has to give. You don't know what it's like to be in my shoes. Neither does Granddad. All you ever say is, 'You can walk if you want to.' I've heard it a million times, Katarina. Is your vocabulary so limited you can't find anything else to say? So don't bother saying it again. Just go on your way and leave me alone."

She winced. He never called her 'Katarina.' "Honey, listen." She sat down in the chair beside him, placed her hand on his, and leaned forward. "You have a huge hurdle, but it's not insurmountable. We're all here to help you, but you shut us out. You can do it. I know you can. You're a Kahill."

"I've heard that enough times too." His angry words lashed out at her.

"Maybe it bears repeating."

"No! You don't know how it is. Nowhere near it." He turned his head from her. "And don't ever call me a Kahill again."

"It's who you are, Dawson. You can't change that. But you *can* change your morose attitude toward life in general and your family in particular. And thank you for finally being open with me about how you feel." She grimaced at the bitterness in her own words. Tears stung her eyes. She blinked them away.

"I disown the name. Now just leave me the devil alone."

She stood and looked at him. Anger rose in her chest. It forced out any remnants of sympathy she had left.

He laughed at her expression and pulled his callused hand away so violently that she fell back into her chair. She blinked hard. He had never talked to her like that before.

"What in the world is wrong with you? Why are you acting like this? It's so out of character. I'm sorry to have to say it this way, but there's not a damned thing wrong with your leg, Dawson. You're a cripple because you want to be." She pointed her finger at him. "You were a stronger person when you were twelve years old. You didn't need babying then, but you sure expect it now. I'm sick and tired of it. So is Granddad." She stood and paced in front of him. "We all love you, but you don't care about that either. You've neglected us all, as well as the lodge." She stopped and glared at him. He diverted his eyes away from her. "Do you think you're the only person in the world with a rod in his leg? At least you still have your leg. You blame everyone else for your misery. It's never you. If it isn't me, it's Granddad. If it isn't the hospital, it's the physical therapist. If it isn't the physical therapist it's . . . oh, never mind. Your misery is self-inflected, Dawson Kahill. Get off your backside and act like the man you used to be."

She wiped her eyes. Her heart pounded. She felt like vomiting, but she swallowed hard and continued. "You're defeating yourself, but I won't stay around and watch. I will not allow you to drag me down with you."

They stared at each other in cold silence for several moments. She tried to soften her words. "I try to understand how you feel, but I can't reach you, no matter how much I try."

He lowered his gaze. His jaw stiffened.

She walked to the other side of the room and turned to look at him. "I've taken a job with Rebecca Wolf. She wants me to orchestrate the January Fashion Show for Wolf International. It will be in Paris this year. I'm excited about the opportunity to get my fashions out again on the world stage." She hesitated. "I need you to be happy for me."

Yeah right. Happiness wasn't something he allowed in his life anymore. If looks could kill she'd be dead. His gaze locked onto hers and held it fast. His incredulous expression took her by surprise.

"If you go, Kat, don't bother to come back. We went down this road once before with Lincoln and his company. I warned you then about the fashion industry being corrupt, but you didn't listen. And that slime ball, Lincoln Wolf, hurt you. My mind hasn't changed."

"Good grief, Dawson, you've got it upside down. The *man* hurt me, *not* the industry. You even supported me, or have you forgotten? Fashion's what I know, what I trained for. It's my career." She lowered her tone. Her hands shook. "Dawson, it's what I love most after you and Joey and Granddad. Joey will do fine without me for a little while, and I'll be making regular trips home during the few months I'm gone. You don't need me. Your actions tell me every day that you don't even want me around. I need to be needed. I need something productive, and I'm going to do this."

"The boutique is not enough for you? Willow Walk is not enough for you? Joey is not enough for you? What more do you need to be productive? I should think that would be plenty to keep anyone busy."

She rose and walked to the window across the room. "I can tell you what I think, or I can tell you what you think I should think. Which shall it be?"

"Forget it, Kat. Don't worry about me. I'll get along. I may still be breathing, but I've been dead since the accident. So leave it that way. And leave *me* alone. I don't need you or anyone else. And I don't give a damn where you go or what you do or who you do it with."

She whirled around to face him. "I may share your name, Dawson Kahill, but I don't share your views."

"If my name makes you ashamed, leave it here when you walk out that door. Just don't ever come back for it."

She tried not to believe what she had just heard.

"Please, don't make this harder than it is. I'm already having nightmares about leaving Joey."

When had he had become so self-absorbed? When had the love and marriage they both treasured become of no value to him? Other people had accidents a lot worse than his, and their lives didn't fall apart. Why did Dawson's?

"I wasn't going to, but I think I'll hire a nurse for you since you're hell-bent on being helpless."

His eyes looked as though they would pop out of his head. "The hell, you say! I'll not have a nurse in this house. You leave me helpless and expect some stranger to take care of me? This is the Kahill house. *I'm* the boss here. How *dare* you even think you can do that?"

"Dawson!" she screamed and threw her hands up in front of him. Her palm itched with the desire to slap him. She could almost hear the sound the slap would make, exploding against his jowl. "What a hypocrite you've become!" He turned his head away from her, but she flew in his face. "You said you were dead, so what does it matter? And you disowned the Kahill name, so Willow Walk is no longer your concern, right?"

"I'm still the head of this household and I'll tell you one last time, there will be no nurse in this house."

She glowered at him for a long moment. Then she turned and walked out without looking back. He could sit in front of that window forever if that's what he chose to do.

If he wants things to be different, he'll have to make the first move.

CHAPTER TWENTY-ONE

The Boeing 747 split the clouds and climbed gracefully sunward. Kat leaned back in her seat, one ear tuned to the sound of the engines that kept the mammoth plane aloft. She gazed out the window. A slow smile crossed her face. Paris, France. Never in her wildest dreams had she imagined going to Paris.

She still worried about leaving Joey and Granddad at Willow Walk. She couldn't bring them with her, but she would miss them terribly. Leaving Dawson, on the other hand, may have been the best thing she'd done in a long time—and not just for his sake.

I'm sorry, Daw, but you don't seem to care about the lodge, your son, Willow Walk, Granddad, yourself—even me. Maybe time and distance will heal the rift between us. If it doesn't, I'm so afraid our marriage is over. You've lost your zest for life, your spark, but I haven't. When this plane took off and I looked down at the disappearing landscape, I felt a rush of adrenalin, an invigoration I hadn't experienced since your accident. I won't let you kill my joy, Daw . . . not now, not ever. And I won't let you kill Joey's.

Rebecca stood, waving, as Kat walked toward her. She looked as though she'd stepped out of a recent issue of *Vogue*. With her wide-brimmed black hat dipped over one eye and enough sensuality to turn almost any man's head, she could have doubled for Ingrid Bergman in the plane scene in *Casablanca*. The woman fit into the fashion world like it had been designed for her. Kat smiled. This new venture could once again connect her with the rich and the famous, the elite of the lot.

Can I do this again? I did it once—an unknown competing with the leaders of the fashion industry and beating them at their own game. A lot has happened since then . . . Don't doubt yourself. Don't be like Dawson. Oh, stop it! I know what I have to do, and I can do it.

She knew what lay ahead. Hundreds of sketches tucked in her briefcase had been destined to celebrate her boutique expansion, but they were needed now. And the new ones she'd committed to paper in the last few weeks still excited her. Were they good enough to catch the eyes of the judges? *Yes, I think so . . . because there's nothing like them out there.* Rebecca wanted classic Katarina—*elegant whimsy,* she had dubbed her style. Well, she wouldn't be disappointed. Kat had brought exactly that, trendy fashions that would form a collection so powerful it would propel Wolf International back onto the pinnacle of the industry.

"You do realize that in this show, fashions can be bought right off the runway?" Rebecca asked in the taxi on their way to Kat's new home away from home.

"Hmmm . . . I didn't know."

"Yes, my dear. Representatives from the fashion houses will take orders on the spot. Boutique and specialty fashion buyers, socialites, and corporate sponsors will also grace us with their presence. It's an exciting time."

"Oh, I remember the excitement. It's not a bell you can stop ringing once it's started."

"Well put." Rebecca straightened her shoulders and looked at Kat. "I hope you'll like the studio I've rented for you. The view of the Seine River is breathtaking."

"If you chose it, I can't imagine that it will be any less than perfect."

They passed boutiques, landmarks, and the most important business centers. Kat gazed out the window, taking in the sites she'd heard about but never dreamed she'd be seeing in person.

"Breathtaking, indeed," she whispered.

"Wait until one of those gorgeous suave Frenchmen gives you the eye." Rebecca raised an eyebrow and smiled. "Oh, sorry, you have a darling at home."

"He's not so darling at present."

"What's wrong, Katarina? You didn't tell me much about Dawson's accident."

"He's given up, Rebecca. The doctors told him that physical therapy was all he needed to walk again. They say now his problem is psychological, but he doesn't believe them. He blames everyone and everything for his accident, and I'm supposed to throw my life away, waiting for him to buck up and be the man I married. How do you find a silver lining in that?"

"You don't, Sweetheart. You detach yourself from his denial, and you don't go to his pity party. But you don't give up on him either. Carry on with your life. And when the day comes for you two to reconnect, you'll have nothing to be sorry for. Time takes care of everything." She took Kat's hand and laughed. "Listen to me. Giving you advice when for so many years I couldn't do just what I'm telling you to do."

"But you're so right, Rebecca. I'll tell you all about it later. Right now I want to know where the Wolf International office is located. I have so much to show you." Her head overflowed with dazzling ideas just waiting to embellish her sketchpads.

Rebecca smoothed a loose strand of butterscotch hair from the side of her face. "Not today. You've been traveling for hours, and I want you rested for tomorrow. That's when we begin in earnest to get down to business. I'll order a limo for us in the morning. The crew has everything ready. We'll have plenty of room to work—and Lillian is dying to see you again."

"Sounds good. What about the catwalk for the show?" Kat persisted.

"Whoa! Slow down, darling. I'll show you everything soon. First you need a nap. Then you can freshen up for dinner."

"I'm just so excited. I can't wait to get started. And I can't wait to see all of Paris." She felt like a little kid pressing her nose against the window of a candy store.

Rebecca raised her eyebrows. "All in due time, my dear, all in due time."

At times Rebecca seems much older than me, but she's only five years my senior. She knew all too well the life Rebecca had led with Lincoln. He was as corrupt and evil as he was drop-dead gorgeous. She shuddered. *I came so close . . . too close . . . I'd never have forgiven myself if I'd gotten physically involved with that man and then found out that Rebecca was his wife . . . Forget it, Kat. It didn't happen. You don't have anything to regret. But you do have a wonderful memory of being the dark horse who won the race and catapulted Wolf International back into first place in the world of fashion.*

The taxi stopped at the enchanting entrance of the Maison St. Pierre Hotel and Apartments. The opulent lobby took her breath away as they entered the most magnificent building she'd ever stepped foot into. Ornate columns of marble and gold led the way to the front desk. Magnificent urns held sprays of roses, tulips, delphinium, and stems she'd never seen. Brocaded drapes and furnishings complemented the paintings that graced its walls. Matching Aubusson rugs of various sizes protected the marble floors in high-traffic areas.

"Oh, my goodness." Her voice was barely above a whisper. "I've never seen anything like this."

With one perfectly plucked raised eyebrow, Rebecca gave her a look. "I'm so happy you like it, Katarina."

"What's not to like? I'm not sure I'll be able to get any work done for bathing in all this luxury."

Rebecca laughed. "Wait till you see your studio."

"If it's anything like this lobby, I'll never want to leave it." Kat laughed as she signed the register. Luggage in hand, the bellboys led them into the elevator.

The numbers climbed—four, five, six, seven. The door opened. They stepped out onto the rich wine-colored wool carpet. *This place screams elegance, glamour, romance.* "I'm trying to curb my excitement, Rebecca, but it's not easy. Maison St. Pierre is outrageously gorgeous."

"Yes it is. It was built in 1835, and much of the original decor has been preserved. The paintings were hidden in a vault under the floor when the German army approached the city in 1940, and prints were hurriedly hung in their place. Apparently, the Nazis were none the wiser because they never found the originals. The whole place is quite a work of art, don't you agree?"

"Oh, yes, I do." *Get hold of yourself, Kat. You're acting like a country bumpkin.* "Is your studio close?"

She turned the key in the lock and entered a foyer of dark wood, ornate detailing, a dado with gold leaf wallpaper above and a gold gilded mirror atop a mahogany credenza. Luscious, grand, luxurious, magnificent—the placed reeked of all that and more.

"I'm just across the hall in seven-oh-two. The apartment's very similar to this one and quite comfortable. Why don't you unpack, take a warm bath, and sleep for two or three hours? Shall we have dinner around eight?"

"That sounds perfect."

"I'll see you then. And thank you for coming, Katarina."

"Thank *you* for the opportunity."

"Don't mention it, Sweetheart. Your winning the show will repay us many times over." She stepped into the corridor and closed the door behind her.

I just hope I don't let you down.

Kat walked to the living room window and looked out over the city. The maze of streets below beckoned her. *I can't wait to go exploring. Some of the best cheese and wine shops in Paris are on those streets, I bet, not to mention the boutiques, sidewalk cafes, and restaurants. Enjoy it, Kat. You may never have another chance to leave your mark on Paris.*

A hand-carved grandfather clock chimed the hour. She guessed the old mahogany timepiece to be thirty or forty years older than the one in the foyer at Willow Walk. Ornate crown molding and identical trim around the large arched double-paned windows depicted a bygone era.

The fully equipped kitchen was a cook's delight—and a subtle but definite departure from the nineteenth century atmosphere of the apartment. However, the cabinetry's ornate carvings complemented that of the crown moldings, and the decor in general reflected that time period. She opened one of the doors and pulled out a plate. The reproduction of an old Haviland bone china pattern was distinguishable only by the absence of the marks on its bottom.

A basket of fruit rested on the marble countertop next to a bottle of wine nestled in a sterling silver bucket of ice. She read the label on the bottle—Dom Perignon—opened it, poured a glass, and sipped while exploring the studio. The ambience, the furnishings, all the décor transported her to another time when life was simple and elegance ruled. The gas-log fireplace in the living room invited her to slump in an overstuffed chair, one of two sitting on either side of it. She laid her head against its back and allowed the wine and warmth to wrap her in their embrace. Gazing at the aged wood beams on the ceiling, she let her mind wander home to Willow Walk. Already she missed her family. She had promised to let Granddad know when she arrived.

"I here," she said when Jedediah answered. Fatigue from the long trip and inevitable jetlag dampened the enthusiasm in her tone. "How's everything at home?"

"Nothin's changed, Kitten. Dawson's still sittin' just like you left him—twiddlin' his thumbs."

"I didn't expect his attitude to get better, Granddad. It's too soon to talk to him, but tell him hello for me and I—I love him. And Joey and Molly Anna too. Give them a hug and kiss for me. I need to get some sleep. Tell Joey I'll talk to him tomorrow."

"I'll do it. Have a good time. Don't work too hard. Maybe I'll have better news about Dawson soon. Let this old man know what's going on in your world across the ocean. I miss you, Kitten. And I love you."

Tears spilled down her cheeks as she replaced the receiver. Where was the man she used to know who would have been on the phone first to say "I love you"? He had always been like a lamp sitting on a sill, shining and pointing the way for her to go. Words couldn't describe how much she missed what used to be, most of all the intimacy they had shared over the years.

She couldn't think about it anymore. Pushing herself out of the chair, she rinsed her empty wine glass and headed for the bedroom. The nap Rebecca had suggested would make her feel better—and let her forget, at least for a little while.

She took off her traveling suit and hung it in the closet. Pulling a long robe out of her suitcase, she shrugged into it and snuggled into the soft comforter. With the time difference, she knew Joey would be awake. Her eyes filled again at the thought of someone else reading him a nursery rhyme before he went to sleep every night. She wouldn't be there when he woke up, but Granddad would and so would Carla. Months ago, Joey had quit asking his father for anything.

She stretched out and closed her eyes. The Dawson she had married flitted through her mind as she drifted toward sleep. The outline of his mouth. The sweep from his shoulders to his hips. His arms reaching out for her. They were so good together . . . She remembered . . . she remembered . . .

She remembered.

CHAPTER TWENTY-TWO

Streaks of the rising sun slanted through the high east window. Dawson squirmed in the wheelchair and looked in the mirror. One side of his robe hung off his shoulder. He jerked it back up where it belonged and stared at his reflection.

"Who are you?" The disdain in his voice shocked him.

The man in the mirror stared back. *What do you mean, who am I? I'm you, you stubborn fool.*

He shook his head. The eyes looked vaguely familiar, but that shaggy beard and stringy hair didn't remind him of anybody he knew. His sandy brows drew down in a scowl.

"Dawson Kahill, is that you?"

The reflection in the mirror didn't respond.

He rubbed the back of his head with his hand and turned his chair away.

That's right, Mr. DoNothing, run away like you always do. You put me in this chair and turned me into an invalid when all I had was a broken leg.

He wheeled the chair around to face the mirror again. "Hey! Don't talk to me like that. You don't know what I'm feeling."

I beg to differ, DoNothing. I know exactly what you're feeling. I'm glued to this chair with you, remember? I'm an invalid because you're an invalid, but it seems I like it a whole lot less than you do.

"Are you implying that I like my life the way it is?"

Who's the person here who's been sitting around in a wheelchair for almost a year, letting other people take care of his responsibilities? Who doesn't even have the good grace to say thank you to everybody who waits on him day and night?

"I don't like you."

"That makes us even. I don't like you either."

"How dare you—"

You don't get it, do you? You're a jerk, Kahill. Oh, pardon me. You disowned that name, didn't you? We'll go back to DoNothing. It fits you better anyway. So, DoNothing, you know the lodge needs your attention, but here you sit. That sweet little boy of yours is growing up without his dad, but here you sit. Willow Walk could be going to pot, and here you'd sit. And then there's Granddad. Have you taken a look at that old man lately? The strain of your self-willed disability is killing him. And here you sit.

"Joey doesn't come to see me anymore. And Granddad would rather be in the swing than talk to me."

I wonder why. You really are dense, aren't you? Who do you think is to blame for the way they are with you? How many times did you push your son away before he quit coming to you? How often did Granddad try to start conversations and you ignored him or answered with a grunt? And what about Kat?

Dawson winced as though the question had pierced his flesh. "She left me."

In the conversation I heard, you told her if she accepted that wonderful opportunity to show her designs in Paris and make a name for herself again in the fashion world, she needn't bother to come back.

"She knows I didn't mean that."

Does she now? Just how is it she knows? Is it by the loving way you've responded to her tender care ever since your accident?

"Uh . . . um . . ."

Uh, what?

Tears welled up in his eyes. "She's gone."

And you told her not to come back.

"I know Kat. She'll come home to Joey and Granddad."

Is that so? You ran her off with your simpering, whimpering 'poor me' routine, and you think she'll hurry back for more of it? Get a clue, DoNothing. I don't know where your head's at, but I love that lady who just flew off to France. Why don't you just admit this is all your fault and get her back here?

He glared at his reflection in the mirror. "Oh, yeah? My apologies if I don't share you opinion about that." He watched the man's mouth move, spewing out words he didn't want to hear, but he couldn't turn away or shut them out.

Forget walking, Iron Leg . . . excuse me, DoNothing. You might as well sweep sand off a beach. Besides, what do doctors know about fixing broken legs? You're so much more knowledgeable than they are, after all. They said you'd be almost as good as new with a little physical therapy, but hell, it's not their leg and their pain we're talking about, is it?

"Shut up. My life's in the toilet."

So I guess you'd better hope somebody doesn't come along and flush it. C'mon, DoNothing, if that's where your life is, you jumped in all by yourself. You've got it made. You don't have to work. All you do is watch TV, drink, eat, and ring for your servants with that bell that's attached to your throne.

"You make it sound like a choice. I'm an invalid. I can't walk."

Can't walk or won't walk? Let me see now, how long has that cast been off? You're the voice of doom, DoNothing. You could walk if you wanted to, but you're too damn stubborn to try. Take a real good look at me . . . at us. Not a pretty picture, are we?

He sniffed hard. "You think I don't want to walk? I can't!"

Cut the crap! Sure, rehab's tough, but there was once a man named Dawson Kahill who would've met that challenge head-on and whipped it in no time. But you, gutless wonder, have been running from it since day one. Oh, excuse me, rolling from it.

"That's not true! Nothing you say is true."

Boy, you're some piece of work. I'm tired of your bellyaching. If you wanna stay in that chair, go ahead. I'm done with you. Good-bye, DoNothing. Don't call me, and I won't call you.

He glowered at the mirror in silence. How dare that . . . image . . . say he didn't want to walk? What did it know? He did want to walk . . . more than anything else in the world, he wanted to walk. Tears streamed down his face and disappeared in his scruffy beard. *What's wrong with me? I've chased my family away . . . my granddad, my son, my Kat . . . my darling Kat. I sound just like my father . . . like my father . . . like my . . . Oh, no! Oh, God, please no!"*

He put his hands on the arms of the wheelchair and pushed himself upward. His leg shook with pain. His head throbbed. The room began to spin. He reached forward and picked up the electric razor from the table in front of him. Raising his arm, he hurled it at the mirror.

He and the glass hit the floor at the same time.

"Granddad. Granddad!"

He could hear the old man coming down the hallway, feet shuffling and cane tapping.

"What is it, Sonny? What's wrong, boy?" Jedediah's knees creaked audibly as he knelt at his grandson's side.

Dawson forced his eyes open. The room had stopped spinning.

"Granddad, please help me."

CHAPTER TWENTY-THREE

Kat stood and stretched. She poured a cup of coffee from the coffee maker near the bar sink and walked over to a window that looked out on the sidewalk cafe below.

"Ready for lunch?" Rebecca stood at the drawing board and nodded her approval. "O-o-o-oh, I like this one." She pointed to a sweeping gown that stepped out of elegant whimsy and into elegant allure.

"Paris is such an inspiration. And yes to lunch. I'm famished."

Kat welcomed the opportunity to get away from the backbreaking work of hunching over sketches for hours on end to meet the deadline they faced. The time for designing was running out. Fabrics had to be selected, garments made and fitted to models, staging designed and created.

Rebecca had chosen several designs Kat had brought with her, but this show required more than the usual number. More trendy and daring than that in the States, the European market challenged her with the need for a number of new lines. Bold bikinis and maillots must be added to the collection, the daywear line expanded, and new suits and dresses designed to take a businesswoman from office to nightclub with minimal fuss. Rebecca had given her free rein—and applauded her new sketches—but gowns were Kat's forte. Worn by Lillian Rae and Silka Sinclair, her latest creations would debut at the climax of Wolf's presentation. Silka's temperamental personality lent itself to the flashier fashions, which were beautifully balanced by the classic styles and graceful gowns so well suited to Lillian's willowy figure and sophisticated maturity. Silka's initial reluctance had melted away when she saw some of the designs she'd be wearing. Lillian's class, rhythm, showmanship, and burning desire to win made her a runway favorite. She'd come back on the scene after years of absence and again graced the fashion world as one of its top ten models.

Kat stood at her easel and stared. She'd just sketched what she knew was the most gorgeous gown she'd ever envisioned. Rebecca looked over her shoulder.

"It's breathtaking, Katarina. That piece alone will make us a top contender for first place."

"I've been working on it ever since I arrived, but the idea first came to me a few years ago. Somehow, neither time nor place made me commit it to paper and fabric, but Paris has changed all that."

"I have to say, my dear, it's certainly come into its own today." She gazed at the simple, yet majestic lines of the flowing white gown. "That's it, Katarina, the inspiration for the grand finale. We'll call it . . . 'Castles in the Air.'"

Kat nodded. "Yes, that's perfect. 'Castles in the Air.' We'll need to modify our backdrop, but set against a cerulean blue sky, this gown will look like a wispy cloud. Our model will appear to be floating down the runway."

She recalled another time, another runway, another show. Lincoln had said, "We pulled it off. We won." *We?* she remembered thinking, *I worked sixteen hours a day while he played, and he says 'we' pulled it off? I don't think so.*

"Do you happen to have an aspirin, Darling?" Rebecca's voice interrupted her reverie. "I have one of those awful headaches again."

Kat reached for her purse and handed the pills to Rebecca. "These are extra-strength, so don't take more than two at a time. You really ought to see a doctor, you know."

"This is nothing. I know. I used to have migraines."

She looked at the dark circles under Rebecca's eyes. "I still think it wouldn't hurt to see a doctor. There might be something more effective than aspirin to get rid of the pain."

"It's just all this work and little rest. Two days of peace and quiet and two good nights of sleep would make all the difference in the world, and no physician can make that happen for me. We've got a show coming up. I'll be okay once it's over." Rebecca closed her eyes and leaned back against her chair.

Kat stopped sketching and pointed her drawing pencil at her friend. "I'll make you a deal. You go see a doctor, and I'll stay in Paris and help you win this. You don't go to a doctor, and I pack my bags and go back to Willow Walk."

Rebecca's eyes popped open. "That sounds more like a threat than a deal. Or maybe blackmail."

Kat laughed. "Call it what you will. That's it."

"Okay. Okay! I'll make an appointment. And I'll make sure he's a good-looking, sexy Frenchman."

They laughed together. Kat reached for the telephone and called the desk at Maison St. Pierre. "Just in case it slips your mind." She grinned at Rebecca while she waited for the clerk to answer. "Hello, Jean-Paul, this is Katarina Kahill in apartment seven-oh-one. A friend of mine needs to see a neurologist here in Paris. Do you happen to know the name of a good one?" She jotted a note on a piece of paper. "Your mother was happy with Dr. LeBlanc? . . . Excellent. Thank you for the recommendation."

She dialed the number. A female voice answered in French.

"*Parlez-vous anglais?*" Kat asked.

"Yes, I speak English," came the response.

She explained the need for an immediate appointment.

"Madame Kahill, Doctor LeBlanc is not accepting new patients. I will be happy to give you the name of someone else."

"Allow me to speak to Dr.LeBlanc, please," Kat persisted. "This is very important."

"He's with a patient. May I have him call you?"

Kat gave the receptionist her number and jotted down the name of the referral in case the man didn't return her call. Her cell phone rang several hours later as she was about to quit working for the day.

"Sorry to bother you, Dr.LeBlanc. Your receptionist said you were not accepting new patients. I wanted to ask you to please make an exception. Rebecca Wolf, my employer, is in dire need of a doctor. You see, Wolf International Fashions Inc., which she owns, has a spot in the world-wide fashion show beginning—"

"Madame or Mademoiselle?" Before Kat could respond, he continued. "It doesn't matter. I'm not accepting new patients." He spoke perfect English.

"But . . . but Doctor, this is an emergency. Please reconsider. Rebecca is having excruciating headaches, and she looks so ill at times. I *know* something's seriously wrong. She doesn't want to jeopardize the show, but it will go on even if . . . Oh, I'd be so grateful if you would see her. In fact—"

"You win. It seems I cannot, with any measure of decency, turn you down. If your friend can come at eight-thirty in the morning, I'll see her before my office hours begin at nine."

"Thank you so much, Doctor. We'll see you tomorrow."

"You're most welcome, Madame Kahill. Now I must go. I have patients waiting."

"Yes, of course. Good bye, Doctor LeBlanc."

Rebecca should be pleased. If he looks anything like he sounds, he's going to be the French version of James Bond. For a brief moment, she almost regretted that she had a husband at home in West Virginia—a husband who'd been one in name only for the last nine months.

Kat and Rebecca walked into the empty waiting room at eight-fifteen. Within moments, an outrageously handsome man who put James Bond to shame appeared from the back of the office.

"I'm Dr. LeBlanc." He looked straight at Kat out of the bluest eyes she'd ever seen. "Madame Kahill, I assume?"

"Uh . . . y-y-yes." Where was her voice? "And . . . this is the friend I told you about . . . uh . . . Rebecca . . . Rebecca Wolf." She felt like an idiot, like thirty-something going on fifteen. The warmth rising in her cheeks confirmed her discomfort.

"Madame Wolf." He smiled at Rebecca. "Please come back to my office." He turned his smile to Kat. Her knees felt like putty. "You may join us, Madame Kahill, if your friend doesn't mind, that is."

Rebecca grabbed her hand. "Yes, Katarina, please do come."

They followed him down the hall and into a well-appointed room. A large cherry desk sat in front of a wall of shelves. *Are those all medical books?* Somehow, Kat doubted that.

"Please sit down, ladies." He indicated two plush chairs in front of his desk and strolled around it to his dark leather one.

Kat couldn't take her eyes off him. Blond hair the shade of summer wheat, perfectly balanced features, and broad shoulders made her much too aware of the absence of a loving man in her life. Like a magnet, he was drawing her to him. She couldn't think straight. *Stop it Kat. What's wrong with you? You have no right to . . . to . . .* Thank goodness Rebecca was the one who had to answer his questions. Her tongue would have been tied in knots.

Thirty minutes later the two women emerged from the office, scheduled tests at the front desk for the following day, and stepped out onto the rue de Courcelles.

"Let's stop and have a drink, and I don't mean coffee," Rebecca said.

"Sounds good to me." Kat glanced at her watch. "But I think I'll go for the coffee."

"Whatever suits your fancy."

"So tell me, was Dr. Mason LeBlanc handsome enough to meet your requirements?" Kat said as they sat at a small table.

Rebecca laughed. "That seems like a strange question coming from a lady whose gaze was glued to the man. And I'll answer your next one before you ask. Yes, he was sexy enough for ten men. *But* I don't think that was lost on you either."

"I did notice a certain sensual quality in him." She thought Rebecca was going to choke on her drink.

"I'll say you did. The vibes flying back and forth between the two of you are probably still bouncing around that room. I'm almost sorry that I'll be seeing him more often that you do. Just the luck of the draw, I guess."

"Didn't I mention that I plan to accompany you on all your appointments? You never know when one of those headaches might hit, and you'll need my help."

"Oh? And who will be working on preparations for the show?"

"Lillian can oversee things for an hour or so." Kat grinned. "She knows the drill, she's well acquainted with our schedule, and she's an exacting taskmaster who knows how to get people to do her bidding."

Rebecca watched her for a moment. "Okay. Just remember that you have somebody—several somebodies, in fact—waiting for you back in the States. If this Frenchman is in the market for romance . . ." She left the thought hanging. "Other than a few details about Dawson's accident, you haven't shared much of your personal life with me, Katarina. If ever you need a shoulder, you can be certain that your words will go no farther than my ears."

"Thank you, Rebecca. I do love Dawson very much. He's just a little lost right now. I'm hoping by the time I go home after the show, he will have found himself. Meanwhile, a girl can look if she doesn't touch, can't she? I'm not a flirt, and I won't cheat on my husband. It's just that . . . Dr. LeBlanc awakened something inside me that's been dormant for a long time. It caught me quite off guard."

"Just be careful, Katarina. I suspect the good doctor has much more experience in matters of the heart than you do."

Two days later, Kat and Rebecca sat facing Dr. LeBlanc. He leaned forward, his arms resting on the desk. An open file lay in front of him. A frown formed on his forehead. He shifted his weight in his chair.

Kat held her breath. *This isn't good.*

"Madame Wolf, I have the results of your tests."

Rebecca sat straight up and crossed one knee over the other. Her black linen sheath with three-quarter length jacket showed just enough leg to hint at interest. She nodded at the doctor.

"Your CT scan shows that you have a cerebral aneurysm at the base of your brain. That area is called the circle of Willis."

Rebecca's face paled. She put up her hand and closed her eyes. "A what? How . . . ?"

"An aneurysm is a bulging weak area in the wall of an artery—in this case, one that supplies blood to the brain. It's more common in women and can be caused by hypertension, smoking, or even heredity. Has anyone in your family had this problem? Or do you smoke?"

She shook her head. "I've never smoked, and I don't know of anyone in my family who's had an aneurysm. But this makes no sense. I've only had the headaches since I arrived in Paris."

"Symptoms of a ruptured brain aneurysm often come on suddenly. Your complaints are consistent with those of a subarachnoid hemorrhage."

Rebecca's hand went up again. "Whoa. Wait a minute, doctor. You confuse me. One minute you say I have an aneurysm, and now you say it's ruptured. How do you know it ruptured?"

"The scan showed that blood had been released into your skull, and that is what's causing your headaches. If it hadn't ruptured, you probably wouldn't be aware that it's there. Now, Madame Wolf, we must talk about surgery. There are—"

"Surgery!" Rebecca interrupted. "That's not possible. Not now. I have a show to do."

Kat reached over and took her hand. Rebecca gripped her fingers so hard, she had to clench her jaw to keep from crying out."

"I know this is frightening, but consider the fact that you are very fortunate that it occurred the way it did."

"How do you figure that, doctor? It couldn't have come at a worse time as far as I'm concerned."

"I don't think you understand the severity of your situation, Madame. The scan indicates the bleeding has subsided . . . for the moment. It can return at any time, and very likely will. If and when it does, the hemorrhaging could cause brain damage, a stroke, and/or death."

"Oh, no!" Rebecca's free hand flew to her mouth. She squeezed Kat's hand even harder.

"We treat this condition with one of two types of surgery," Dr. LeBlanc continued. "The one I wish to use in your case is called coil embolization. I'll insert a small tube into the artery near the aneurysm, relieving the pressure on the weak spot. It's a less invasive procedure, and recovery time is reduced. If you do it right away—which I strongly recommend—there's no reason you can't be there for your show." He handed her some information. "This literature will give you a complete explanation of the problem and the corrective surgery. Read this tonight, and let's talk tomorrow. I don't wish to alarm you, but we have no time to waste."

Rebecca stared at the doctor for a long moment before turning to Kat. "What do I do, Katarina?" The life had drained from her voice.

"You have the surgery, Rebecca. I'll be here for you, and I'll see that everything for the show proceeds as scheduled." Her lashes flickered in a vain effort to staunch her tears.

Dr LeBlanc smiled. "This cloud does have its silver lining, ladies. The condition is treatable, and the success rate exceeds sixty percent."

"And if I don't have the surgery?" Rebecca's eyes never wavered from the doctor's face.

His smile faded. "I'm afraid it will kill you."

CHAPTER TWENTY-FOUR

Kat and Rebecca sat in front of the fireplace in Kat's studio. Rebecca pored over the packet of information from Dr. LeBlanc. Kat enhanced some sketches she'd brought home from the office.

"I think we could use some wine." Kat laid the drawings on the floor beside the chair. "What's your pleasure, Rebecca?"

"Chardonnay would hit the spot, I think."

A few moments later, Kat set a tray on the table that sat between the chairs. A small plate of cheese and crackers separated the wine goblets.

I can't even imagine what's running through your mind right now, Rebecca. If I were in your shoes, I'd want to be surrounded by my family and close friends. All you have is me. And you barely know me. A teardrop fell onto her cheek as Rebecca turned to look at her.

"Oh, Katarina, you're sad and it's my fault. But you needn't be. I've come to a decision. Tomorrow I'll tell Dr. LeBlanc to schedule the surgery as soon as possible. I intend to be back on my feet and at that show, come hell or high water as the expression goes."

Kat lifted her wine goblet off the tray and grinned through her tears. "I'll drink to that."

Rebecca picked up her drink and nodded. She brushed a stray lock of hair from her face and looked straight at Kat. "We have some serious planning to do tonight. I know you want to be there for the surgery, and I want you there. However, I'm counting on you to keep the ball rolling at Wolf. I hate to dump the whole thing in your lap, but you're probably better suited to this than I am. Believe me, I have the utmost confidence in your ability. If I didn't, my decision about the surgery would have been

124

quite different. The future of Wolf International—your future—is in your capable hands."

"I appreciate your confidence, but—"

"Please let me finish. If I don't make it, I want you to promise to do the show. My problem must not be the reason all the people who have worked so hard to make this happen are suddenly out of work. Are you up to the task?"

"Let's not be negative, Rebecca. You need to think only good thoughts. Why not begin with being happy that the aneurysm was discovered in time to treat it? You and Wolf International have a great future together."

"I don't think so, but that's a conversation for another time."

What does that mean? She didn't ask. "You know I'll take care of creating the fashions, and I'll make sure everything is done just the way you want it to be. We've talked so much about this that I think I know it almost as well as you do. Lillian will help me wherever I need it, so you can stop worrying about everything except getting well. We all want you to walk up on that stage and accept the award when your name is called. And here's one other thing you can think about that'll keep your spirits up: There's one hunk of a man who will be focusing on nothing but you . . . Dr. Mason Leblanc."

Rebecca's laughter filled the room as she threw a velvet pillow in Kat's direction. "You're right, Sweetie. He *is* a hunk."

"Yes, but I wish he'd quit popping into my consciousness when I least expect him. That man could stifle my creativity."

"Oh, no, you mustn't let that happen. You know, Katarina, I never realized what a special person you are. I know why Lincoln was attracted to you. You're everything he wasn't, and he wanted to be everything you were and still are. Only he didn't want to make the changes that required. In a way, he was living vicariously through you. I can assure you that he never understood why you walked away. I imagine that was a first for him." She stared at the flames. "That man jabbed at me until he made a huge hole in my heart, then almost killed me with drugs. He stole my inheritance, cheated on me more times than I can count, and would have divorced me had he lived. I'm sure he had a scheme devised to get the rest of my money because he was a man who never intended to be broke."

Kat refilled their wine glasses and turned up the fire.

"He even convinced me to change the name of my company from Winslow International Fashions. My great-grandfather founded that company. But *dear, sweet* Lincoln came to me one day and said, 'Rebecca, a name like Wolf will carry the company to new heights, and that's what it needs to get on top and stay there.' On and on and on he went until I yielded and allowed the change. Lincoln Wolf was a treacherous man. He always got what he wanted—except you."

"Lincoln's not here anymore, Rebecca. And all that he took from you is yours again."

"Not quite. That gaping hole in my heart hasn't healed. I realized that when the debonair Dr. LeBlanc made me want to run *away* from him rather than toward him. He can fix my brain, and I'll be eternally grateful. But that's the only part of my anatomy I'll let him touch."

"Oh, Honey, please don't talk that way. What did we just say about negative thinking? The past is exactly that . . . past. You're going to make it. This little bump in the road is a molehill, not a mountain."

Rebecca's expression reflected the turmoil of her thoughts. "I know. And I plan to be sitting in the front row next to you at the show, ready to accept that trophy and bring it home for us. Now let's go across the hall to my apartment and pick out a few gorgeous negligees for me to wear while I'm recuperating. I can't have Dr. Handsome seeing me in one of those hideous vented hospital gowns.

"*That's* the Rebecca Wolf I know. You go ahead; I'll be there as soon as I call my son. And by the way, I'm designing a special outfit for you to wear to the show. I'm seeing you in something very bold, yet totally sophisticated. You have to exemplify the arrival of the new, invigorated Wolf International."

Rebecca rubbed her hand over the back of her head and smiled. "While you're at it, be sure to create a matching turban or some kind of head covering. The good doctor didn't mention the part about shaving part of my hair off, but the brochure clued me in." She got up and was gone before Kat could answer.

Oh, dear. I didn't think about her glorious butterscotch hair.

The next morning Dr. LeBlanc greeted them both with a big smile. "How are you two beautiful ladies this morning? I hope you slept well, Rebecca."

"Thank you, doctor, I did . . . for a change."

"Could that mean you've come to a decision that you're at peace with?"

She returned his smile. "Yes. I want this little procedure done as soon as possible. I still have that show to make."

"Let me see when we can schedule you." He turned to the monitor on his computer. "Oh, I see one of my patients that was supposed to check into the hospital today for surgery tomorrow has rescheduled for next week. This is perfect. Can you be at the hospital around three o'clock this afternoon?"

"Oh, my goodness. That's a little sooner than I expected, but—"

"She'll be there." Kat turned to Rebecca. "Don't worry. I have everything about the show under control. You concentrate on getting well."

Doctor LeBlanc buzzed for the nurse to come in and take Rebecca for pre-op tests and the necessary paperwork. He turned to Kat when Rebecca had gone. "We do all the preliminaries here so the patient isn't overwhelmed when they arrive at the hospital. They're apprehensive enough, and I prefer that they relax and rest as much as possible before surgery."

"You're very kind, doctor. Thank you so much for seeing Rebecca on an emergency basis. It's very apparent now that we could have lost her."

"Oh yes, Madame Kahill—may I call you Katarina?"

"Uh . . . yes, of course."

"I've tried to prepare Rebecca for the worst without terrifying her. Her situation could quickly become critical, and the surgery doesn't always work."

"I understand." *Why doesn't he turn those incredible blue eyes in a different direction? Don't be ridiculous, Kat, it's you he's talking to. You think he should be looking out the window?* Apprehension tugged at her. "Is there something else you haven't told me about?"

He leaned back in his leather chair, folded his arms, and stared at her. She averted his eyes, but his scrutiny confused her. She felt the flush rise in her cheeks. *Stop looking at me. I haven't blushed since I was in high school. This is beyond embarrassing . . .*

"Only that after her release, she'll need rest and quiet. I don't want her going from the hospital to the office. Nor do I want her staying alone. However, I've gotten the impression that Rebecca might do both of these."

She couldn't help laughing. "I see you've got her pegged. We have a great staff here. I will personally see that she stays home—or with me—until you say she can come back to work. The show's still a little over two months away. Do you think she'll be well enough by then to take charge . . . or at least attend?"

"At this point, I can't say. A lot depends on whether we have complications and how well she heals. I admire your willingness to help and your loyalty to your friend, Madame . . . Katarina. Those are very admirable qualities, particularly in a woman who has achieved your obvious level of success." His long, hard look didn't waver. "If you need anything . . . anything at all . . . please don't hesitate to call on me, *oui*?"

Keep your cool, Kat. She stood. He walked around his desk and reached out to shake her hand. The moment he touched her, she knew that had been a mistake. "If you have any interest in such events, I would like to give you and . . . Mrs. LeBlanc . . . tickets to the show. Is there a Mrs. LeBlanc?" *How mortifying. Why did I ask that?*

The slight upturn at the corners of his mouth widened into a full-fledged smile. "No Madame LeBlanc, Katarina. Not anymore. What of your husband? Did he not journey here with you? Such a lovely woman as you should not be in Paris without her love."

There came that blush again. *I can't believe you're doing this, Kat. Say your goodbyes and get out of here before your foot gets caught in your mouth permanently.* "I'm so sorry. It was rude of me to inquire about your personal life. As for my husband, he was injured in an accident several months ago and didn't wish to travel with me. He's at home in West Virginia with his grandfather and our son." *Quit babbling and get out of here.* She looked down. He was still holding her hand. "I really should be going. Please tell Rebecca that I . . . I'm waiting for her outside."

He pulled her to her feet, but kept her hand in his. "I'm so sorry for your friend's illness, but I cannot regret having met you." His gaze never left her face. She tried to stop the warm tingling his touch sent sweeping over her body. "I'll stop by to see Rebecca after she checks into the hospital. Will you be there, too?"

"I . . . uh . . . it depends on my work schedule and whether Rebecca wants me to stay with her until . . . after the surgery."

His eyes twinkled. "I see. Oh, I didn't answer you about the ticket to your show. After the surgery, you can give me the date. I'll see if I can clear my calendar for that evening." He gave her hand a tiny squeeze and was gone.

Oh my goodness, I think Mason LeBlanc just made a pass at me. Shut up, Kat. He's a Frenchmen. Now get your heart back where it belongs. And where's that? Dawson doesn't seem to want it anymore. What had he said when she told him she'd accepted Rebecca's offer? 'If you go, don't bother to come back.' Well, Daw, this is Paris, the city of love. But thanks to you, my heart has no one to love.

CHAPTER TWENTY-FIVE

"How's it look, Sonny?" Jedediah adjusted the new mirror on the wall in Dawson's room and picked up his tools. He stepped back to admire his handiwork.

Dawson stood in front of it, leaning heavily on the crutches under his arms. With one hand, he rubbed first his unshaven face and then his scraggly hair. "It's good, Granddad. Thanks."

"Glad to see you up on your feet. Been practicin' with those crutches, have you?"

"You've seen the new physical therapist. He doesn't take 'no' for an answer."

"Good for him."

"That's your opinion. I've got mine."

"Hmmm. I best be gettin' down to the kitchen. Carla was makin' a coffee cake when I came up here." He turned to leave. "Oh, I almost forgot. Had a funny phone call first thing this mornin' from a James Harrison. Said he's your accountant."

Dawson turned his head toward the old man. "I know Jim Harrison. What was so funny about his call?"

"He said somethin's wrong with the books?"

"What books?"

"The books for the lodge. Said he'd be here at eleven-thirty to talk to you."

"I'm not seeing *anybody* today." He looked back at the mirror. "Do I look like I'm ready for visitors?"

"I think you'd better *get* ready. He said it was important, but he wouldn't tell me what's goin' on. I'll be bringin' the man up here to see you if you're not downstairs when he comes." He shuffled out of the room.

Dawson glared at his image. *Don't you say a word, you worthless . . . Never mind.* He looked away.

What could be wrong with the books? He hadn't paid any attention to the lodge since the accident, but he trusted his staff. They'd been running the place for almost a year. Oh, well, maybe this one time, he'd make an exception and see Harrison. He'd make it plain, though, that in the future the man would be dealing with Polly Dee.

He hobbled into the bathroom and turned on the shower. The room began to spin. Closing his eyes, he leaned against the wall until the dizziness disappeared, then maneuvered himself under the gentle spray. After a few moments, the warm water began to ease the tension in the muscles that were complaining about being put back into service after months of disuse. *At least I didn't yell at Granddad. I can't believe how hard it is to be civil. I didn't used to be that way.*

An hour later, clean-shaven and with his hair washed and combed, he sat at the large dining table with James Harrison, reviewing the last ten months of debits, credits, and balances for Willow Walk Ski Lodge.

"How can anybody steal money? Don't our guests pay with credit cards?"

"As a rule that's true, Dawson, and it doesn't appear that there's any credit card theft here. But some people still use cash. I didn't find these discrepancies at first because there's no problem with the credit card payments. But when my assistant balanced the reservations against the receipts, they didn't match. I asked Polly Dee to let me know which reservations had cancelled. Only three or four had, and the rooms had been rented to other guests within a day."

"Did she say some of the guests paid with cash?"

"Yes. She told me her son handled the reservations. She promised to have him call me, but I haven't heard from him."

Dawson rubbed his neck with the palm of his hand. The headache was coming back.

Barefoot and shirtless, Cabe sat on the beach in Tampico, Mexico. Waves rolled toward the shore, an endless succession of ridges moving across the water's surface. Whitecaps tapered off as they approached, leaving behind their white foam to disappear in the sand. The sun slipped below the horizon, taking with it the warmth and light of the day.

Except for the birds, he was alone. Sandpipers skittered back and forth, searching for coquina clams buried just below the surface of the wet sand. Gray and white seagulls with outstretched wings sounded their call and swooped down for tasty morsels.

A soft mist of salt air blew into his face and mingled with the saltiness of his tears. Wasn't she coming? She should've been here by now. To get back to her, he'd done something awful, something he'd never done before. *I know I hurt Mom and Dad by taking that money. They know I'm not a thief, so they won't understand. But it was the only way.*

His fingers sifting absently through the sand, he tried to ignore the battle that raged inside him. *Mom told me about the Kahills after I turned eighteen. Said I had a whole family I didn't know. That was some big shock. Then we got the chance to go to Wheeling and meet them and have work. I didn't want to go. I didn't want to leave her behind.*

A seagull squawked and landed a few feet away. It gave him a long, wary look before it began scavenging for food.

We needed the money because the inn wasn't supporting us anymore. Dad stayed here to try to keep it going, and I wanted to stay with him. He asked me to please help Mom at the lodge. When he joined us a few months later, I wanted to come home. I couldn't . . . the inn was closed.

The gull strutted back and forth in front of him, let out a call, and took off. If only he could have been that free. He wouldn't be sitting here now, wondering how his long-lost relatives would react when they found out what he had done.

I know what Granddad'll do. He'll try to talk them into hanging me from the highest tree. That old man hasn't liked me from the first time he saw me. No matter how hard I tried, he scowled at me like I was up to something. Now I bet he thinks he was right all along. But he doesn't know the reason. None of them know the reason.

Jedediah stared out the large window in the guest drawing room at Willow Walk. *I knew that boy was no good from the beginnin'. I could feel it in my bones. I'm most often right about folks, but I take no joy in it this time.* Wrestling with the urge to speak his mind, he mulled over the pros and cons of blurting out the words that would only cause pain to the innocent people in the room. He turned to look at them.

Polly Dee and Darrell sat in front of the fireplace, their gazes fixed on the orange and blue flames that flickered up the chimney. Dawson poured a cup of coffee for each of them from the large carafe Carla had set on the coffee table.

"Are you sure the money's gone, Dawson?" Tears welled up in Polly Dee's eyes.

"Jim's been my accountant for years. I saw the books myself. There's no doubt, Polly."

"What are we going to do?" Darrell asked.

"We need to find him and bring him home," Dawson said.

Polly grabbed Darrell's hand and held it tight.

Jedediah spoke not a word. *We gave that boy a good home and a job with a future. What's he do? Throws the good Kahill name in the dirt and stomps on it just like his daddy did. Only difference is his daddy had an excuse. He was a sick man who didn't have control over his actions. The boy's healthy. Sure glad we got little Joey to carry on the family name.* He shook his head and turned his attention to Polly Dee.

"I can't believe Cabe would do such a thing. He's never stolen anything in his life," Polly said.

"Believe me, Polly. I'm so sorry, but . . . if you want to see the books, I'll show you."

"I know nothing about bookkeeping, but Darrell does." She gave her husband a pleading look. "You want to go over the books with Dawson?"

"No . . . uh, on second thought, yes. I want to know exactly what the boy did. We didn't raise him to be a thief, Polly." He put his arm around her as she began to sob. "Then I'm calling the law."

"On your own son?" Polly sat up straight and stared at him.

"I raised him as though he were mine, but he's a Kahill. So he has stolen from his own, and he knew it. That's even more inexcusable."

Granddad shuffled over to stand in front of them, his cane resounding against the hardwood floor with every step. "Now let's think about this before we drag the Kahill name in the mud again. I'm not one bit interested in readin' about young Cabe's misdeed in the local newspaper, and that's what'll happen if you turn him in. There's got to be another way."

Darrell stood up to meet the old man's steady gaze. "What if I report him as a missing person? Can you live with that, Jedediah?"

"I suppose so."

"Just remember that this isn't a naughty child we're talking about. Cabe needs to take responsibility for his actions." Darrell frowned.

"I agree," Dawson interjected. "However, it's pretty much a family matter at this point because no credit card theft was involved. The law doesn't need to know about the money."

"Thank goodness for that." Polly sniffed. "Are you going to press charges, Dawson?"

"I'd rather not do that. We've got to find him, though. Any idea where he may have gone?"

"He didn't want to leave Mexico when we came here, so he might have gone back," Polly said. "I think he was interested in a girl . . ."

"In Tampico?" Dawson wrinkled his brow, rubbed his chin, and glanced at the clock. "It's late. Why don't we retire for the night and discuss this tomorrow?"

Darrell shook Dawson's hand, and Polly smiled a little before they turned to go.

"So, you gonna traipse all the way to Mexico to find him, Sonny?" Jedediah asked.

"I don't know yet, Granddad. I might try that before Darrell reports him missing. That would keep the matter altogether private."

"How much did the scoundrel take?"

"A little over three thousand. Not enough to put us in the red, but enough to keep him going for a while in Mexico if he's careful what he spends."

"Thievin' is thievin'. That boy needs to be taught a lesson. He needs to pay for what he's done."

"That boy's a twenty-four-year-old man, Granddad, and he's my brother."

"*Half*-brother," Granddad corrected.

"Doesn't matter. Blood is blood."

"That no-account boy . . . man . . . bit the hand that was feedin' him. I could've told you this would happen. You know the apple and the tree sayin'. Why was he handlin' the money, anyway?"

"Don't get started on my father, Granddad. "We both know he couldn't help the way he was."

"Humph. I suppose that means you're sayin' what the boy did weren't hereditary."

"Let's see now." Dawson grinned. "If it *was* hereditary, which side of the family did it come from? Yours or Grandma Emma's?"

Jedediah stomped his cane on the floor. "See here, Sonny, we'll have no talk like that. Our families didn't sprout no criminals.

"Oh, really? How about Grandma Emma's brother Hiram. Seems he spent some time in jail for something or other."

Granddad scowled. "We always figured he was adopted."

"Yeah, right."

Jedediah raised his cane.

Dawson leaned forward on his crutches and swung himself out of reach. He almost collided with Carla as she came in for the carafe. "Is Joey in bed?"

"I just finished his story. He was awake when I turned out his light."

Dawson started out of the room. "I want to tell him goodnight."

"You want one last cup of coffee?" Carla asked Jedediah, reaching for the carafe.

"Only if you put a jigger of brandy in it and have one with me." He looked at her ageless face beneath a full head of curly salt-and-pepper hair. *How old are you, woman? Could be anywhere between sixty and seventy-five. But it wouldn't be gentlemanly to ask.*

"Oh, Jed, you are *so* bad, but yes. A little brandy never hurt anybody. Good sleeping tonic." She laughed and went off to get the brandy.

He sank into a wing chair beside the fireplace. Flames rose and fell, flickering in all directions and creating just enough light and warmth to take the chill off the night and the family drama. *All that's missin' is my Emma.* He wiped as his eyes when Carla's back was turned to keep her from seeing their mistiness.

"Jed?" She handed him his coffee and sat down in the chair across from him. "Penelope Weatherbush was here this afternoon."

"She was?"

"Uh huh. She left a mincemeat pie. I think she mentioned that it's your favorite."

He didn't say anything.

"She's becoming a regular visitor to my kitchen."

"*Your* kitchen?"

She grinned. "Only when I'm in it."

"Humph. That's better."

"I've been thinking."

"I thought I smelt somethin' burnin'."

"You're in rare form tonight, aren't you?" She paused and watched him for a moment. "You and Penelope might get something going."

His eyes widened. "Excuse me?"

"Women read women. She wants more than your company."

"What are you talkin' about, woman?" he sputtered. "I've never led her on so'd she think something like that."

"Obviously, you never turned her off, either. You don't know much about women, do you?"

He coughed and spewed coffee down the front of his shirt. "What did you say?"

"I said you don't know much about women. No offense intended. I'm just letting you know what she's thinking."

"I'm real flattered if she has an interest in this broken down old man. I even like her—a whole lot, but I'm still stuck on my Emma. She's the only woman I ever had or ever wanted."

"That's what I thought." Carla stood up and took his empty cup. "Just be careful. You're a bit of a flirt, and she's reading more into it than you may intend."

He swallowed hard and cleared his throat. "I'll be watchin' my p's and q's from now own, you can be sure. I . . . I do thank you for bringing this to my attention."

"Good night, Jedediah."

"Good night, Carla." He watched her walk out of the room. *Whew, I'll be danged. Oh, Emma Baby, you know I'd never be unfaithful to your memory. I knew that woman was takin' a fancy to me, but I was just funnin' with her. You hold the key to my heart. And don't you go givin' it to nobody else, you hear now?*

He trudged up the stairs to his room, went to the new desk Sonny and Kitten had given him, and retrieved a skeleton key from one of its cubbyholes. After taking a moment to catch his breath, he walked over to a door on the back wall of his room, inserted the old key in the lock, and gave it a half turn. The door opened. He pulled the chain on the wall light just inside and sat down at the antique table under it. Opening up the journal that rested on one corner, he picked up his pen and began to write. The words flowed like water over a dam. Danged if they didn't have a mind of their own.

> I love you, my Emma—I dearly do,
> You with lips of red and eyes so blue.
> My boots are shined, my shirt is new.
> Hold on to your broom, I'm not cheatin' on you.

Satisfied, he nodded and put his pen down. Then, he pushed himself up and walked to the other side of the large room, where two overstuffed chairs from the early days of their marriage rested against the far wall. They sat side by side, a small, plain table between them. He settled into one of them. *Your chair's empty, Emma, but I can still see you there.*

He opened the decanter on the table next to him and poured a peach brandy. He'd barely tasted that little dab Carla had put in his coffee. After downing the first glass, he poured himself a second one and picked up the small teak box sitting next to it. His fingers traced the letters: ETK. Emma Theresa Kahill.

How well he remembered the day he'd given the box to her. He opened the lid and picked up a cameo pendant, then pressed it to his heart. His eyes closed. His chin fell to his chest.

He saw her sitting in her chair, just as pretty as the day they'd met. She gave him that coy smile of hers, and he felt his heart skip a beat.

"I miss you, Emma Baby. My world's so empty without you."

"I miss you, too, my dear Jed. But you need to live your life to the fullest while you can. It'll end all too soon just like mine did."

"I suppose—if you say so. You know how much I love you, don't you?"

"My goodness, yes. You've told me often enough, you silly old man." Emma rocked back and forth, feet barely touching the floor. She reached up to tuck some stray hairs into her silver bun, then grinned that flirty grin he loved so much. "I've got my eye on you and that pushy Weatherbush woman. Why, I've known her since her second husband passed away. You behave yourself, you hear me? If you don't, I'll be taking my broom to your backside. And by the way, I'm glad to see that you're keeping your boots shined." She winked and threw him a kiss.

"Oh, Emma, there'll never be another woman for me." He reached out his hand to her, but she was gone.

His head jerked up. His eyes flew open. Shivering from the coolness of the uninsulated attic room, he looked at his empty hand. Where was the pendant? He squinted, his gaze searching the wooden floor in the dim light. Then he spied it next to Emma's chair. *I didn't mean to drop it . . . and I didn't mean to go to sleep. But when I'm sleepin', you're with me. I want to sleep forever just so I can always have you by my side.*

He put the locket back in the box and walked toward the door. His journal was still open to the poem he had written earlier. He picked up the pen and added a love letter.

My Beloved Emma,

Tonight you sat beside me, wearing your pretty sky-blue dress, the one I gave you to match your eyes. I'm so glad you got to wear it before you left me. How pretty your hair looked, all rolled in a bun at your neck, and those ocean blue eyes always twinkling. I had to laugh when you said you'd take your broom to me. You beat all, and I don't mean just with your broom. I'm thinkin' I may be joinin' you soon. Not sure why that feelin' haunts me, but it could be because the family still needs me. Kat's traipsin' around Paris, and Dawson's made himself an invalid.

Even though he seems to be doin' better, I can't shake the feelin' we're not over the hump yet. Then there's young Cabe. That boy's a worry and a half. Now he's gone and stole from Dawson. I don't know yet what we're gonna do about that one. One day soon, these folks are gonna have to solve their own problems because I'm comin' where you are. Until next time I dream of you, my dear Emma Baby, remember how much I love you.

Love you forever and ever,
Just me—Jed

CHAPTER TWENTY-SIX

Kat and Rebecca sipped Chardonnay in the design studio. Kat busied herself over her latest sketches. Rebecca stared into the fire.

"Are you ready for your surgery tomorrow?" Kat tried to sound cheerful.

"As ready as I'll ever be . . . particularly since you helped me choose some stunning negligees to wear after they let me out of that awful hospital gown. Now let's talk business. I know you want to be there for the surgery, but there's nothing you can do for me while I'm under the knife. So I want you here. I need you here because—"

"But—"

"You *will* do it my way, won't you, Kat?" She looked at her watch and stood up. "I have to leave. Three o'clock is check-in time, remember?" Kat put down her sketching pencil, but Rebecca raised her hand. "I'm taking a cab." She whisked out of the room with the dignity of a queen.

The show will go on, Rebecca, no worries. But if you think I'm not going to be there tomorrow, you've got another think coming.

Kat hurried into the hospital lobby and closed her umbrella. Two days of drizzle had made her even more homesick. Every time she talked to Joey and Granddad—and that was several times a week—she wanted to book a flight to Wheeling. But despite her promises to return for regular visits, she hadn't done so. First the designs had to be finished and fabrics chosen. Details of the show had to be worked out and implemented. Now, with Rebecca's pending surgery, she couldn't leave.

138

Rebecca's complications kept her hopping from the studio to the hospital and back again. Dr LeBlanc's sober expression and guarded words came back to her every time she walked through these doors.

The embolization coil didn't work for Rebecca. Once I had access to the aneurysm, I found the bulge was so large that I had to cut it out and stitch the blood vessel together. I think she'll be fine, but her hospital stay will be longer than I originally anticipated.

Out of breath, she rushed in Rebecca's room and sank into a plush chair beside her bed.

"I told you that you needn't come here every day, Katarina."

"Everything's going great. We're several days ahead of schedule."

"At least that's good news."

Kat reached for her hand. "What's going on, Rebecca?"

"Leaving this world so soon is not exactly what I'd planned?"

"You're not going anywhere except back to work when Mason says you're well enough."

"Whether or not that's the case, I need to share some ideas I have for the company." Rebecca raised her bed into a sitting position.

Kat adjusted the pillows behind her. "That's not something you need to worry about right now."

"On the contrary, now is exactly when I need to worry about it. One never knows when tomorrow may not come."

"Okay, Rebecca, what's on your mind?"

"I don't want Wolf International to fold, whether I'm around or not. I want to leave Wolf International to you, Katarina. The glitz and glamour of the fashion world is not as important to me as living whatever time I have left without the hassle of running the company. Lying here in this bed has changed my perspective. What good is fame and fortune if it kills me? I have no one else to leave it to. My only relatives are an elderly aunt and uncle. Besides, all the staff loves you. I know you'll do it and them justice, and I think you'll love doing it."

"What about Lillian Rae? She knows the company inside out, and she's a great designer as well as a supermodel."

"Lillian has many talents, and you can use her talents to the fullest. But the person who can take Wolf to the top and keep it there is you, Katarina Kahill. I know you had plans to expand your boutique before I dragged you off to Paris. Do it under Wolf's umbrella—and I'm not talking about that dripping thing you carried in here."

Kat chuckled and took a deep breath, her chest and shoulders rising as she inhaled.

"This is the perfect solution for everybody. Wolf will be in the best possible hands. Deb and Bonny can work in any of your shops they choose. It'll be the New York expansion you all want."

"I . . . I don't know what to say. May I think about it?"

"Take whatever time you need. Just know that my heart is now elsewhere. The house in the country is once again in my name and that's where I want to go—soon. I want to live where I can see green things growing and smell the earth soaking up the rain, do some gardening, walk in the woods, hear a rooster crow in the early morning and not be too tired from work to sit on the porch and watch the sun come up."

The vision of a rooster crowing in the distance reminded her of Willow Walk. She sniffed back the tears and made a desperate attempt at humor.

"Roosters live in Paris?" she asked with a serious look.

"Of course, silly. Where do you think they get chickens and eggs?"

"It just seems like they don't belong in such a glamorous city."

Rebecca raised an eyebrow and continued. "Aunt Mary and Uncle Bill live close, so we'll look in on one another." She paused, but not long enough to allow Kat to interrupt her. "Don't give me any backtalk now. If my health worsens—and it could—I'll hire a live-in nurse. They say money can't buy happiness, but it can buy a lot of other things . . . like great help when it's needed. Now don't argue with me, please, Katarina. Say you'll accept. It's what I want."

"That is not a simple decision."

"Why not? It's what I want. It fits into your plans." Rebecca appeared close to tears. "I've loved how it felt to be special, to own a famous fashion house, but it no longer works for me. Don't you see that what I'm offering is not just a gift to you? It's also a gift of peace of mind that I'm giving to myself."

I should talk this over with Daw . . . except he doesn't talk. If he were himself, what would he say? Would he encourage me to hitch my wagon to that fashion-world star? Or would he remind me that I have a husband and son at home who need me? Probably not. Daw didn't seem to need anybody anymore.

She took Rebecca's hand and kissed her on the cheek. "Thank you, Rebecca. I accept on these conditions."

"Which are . . . ?"

"You retain fifty-one percent ownership of the company. Be my silent partner. The girls and I will continue to own one hundred percent of Fashions by Kat, and it will remain a separate legal entity from Wolf International. Can your attorney draw up that agreement?"

"I don't see why not. Now that that's settled, I want to address something of a personal nature—your relationship with Dr. LeBlanc."

"We have no relationship, Rebecca."

"You may think you don't, but remember the old saying that actions speak louder than words. Your actions . . . his actions . . . they all scream something else."

"Really, Rebecca," Kat stammered, "I . . . love my husband. I am . . . not involved with Dr. Mason LeBlanc."

"I know the two of you have spent time together discussing my progress. But I also know you're seeing each other socially."

"How could you know that?"

"It seems the social life of the handsome doctor is a daily conversation topic for many of the nurses. More than once, I've overheard them talking about the two of you. While I rarely speak French and am far less than fluent, I do understand it fairly well. My nurses don't know that, so they talk freely in front of me."

"I don't understand."

"Idle chatter rarely interests me, but in this case I have a personal concern. Paris is a romantic city, Katarina. It's ambience can lead you down a path you may not want to travel."

"But—"

"Are you falling in love with Dr. LeBlanc?"

Kat turned and looked out the window. In the distance the Eiffel Tower rose to meet the low-hanging clouds.

"I . . . don't think so." She looked back at Rebecca. "I'll admit Mason's an attractive man . . . *handsome* man. His manners are impeccable, and he treats me like I'm a beautiful woman. Dawson has barely acknowledged my existence for almost a year. Before the accident, we had a wonderful relationship in every way. Since then, we have no relationship at all. So I'm flattered by the doctor's attention. I'm even drawn to him. But I'm not in love with him."

"You're sure about that?"

"I'm sure . . . I think."

Rebecca gave her a long look but said nothing.

"I guess I need to clarify my intention to remain faithful to my husband."

"It's quite possible to remain physically faithful and still have an affair of the heart."

Kat turned again to the rainy scene outside the window. "Dawson hasn't been a husband for a long time, and I'm a normal, red-blooded woman with healthy hormones. I need to be loved. Maybe the good doctor is picking up on that."

"I assure you that he's very knowledgeable about women. And he knows how to get what he wants from them. Trust me, I learned a lot about the way men work from Lincoln Wolf."

"Perhaps I've given Mason a wrong impression by letting him show me the city and take me to lunch. I do so enjoy his company and his attention, but I must let him know that we can never be more than friends."

"I didn't mean to pry, Katarina," Rebecca said when Kat turned back to her with tears in her eyes. "I don't blame you for being taken by such a good-looking, sophisticated man." She grinned. "Besides, his accent drives me wild." They laughed softly. "Now what are your plans for tonight?"

"He's taking me to a new place, Robert and something, I think."

"Robert and Louise?"

"Yes, that's it."

Rebecca raised an eyebrow. "It's a very romantic restaurant, Katarina. A special table next to the fireplace—called the farmhouse table, I think—is very private. His intentions are clear if he asks for that table."

"In that case, the timing's perfect for me to set him straight. Thanks for the warning, Rebecca." Kat rumpled her hair with her fingers. Maybe she was seeing too much of Mason. *I just wish I didn't want to be with him so much.*

Rebecca sighed. "Just make sure you don't wear something so sexy that he won't take no for an answer."

When they arrived at Robert and Louise's, they were shown at once to the farmhouse table. *He must have made a reservation.* The soft light of the candles and the coziness of the fireplace almost overwhelmed her. *Thank you, Rebecca. Without your wise words, I could be walking into something that I would regret for the rest of my life.* She glanced down at the simple but elegant lines of the black wool suit she had chosen instead of the body-hugging blue silk sheath she had intended to wear. *Thank you again, Rebecca.*

They shared a carafe of wine while Mason enthralled her with the story of his life. She tried not the think of the way his gaze held hers. It was almost impossible to look at the blond curls of his hair that lay on the collar of his suit jacket and not want to touch them. It was even more difficult to concentrate on his words rather than the shape of his lips that looked so soft, so sensual, so in need of kissing.

Stop this right now, Katarina Kahill. You're not here to think about how sweet his kisses would be. You're here to say goodbye.

CHAPTER TWENTY-SEVEN

Dr. LeBlanc stared at the patient files on his desk. But their needs lay enclosed within their folders, not in his mind. The need consuming him was his for Katarina Kahill.

He had been drawn to her that first day when she walked into his office with Rebecca Wolf. No, it was before that—when she pleaded on the phone for him to see her sick friend. And how right she had been. Without her persistence, Rebecca would no doubt have soon died.

Now Katarina was juggling her busy work schedule with regular visits to the hospital, and somehow he knew that unselfish giving was part of her character, not a pretense for show. *She's so different from the way my wife turned out to be—selfish and demanding. Katarina is a giver. She is so beautiful, yet totally unaware of it. Dinner with her last night was nearly perfect. I wish I'd had the nerve to kiss her, but I had to settle for a kiss on her cheek when it was all she offered me. One thing I must remember . . . she is a married woman.*

By now she should have the yellow roses I sent. Maybe I should have told her how I feel on the card, but that's something I must do when I'm with her and when I know she can accept my love. To have written 'Thinking of you' is enough . . . for now.

"Are you okay?" Kat helped Rebecca out of the taxi and through the lobby of Maison St. Pierre.

Rebecca adjusted the scarf around her head while Kat carried her single suitcase. "Just tired, Kat. But it's so good to be coming home—to your apartment, that is. I'm glad Dr. LeBlanc agreed that I could recuperate better here. He's even stopping by on his way home in the evenings to check on me. Did I tell you that?"

"No . . . no, you didn't." *Mason's coming here?* Katarina's heart pounded as she carried the suitcase into the bedroom and turned down the covers. "You need to rest, Rebecca. Why not nap until lunchtime?"

"Are you sure this isn't an inconvenience, Katarina? My own place is just across the hall."

"You know Dr. LeBlanc released you early on the condition that you would not be alone. Besides the couch in the living room opens up into a very comfortable bed."

"If you're certain . . ."

Kat tucked her in and kissed her on the cheek. "I brought my work for the next week home, so I'll be at the desk in the living room if you need me. Lillian promised to call me at once if anything comes up that needs my attention."

Rebecca's eyes drifted shut, but she opened them again. "I'm so exhausted, but before I sleep, I must know . . . how did it go when you told Mason you couldn't see him again?"

Kat avoided her gaze.

"Katarina Kahill! You didn't tell him, did you?"

"Not yet . . . but I'm going to, I promise. He's invited me to his family home for dinner in two weeks, and I don't want to be rude by backing out. It'll be the last time . . . really it will. I can't go on allowing him to think that we could have a relationship." The doorbell rang. "Now get some sleep, Rebecca." The bell rang a second time. She pulled the bedroom door shut and answered the persistent ringing. The bellman stood there, a bouquet of yellow roses in his hand. She took them, closed the door, and turned to see Rebecca standing behind her.

"Looks like it's a little late to stop him. Those roses say it all. What did he write on the card."

Pulling it out, she gave it a quick glance and handed it to Rebecca. "Now you're going back to bed and get some sleep." She tempered her order with a smile. "We'll talk after your nap."

"He's in love with you, Katarina."

"Go to sleep, Rebecca."

"I heard the nurses say he's nice to all the women, but it's a known fact he doesn't date. He hasn't since his divorce."

"Good night, Rebecca."

"It isn't night." She softened her tone. "You've got to tell him, Katarina. Otherwise, you'll break his heart just like his wife did."

144

"My goodness, the scuttlebutt around the hospital's full of details, isn't it."

"A lot of the nurses would give almost anything for a date with the man, but he keeps to himself."

"Go to sleep . . . now."

Rebecca's eyelids closed. Kat tiptoed out of the room and pulled the door shut behind her.

She looked around the apartment and began straightening the living room and kitchen. They weren't dirty, just not as tidy as she liked because of the hours she kept. But Mason was coming to see Rebecca . . .

She picked up the flowers and arranged them in a cut glass vase. Each delicate bud was opening into and exquisite rose, the most perfect she had ever seen. She put the vase on the coffee table and sat down on the couch. One of the blossoms seemed to be looking directly at her. She closed her eyes and covered her face with her hands.

What have I done?

November eased into December. Cold, windy nights gave way to days brightened and warmed by the winter sun. With each passing one, Rebecca seemed to gain strength and stamina. Her slow, precise walk disappeared as her usual bustle returned.

"Coffee's made." Kat jumped up when Rebecca came out of the bedroom.

"Sit down, Katarina. I can get it myself."

"You sound like you're feeling well this morning."

"Every day is better. Last night I told Dr. LeBlanc he needn't make any more house calls. By the way, he was obviously disappointed when you weren't here."

"You know I needed to help Lillian and Silka with the fittings of their outfits for the show. We don't want to be doing these adjustments at the last minute."

"I know, but Dr. LeBlanc doesn't understand the fashion business. He probably thought you could have done that earlier in the day and been here when he arrived."

"And he would have been right. But I didn't choose to do that. Besides, you and I had several details to iron out before the fittings."

"Yes . . . but now you're down to the wire. Tonight's the night, isn't it?"

"If you mean that tonight I'm dining with Mason in his home, you're correct. If you're alluding to its being the night when I tell him I can't be any more than a friend, you're also correct." She took a shuddering breath. "I can't tell you how much I'm dreading this."

"You *are* in love with him, aren't you?"

For a long moment she said nothing. "I . . . really don't know. He's been almost everything I needed since we met, and I'm so grateful to him for that. But when does gratitude grow into love . . . or does it at all? I'm so confused, Rebecca."

Kat rented a car and drove to the Maison LeBlanc. Mason had tried to insist that he pick her up, but she'd told him this might be her only chance to drive through the streets of Paris. *You can see more of it if I'm driving,* he'd said. *Yes,* she'd responded, *but then I won't have the exhilarating experience of driving through them myself.* Finally, he had given up. The regret in his voice had almost convinced her to change her mind, but she'd forced herself to remain firm.

Located at the edge of the city but surrounded by considerable acreage stood the LeBlanc mansion. Tourists often passed by to get a glimpse of the six-column French provincial home that had been built in the 1800s.

Mason opened the door to the grand entry hall. "Welcome to my home, Katarina."

She stepped inside and was immediately taken by a beautiful Louis XIV credenza.

"That's Great-grandfather LeBlanc." He pointed to a large oil portrait that hung over the credenza. "Everyone has said he was a rebellious maverick and a prankster to boot."

"Sounds a lot like Granddad Kahill."

His smile sent her heart into a tailspin.

She met his parents and brother and was given a tour of the historic mansion. Just as they returned to the sitting room, dinner was announced. The main course, preceded by hors d'oeuvres and patés, included leg of lamb, tiny potatoes, and French beans. Then came a salad course, followed by a platter of camembert, roquefort and brie cheeses. With each course she felt Mason's burning glances, but she couldn't look in his direction. *If I see the longing in your eyes, I won't be able to say goodbye.*

Mason's brother Jacques kept the conversation lively. "Great-grandfather's favorite joke at parties was to tell everyone about a nude picture that hung in the foyer, then to say it was his lovely wife, Desirée. Funny thing was that the painting did bear a striking resemblance to Great-grandmother."

"Jacques!" Madame LeBlanc's eyes blazed at her son. "This is *not* a proper place to tell such a story."

He gave his mother an impish grin. "But Maman, I'm just a . . . what do the Americans say? . . . a chip off the old block. And the painting *did* look like her—at least in the face."

146

Kat bit her tongue to keep from laughing out loud.

Mason cleared his throat. "You'll have to forgive my brother. He seems not to remember the social etiquette our mother tried to instill in us."

That was all it took. She burst out in unrestrained laughter that seemed to be contagious as, one by one, everyone at the table joined in.

How nice it was to be part of a family gathering. For a nostalgic moment, she longed for her own family. Then she saw his smile . . .

She turned to Madame LeBlanc. "Thank you for making me feel so welcome tonight. I'm a long way from home and from my family."

"This is why we urged Mason to invite you this evening. You must miss your family very much, so for this night we want you to be part of ours."

A lump rose in her throat. She was grateful when one servant cleared the dishes while another brought a platter of fruit tarts and thin slices of a four-layered chocolate cake and five small plates on which to serve the scrumptious-looking desserts. A strong coffee followed and finally cognac.

"I don't believe I've ever eaten so much, yet I don't feel stuffed."

Madame LeBlanc smiled. "That's the secret of French cooking."

"I need to learn that secret and take it home."

Mason stood and reached for her hand. "I want to show you the garden."

She glanced out the window. "It's dark, Mason. I don't think I'll be able to see it."

"Ah, but we have lights. It will be almost as bright as day."

She turned to his mother. "The meal was wonderful and the company even better. Thank you again for including me in your family this evening."

Madame LeBlanc nodded.

Kat followed Mason into the entry hall, where he helped her on with her coat. He opened the door, and they stepped out into the nippy night air. Strolling along the garden path, they came to a place where the ground leveled and they could see the city. A sudden chill made her pull her coat tight around her.

As though sensing her need for warmth, he pulled her against him. She trembled in his arms—not from the cold but from his closeness.

"Katarina, you know I'm falling in love with you."

She pulled away from him. "And you know our love can never be. Oh, Mason, I've been so unfair by not telling you that before. I feel so ashamed to have let you think we could have a relationship. My husband

and I are going through a difficult time right now, but I've loved him with all my heart since I was a little girl. The years have served only to deepen that love. Please forgive me for toying with your emotions."

"There's nothing to forgive, Cherie. It is not my habit to fall in love with someone else's wife, but this time my heart betrayed me. Happiness cannot be built on the pain of others. Were you to leave your husband for me, we would never find the joy that should be shared by a man and a woman in love. You will always have a special place in my heart. I am privileged to have had our paths cross, even if for only a moment in time. Your husband is a very lucky man. I hope he realizes soon what a treasure he has in the loyalty of your devotion." He took her hands and kissed one cheek, then the other.

"I'm so sorry, Mason. I shouldn't be here." She made no attempt to move away from him.

"You *wouldn't* be here if he were taking care of your heart. Just remember that if things don't work out between you, I am here."

With nothing more to say, she walked with him to her car. She pulled out of the driveway and turned toward the lights of the city.

Oh, Dawson, I'd fly home to you tonight if I thought your eyes would shine like those lights to welcome me. You've always been the light of my life.

CHAPTER TWENTY-EIGHT

Kat slipped off her coat and shivered. She'd been gone longer than anticipated, and Rebecca had turned the gas-log fireplace on low and gone to bed. And why not? It was two o'clock in the morning. Kat peeked in on her, watched the even rise and fall of her chest, then pulled the door closed.

She turned up the fireplace, poured a glass of Chardonnay, and turned out the lamp. Spanning the view from the large living room window, she watched the twinkling polka dots of light that covered the city before draining her glass and refilling it.

I may have to finish the whole bottle to escape the sorrow I'm feeling tonight. Trampling on Mason's heart had been bad enough, but her temporary acceptance into the LeBlanc family circle had reminded her how much she missed her own. *Why haven't you called me, Dawson? I've been gone three months, and you haven't spoken a single word to me in all that time. No postcards, no letters, nothing.*

She walked away from the window and let the overstuffed chair engulf her small frame. Placing one leg beneath her, she curled up and dialed the country code and number for Willow Walk.

"Hello?" A pause followed. "Hello! This you, Kitten? I can barely hear you."

Granddad's voice soothed her like a cup of warm tea on a chilly morning. "Yes, it's me, Granddad. This connection isn't very good."

"I know. How's things? Hold on a second, Kat." She heard the children squealing in the background. "Joey! Molly Anna! Stop jumping on the sofa. I'm trying to talk to your Mama in Paris, Joey."

"Lemme talk, lemme talk to Mama in Paris," Joey shouted. Tears filled her eyes, but she was smiling.

"Me too. Me too. I wanna talk." *Molly must still be following Joey's lead.*

"These kids are driving me nuttier than I already am. Hello? Hello! You still there Kitten?"

"I'm here. They're rambunctious so close to bedtime, aren't they?"

"Same as always. But you're up mighty late, girly. We miss you. When're you comin' home for that visit you promised?"

"Does Dawson miss me too?" *Why did I ask that?*

"I . . . I can't speak for Dawson. You'll have to ask him yourself."

Fat chance since he doesn't talk to me. "I won't be home until after the show, Granddad. Rebecca's sick—had an aneurysm in her brain and had to have emergency surgery. She's staying with me until she's back on her feet. Oh, I have so much to tell you."

"You're a good girl—always lookin' after others. We've got lots to tell you, too. Just take care of yourself, Kitten."

"What? You're fading out. The connection is getting worse. Let me say hi to Dawson, and tell Joey I'll call him tomorrow. Love you, Granddad." Other than the background noise of the children, the line was silent for a full minute. *Looks like nothing's changed. Why did I even bother asking.*

"Hello, Kat?"

"Dawson? How are you?" *How are you? We haven't spoken for months, and all I can say is 'how are you?' I never dreamed conversation with my husband could be so awkward.*

"Uh . . . not too bad today. How about you?"

"Okay, but I miss all of you." *So far, so good.*

"Oh. We've had some new developments here, Kat."

"What new developments?"

"When you come home, I'll . . . tell you then."

He was actually talking to her. She didn't know whether to laugh of cry. "Tell me now, please, Daw." She strained to separate his voice from the static on the line.

"Later." His voice crackled and snapped.

"But, Daw, I want to talk to you. I need to tell you . . . how much I love you."

"I . . . I miss you, Kat."

"I miss you, too. I—" A loud buzzing on the line ended the conversation.

Did I hear right? Did he really say he misses me? Why didn't he say he loves me? Something was different. Different? Or wrong? Whatever it is, I can't do anything about it from here. The show's just six weeks away, and I can't dwell on problems at home. They've apparently gotten along without until now. A little longer won't matter one way or the other.

Her alarm went off before the sun came up. She yawned and pushed the snooze button. Four hours' sleep wasn't enough. The aroma of fresh coffee wafted into the living room. *I didn't set the automatic coffee maker.* She forced herself out of bed and grabbed her robe.

"What are you doing up?" She forced a smile for Rebecca.

"Fixing breakfast, night owl. What time did you get in? How did it go with Mason? You did tell him, didn't you?"

She flopped into a chair at the small table. "One question at a time, please. It was a short night."

Rebecca laughed and put two cups of coffee on the table. "Sure, but get started. I'm not letting you out of here this morning until you tell me everything."

"It was wonderful . . . and nostalgic . . . and sad. His family welcomed me with open arms and I got so homesick. The food was more than delicious. Mason and I walked in the garden. And then I broke his heart."

"I take it that's the nutshell version."

Kat sipped her coffee. "It's the best you're going to get in the wee hours of the morning."

"Wee hours? It's six-thirty, Kat. We need to be at the design studio by eight?"

"*We?*"

"The good doctor has given me permission to work half days. Can you believe it? Of course, I've been begging him for the last week. I want to catch up on the staging, lighting, and garments that must be ready by now."

"That's great news. And speaking of news, I have some for you?"

"Other than about Mason, you mean?"

"I talked to Dawson."

"What? I thought—"

"You're right. He hasn't spoken to me since that horrible night when he told me not to bother to come home if I took this job. But this time was different. He almost sounded . . . like the Dawson I married."

"That's good, isn't it?" Rebecca sounded confused.

"It's wonderful . . . except that I can't shake the feeling that something's wrong."

"Now it's my turn to tell *you* not to be a pessimist. Things are looking up at home, and you're thinking something's wrong with that?"

"No, no. It's just one of those woman's intuition things. I'm going to call back this evening just to reassure myself that I'm being silly. It's probably just the shock that my husband not only carried on a pleasant conversation with me, he even said he misses me."

Rebecca got up and began cracking eggs in a bowl. She dumped small ham pieces and julienned vegetables into the skillet. "It's omelettes and toast this morning. I need fuel if I'm going to make it till noon."

"Let me help." Kat pushed herself up from the table and refilled her coffee cup.

"No, this is my day. Why don't you relax while the veggies sauté?" Rebecca stirred the contents of the skillet and moments later added the beaten eggs.

Kat tried to keep her mind on her work, but her thoughts kept turning back to Willow Walk. By midafternoon, she couldn't wait any longer.

"I'm going home. The rest of you are free to call it a day. We'll start at seven in the morning," she told the staff as she hurried out the door.

As soon as she arrived at the apartment, she curled up in the same overstuffed chair and dialed her home number. The call took a few moments to go through, but the connection was good this time. Dawson answered the phone. *What's going on? He hasn't answered the phone since before the accident.* "Daw?"

"Is that you, Kat? Are you okay? I just talked to you a few hours ago."

He asked if I'm okay. Another first. Tears welled up in her eyes. "I'm fine. Are you?"

"Uh . . . why do you ask?"

"Because something's different. Something's changed. And I've just got this feeling . . . Is something wrong with Joey? How about Granddad?"

"Joey and Granddad are fine."

"But you didn't say you're fine. I know something's wrong . . . I can feel it. What are the new developments you mentioned before? Tell me, Daw, please." The tears tumbled down her cheeks.

He didn't respond.

"Dawson, I need to know what's wrong. I'm a long way from home, but I still know something isn't right at Willow Walk. Please, Darling, tell me." She began to sob.

"Please don't cry, Kat. I can't handle that. I'll tell you. I've had some tests run."

"What kind of tests?"

"I have a tumor."

"You have a *what?*" The lump in her throat made her voice crack.

"A brain tumor. Now listen to me, Kat."

"I don't want to listen, Daw. I'm coming home on the next flight out of here."

"Please let me finish."

She took a deep breath. "Okay . . . and then I'm coming home."

"I knew I was treating all of you like I didn't care, but I couldn't figure out why I was so bitter and so angry. The pain in my leg was excruciating, but the pills helped. Then I had a conversation with the mirror. I didn't like what it said, so I broke it.

"What are you talking about?"

"The mirror in the bedroom."

She shook her head. "I don't understand any of this."

"Just listen. I made myself get up out of the chair, and I threw my electric shaver at the mirror. Then I collapsed. Granddad came to help me, and he made me go to the doctor."

"What'd the doctor say?"

"He took the usual medical history and stopped cold when I told him Dad died of a brain tumor. When I described the way he acted for so many years and then my behavioral changes, he ordered an MRI that same afternoon. It seems some types of those things can be hereditary."

"Dinner's ready," Rebecca called from the kitchen.

Kat put her hand over the mouthpiece. "Go ahead and eat. I'll be there in a couple minutes."

"The MRI showed my tumor," Dawson continued, "but it's operable. The doctor said I should have the surgery as soon as possible . . . but I want to wait until you come home. A few more weeks shouldn't make that much difference."

She found her strength. "Stop right there, Dawson Kahill. As soon as his office opens in the morning, you get on the phone and tell your doctor to schedule it right away. I'll be there by tomorrow night at the latest. And don't you say one word to talk me out of it. I need to be with my husband—the man I love with all my heart."

"Oh, yes, Kat, please come home." She heard the tears in his voice. "I need you now more than I've ever needed you."

Rebecca handed her a plate. "What is it? What's happening?"

Kat looked at the food. Whatever appetite she'd had had disappeared. "I have to go home tonight, Rebecca. Dawson has a brain tumor. He's having surgery. I'll explain while I pack, but I need to go right now."

"Of course, you do. I'll arrange for your flight and a car to take you to the airport. I can handle things here. I'm strong enough to oversee the work now."

"I can't believe this is happening. First, your aneurysm. Now Dawson's tumor. If I didn't know better, I'd think it's dangerous to have me as a friend or a wife."

Rebecca laughed. "Maybe you should look at the other side of that coin. It's *good* that we have you as a friend or a wife because we know that we'll get the best care possible. Now eat that food while I make your reservations."

"I'm really not hungry."

"Maybe not, but it'll be the last meal you'll have before you get home. No backtalk now. Just clean that plate."

Kat couldn't hold back her smile. Rebecca was getting even for all the times she'd told *her* what to do.

"I'll keep in touch. If everything goes well, I'll be back in time for the show."

"Don't worry, Katarina. Just go be with your husband. He's the most important thing in your life right now. My prayers and good wishes go with you."

They were all waiting in the reception area at the airport. Granddad and Carla held Joey back. Dawson limped toward her. She dropped her carry-on bag and ran into his open arms. All the pain and rejection of the last year melted away in her tears as he held her tight against his heart. She covered his face with kisses. They didn't move until Joey forced his way between them.

"Mama, don't you wanna kiss me, too?" His cherubic face was filled with so much love. "I missed you, Mama."

She reached down and planted kisses all over the top of his head. "Of course, I want to kiss you. You're my little man, aren't you?"

I'm not so little." He gave her an indignant look. "I'm five now, ya know."

"Yes, my darling. I know you're a big boy now, and I've missed you so much." She looked up at Dawson. "Let's go home."

"I'm glad you flew into Wheeling," Granddad said in a low tone as they walked to her van. "Dawson couldn't have made it any further. He's in pretty bad shape, Kitten. The surgery's scheduled for day after tomorrow."

"Oh, Granddad, why didn't somebody tell me? I would've come home sooner."

"You were needed where you were. Besides, he hasn't known all that long." The old man shook his head. "He refused to bring his crutches to meet you. Said he wanted you to know he was still a man."

Her heart felt like it was going to shatter in a million pieces. *How could I have ever thought that Mason LeBlanc could replace my husband? He's a good man and he saves a lot of lives, but he could never be another Dawson Kahill.*

Kat clung to Dawson's hand as they strolled toward Grandma Emma's greenhouse. They passed the old swing where they used to play as children.

"Wait!" She pulled him gently back toward it and sat down on its still sturdy seat." A moment later he was pushing her like he had some twenty years before.

"It feels so good to be home," she said as they continued on to the greenhouse.

"It's good to have you home. I was so afraid you'd meet somebody in Paris and fall for him after the way I'd treated you for months."

Her breath caught in her chest. "You're the only man for me, Dawson Kahill, and don't you forget it." She reached up and kissed his cheek. *Does he know? When we were kids, he could always tell what was in my heart. But we're not kids now. And I'll never tell him . . .*

They cut flowers for the dinner table. Dawson snipped an exquisite red rose, clipped the thorns, and slipped it behind her ear.

"For you, my darling. It's beauty pales beside yours."

His kiss was as soft and silky as the tender blossom he'd placed in her hair.

"Let me help," Kat said to Carla when they entered the kitchen.

"Not on your life, Missy. You just got home, and your family's been missing you something awful. Now you go and spend time with them. I hear you'll be going back to Paris before long, so you'd best not waste a minute. Now if I need help, I can ask Jedediah." Her skeptical look was answered by a wink from Carla. *Wonder what's going on with those two. Come to think about it, Granddad hasn't said one bad thing about her since I got back. I bet Penelope Weatherbush isn't a happy camper right now.*

She was almost too tired to eat, but she forced herself. Carla had outdone herself with roast beef, sweet potato casserole, honey-buttered carrots, and the best Waldorf salad she'd ever tasted. Joey had insisted on helping with dessert, and he and Carla concocted a gelatin mold that he topped with whipped cream.

Looking around at her family, she was overcome with love. The lovely dinner at Maison LeBlanc hadn't begun to compare with this simple family meal she was sharing with those she loved most. *This is how every night should be at Willow Walk. How fortunate I am to be here. Thank you, God, for giving me this time with my loved ones. Please take care of Dawson, and protect him if it is Your will.*

Joey and Jedediah helped Carla clean up. Kat and Dawson headed upstairs to bed. She had barely closed the door when he reached for her. His gentle kisses teased her. His urgent ones drew her. With happy tears she surrendered to the man she had married.

"No word yet, Kitten?" Jedediah called for the second time in thirty minutes.

"Not yet, Granddad. The doctor said it could take a while. This is worse than waiting through Rebecca's aneurysm surgery. If anything happens to . . ."

"Now, Kitten, you get them bad thoughts out of your head. Pray like I been doin' and have some faith. Sonny has everything to live for, and he knows that now. Besides, I ain't got that new grandbaby Emma yet. I told that boy he'd best get back on his feet quick and get to work on that."

She stifled a giggle. It wouldn't do to tell Granddad that the problem was in Dawson's head. The rest of him worked just fine. "Okay, Granddad, I'll remind him when I see him. I'll call you as soon as I know something. I love you. And tell Joey I love him, too."

He always makes me feel better. I think having a new baby around might be just the thing we need at Willow Walk. I'm not sure how I'll juggle that with my work for Wolf International, but it might be a great incentive to create a line of chic maternity wear. I could call it 'Waiting in Style.' With the right computer set-up, I could work from home. It would have to be from home. Family comes first.

"Kat?"

She looked up from the magazine she was reading. "Deb! Bonny! I can't believe you're here. How did you know." She jumped up and gave them both a hug.

"Granddad called a while ago. He thought you might like some company since he's home taking care of the kids," Deb said.

"I have to say, those two are keeping him young. He looks better than I've seen him in months," Bonny added.

"Dawson's ordeal has been very hard on him. He'd pinned all his hopes on his grandson, and when Dawson began acting like Cable, he almost lost that hope."

Deb and Bonny sat on either side of her. "How's the surgery coming? Have you heard anything?"

"No, but I'm hoping to soon. He's been in there a long time."

"Mrs. Kahill?"

They all turned toward the man in scrubs.

"I'm Katarina Kahill." Kat stood and walked over to him.

He reached out and shook her hand. "I'm Dr. Barton."

"How's my husband?"

"He's in recovery now. The surgery went well, even better than expected. Dawson had a meningioma tumor at the base of his brain. It was fairly large and covered part of the base of the cerebellum and had invaded the top end of the spinal column. We were able to get it all, and the preliminary tissue examination indicated it wasn't malignant. Of course, we'll have to wait for a full report on the biopsy, but based on what we know now, he has a good chance to recover completely."

"When may I see him?"

"It'll be a little while. I'll have somebody come for you when he's out of recovery. He shouldn't have any more problems with his balance."

"His balance, doctor? I wasn't aware that he was having problems with his balance." *That means . . . maybe Dawson was right. Maybe he really couldn't walk. And we all chastised him.* She felt sick to her stomach.

"This type of tumor affects balance and mood. Dizziness and nausea are also common symptoms." He checked the clock on the wall. "I have another surgery, but I'll be checking on your husband daily."

"That's what we wanted to hear." Deb stood up and smiled.

"Our prayers have been answered." Bonny gave her a big hug.

Deb pulled on her coat. "Now it's time to go back to work. We closed the boutique for an hour so we could be with you, but it's time to open up again."

She watched them leave and flipped open her cell phone to call Granddad with the good news.

"I'm so glad to hear that." She heard the concern in his voice disappear. "Now when are you thinkin' on bein' home, Kitten?"

"Not until I've seen Dawson and know first-hand that he's okay. Then I may sit with him for a while so when he opens his eyes, he knows he's not alone."

"That's my girl! We'll see you when you get here."

"Bye, Granddad."

She closed the phone and stared at the wall. *Oh, Dawson, please forgive me for the times I scolded you for sitting in that wheelchair. I thought you just didn't want to walk. I didn't know . . . you never let on . . . I can't imagine how difficult it must have been for you to stay on your feet since I've been home . . .*

and to meet me at the airport. Granddad said you wanted me to know you're still a man. My love, you are all the man I will ever need and so much more.

"Mrs. Kahill?" A portly male nurse stood in the doorway. "You may see your husband now if you like."

"I'd like." She followed him to ICU and stood beside Dawson's bed. He didn't seem to hear a word she said, but she knew he felt the warmth of her tears as they fell upon his hand because his fingers curled around hers.

When he woke up, she told him about the fashion show and about Rebecca's surgery. She had a captive audience and a husband she'd missed for many months, so he got an earful about the fashion world, whether he wanted to hear it or not.

Several days later, he held her hand as they sat in the sunroom with other patients and their visitors. "I had no idea what you were dealing with in Paris. Taking care of Rebecca, working on the show, trying to stay in touch with your family at home, and now you're here taking care of me. Maybe you should've been a nurse instead of a famous fashion designer."

"I'm not cut out to be a nurse, but Rebecca didn't have anybody else to care for her. As for you, I'm your wife. I'm doing for you what you did for me after Joey was born. We take care of each other. And as for the famous part . . . you've got to be kidding. I'm Mrs. Dawson Kahill, and I've never heard of her in the fashion world."

He chuckled.

"If you hadn't told me what was going on, I wouldn't be here now. That scares me, Daw. What if something awful had happened?" She grasped his other hand as the tears started to flow.

"Shhh, my darling Kat." He pulled her to him.

"If I hadn't gotten the feeling that something was wrong, would you have called me?"

"I . . . I don't know. Granddad was after me to let you know, but you remember what a jerk I was being. The only thing that matters now is that you're here and our lives are back on track . . . together."

She sniffed.

"I've been thinking."

"Oh, oh. I'm not sure I like the sound of that."

"I know how much your career means to you, and—"

"My family means more."

"I understand that, but please hear me out. You spent three months in Paris, working on this show. I think you need to go back and finish what you started."

She shook her head.

"Rebecca's counting on you to be there, and I feel so much better since the surgery. I can't believe what an ogre I was for all those months, but I'm not one now. Even the headaches are easing off. So I'm going to get my rear in gear, get back to my physical therapy, and work on becoming the husband that my beautiful, loving wife deserves. When you get back from winning that show, I'll be a new man."

"I don't need a new man." Her heart shuddered. She kissed his fingers. "I love the one I've got. So let's do this. If you still feel the same way a week after you get home, I'll go. The show's just three weeks away now, so I'd only be gone for a couple of weeks. How does that sound?" She searched his face for approval.

He nodded. "Sounds like a plan. Now let's get back to my room so I can kiss my sweet wife without all these prying eyes watching."

She laughed and blushed. "I would say you're recovering quite nicely, Dawson Kahill, maybe a little too nicely."

"Hey, woman, I've got almost a year of catching up to do. You'd better get prepared."

A week later, she and Granddad sat on the porch swing while Dawson and Joey napped on the couch.

"I've been meaning to ask you about Cabe," she said. "Have you heard anything?"

"Not much. The scoundrel's in Mexico, chasin' a skirt just like his old man."

"C'mon, Granddad, you know Cable was a sick man. As for his boy, I'd be willing to bet you don't know the whole story."

"I don't care to know it neither."

"Granddad! At least give him the benefit of the doubt."

"I'll be doin' that . . . the day he returns with all the money he stole."

"Has he admitted stealing it?"

"Yep. Told Polly Dee he had to get back to some Mexican girl. Said he loved her, but I kinda doubt that."

"Why would you doubt it?"

"Because he's the worst kind of thief. I don't think anybody who stoops so low as to steal from family has the ability to love."

She gave him a hard look. "You've got to be kidding."

"Nope."

"Did he make arrangements to pay back what he took?"

"Told Dawson he would, but he hasn't put his money where his mouth is up to now."

"So let's not give up on him just yet. Polly Dee told me he was always a good kid. Let's not assume that he's a rotten adult just because he made one mistake."

"I'll not give up on him. But he'd best stay in Mexico till he's paid his debt to Dawson . . . with interest."

She shook her head. He was a stubborn old soul, and he expected everybody to march to his drummer. "Granddad, I'm going back to Paris."

"No." He scowled at her. "We just got you back, and we're not lettin' you out of our sight again."

"I already have my ticket."

"Does Sonny know about this?"

"It was his idea. I leave tomorrow morning."

"You two have a fight or somethin'? I thought things was hunky-dory between you now."

"Everything's fine between Dawson and me. I have a contract with Wolf International, and he says he's feeling much better now so I need to fulfill it."

Jedediah gave her a long look. "You best go, then, and do what you set out to do, Kitten. You show them high falutin' folks that my Kitten from West Virginia is the best in the business. Then you hightail it back home to your family. Meantime, we got everythin' under control here."

"Thanks, Granddad." She hugged him tight. "I've got to finish packing before my men wake up and want something to eat.

"You're missing your family, aren't you, Katarina? I can see it in your eyes. A faraway look has replaced the sadness that was there before." Rebecca's question came a few days after her return to Paris.

"Oh, yes, but I'll be home soon. And this time it's with joyful anticipation rather than dread. But before that we have a trophy to win, lady, so let's get busy an put the Wolf name back on those wagging fashion tongues."

"I couldn't believe how much you had accomplished when I came back to work. Why, everything was practically ready to go. I don't know how you managed with all the time you were spending with me."

"Would you believe a lot of long days and short nights?"

"I'd believe. But you know you don't have to keep those hours after the show."

"I know you wanted me to take over at Wolf, but you're doing so well, and—"

"Stop right there, Katarina. I haven't changed my mind about retiring. After the show I'm kissing the world of glamour goodbye and going off to the countryside to begin my life of leisure. If I ever feel the urge to wear silk and brocade, I can do my gardening in them." Rebecca paused and they both broke out in laughter.

"I'll be forever in your debt for the faith you've put in me and my designs, even more so for the opportunity to put Wolf International back on the map and keep it there." She paused. "How do you think the industry will feel about my moving its executive office to Wheeling? The rest of the staff could be in New York, of course."

Rebecca raised an eyebrow. "You don't want to stay in Paris? Your family could join you here, you know."

"Ummm . . . I don't think so. Dawson's just getting back to the ski lodge that was his dream for years before it became a reality. Besides . . . I'd rather not run into Mason. It would be awkward at best, catastrophic at worst. And I certainly don't ever want to see him and Dawson together."

"You really did care for the man, didn't you?"

"Yes, but not in the same way that I love my husband. Mason's a very special man. I was wrong to let him think we could have a relationship, wrong to lead him on—however unintentionally. I was lonely, starved for affection—and in this city where romance rules. Aren't those pitiful excuses for playing with a man's heart?"

Rebecca nodded and smiled. "I had a follow-up appointment with him while you were gone. He asked about you, and I told him of your husband's problem. It did, after all, fall into his field of work."

"What did he say?"

"He wanted to know the outcome. I haven't told him yet."

"I hope that doesn't mean he'll be popping in to find out."

"I don't know. But enough of this. We've got a show to do."

CHAPTER TWENTY NINE

"It's show time," Kat whispered to herself. She bit her lip while she put the final touches on her makeup. *I'm as nervous as a fly caught in a spider's web. Before this night is over, Wolf International Fashions will be famous around the globe once again.* She felt a certain satisfaction in helping to undo the damage Lincoln had done to Rebecca's business. *The atmosphere for this show is so different from the last one. Lillian has been invaluable. Last time, she despised me. I had no idea she was romantically involved with Lincoln, and she had no idea I intended to be no man's mistress.*

"You look stunning, Katarina," Rebecca said as they rode the elevator down to the lobby.

"Thank you, Rebecca. But tell me, who will be looking at the models when you show up in that outfit?" Kat smiled as Rebecca posed in the dress Kat had designed for her.

"You really meant it when you said you'd make something special for me. I love it. Too bad you didn't design it for one of the models. It really should be part of the show."

"Oh, no. You were the inspiration for it. You should be the only one to wear it."

"I once aspired to be the belle of the ball. That day has passed, but I think that aspiration may be fulfilled tonight."

"Better late than never," Kat reminded her.

She viewed the three-piece ensemble with approval. The suit, a deep shade of jade green brocade, had a quilted collar and cuffs trimmed with the same jet beads as the black satin camisole. In keeping with Rebecca's trademark of brimmed hats, she had fashioned a black satin one for her, lined with black tulle that hid the back of her head where the hair had not yet grown in. Thick blonde waves framed her face, giving the illusion of a full head of hair. No one would ever suspect that she had just undergone the ordeal of brain surgery. Just before they left the apartment, she had given Rebecca a single strand of jet beads interspersed with Florentine gold balls.

Kat's own knee-length dress, also one of her original designs, had been crafted from deep blue silk chiffon with a dropped waistline and flared skirt. Deco-styled beading trimmed the waistline and edged the matching bolero jacket. Her only jewelry, a diamond heart pendant with matching earrings, had been a gift from Dawson on the night before she returned to Paris.

Their limousine parked at the arena entrance, and the chauffer helped them out. Kat beamed as every passerby stopped to stare. As they entered the pavilion, all eyes turned their way. One was blonde and one was brunette, but both exuded an air of elegant confidence that couldn't be ignored.

McCarron Designs took the runway first. All their models were made up to look like dolls. Heavily rouged cheeks, overdone eye shadow, and straightened hair gave credence to the whimsical clothing they wore. This theme carried over into the evening wear. The backdrop depicted an open book of paper dolls. Each of the first three models stepped off the page, leaving behind only the tabs used to hold their clothing in place. Their simple gowns in pastel shades further emphasized their characters. Spectacular fabrics in subtle paisley prints—pink, lilac, and blue—created a rainbow of colors that led to their grand finale gown. The paisley theme was captured in the shape of the peacock feathers that filled the voluminous skirt. The tightly fitted bodice in a deep aqua tone was accentuated by the same tone in the spray of peacock feathers in the model's hair. The bold colors of the gown, in striking contrast to the others, struck an instant chord with the cheering audience.

Rebecca let out a soft groan. Kat looked at her and smiled.

The next presentation was staged by Flair, last year's winner. Purple, green, and gold banners—the colors of Mardi Gras—decorated the stage.

"How clever," Rebecca whispered. "Mardi Gras was started by the French. Look at that gold lamé fleur-de-lis flag. The French media will love it." Once again she gave Kat a worried look.

Kat rolled her eyes. "Rebecca Wolf, since when are you afraid of a little competition?"

Flair's models wore elaborate carnival masks to match the colors of their purple, green and gold gowns—a gorgeous purple velvet, a delicate green voile, and a striking gold lamé. The finale gown of silk taffeta combined all three colors in a diagonal swirl design. Kat was sure the strapless top and bell-shaped skirt must have taken yards of the unique fabric. As the model walked the runway, jesters ran through the audience, handing out colorful beads. The entire presentation was beautiful, outrageous, and an obvious crowd pleaser. The cheers went on so long that the emcee asked the models to take another turn down the runway.

Kat winced when Rebecca looked at her for reassurance. *I'm not sure how we're going to beat that one. It's magnificent.* Kat's palm was cold and clammy when Rebecca reached for it, but Kat didn't return her stare. Her gaze was glued to the stage as the emcee announced the next participant —Wolf International Fashions.

Lillian, Silka, and two other models they'd hired for the show moved rhythmically to the music they'd chosen to fit each category of clothing. Everything came off as planned—no slips, no missed cues. When the moment for the evening gowns arrived, Kat closed her eyes. *I can't breathe. What if we don't win? What if . . .* She felt Rebecca's hand touch her arm and opened her eyes to see her smile and wink.

"Ladies and gentlemen," the emcee announced, "may I present Wolf International's evening entries, 'Fit for a Queen.' First, we have Guinevere, King Arthur's queen."

She looked like a delicate flower in iridescent silk chiffon, hand brushed in shades of blue, mauve, and violet. A blue and gold cord of braided silk surrounded her waist. From its ends hung beads of Austrian crystal. A matching headband encircled her pale blonde curls. She wore no jewelry. The breathtaking gown needed no additional enhancement.

"Next we have a gown based on the style of Queen Victoria, but softened to meet the sophisticated taste of today's woman," the announcer said.

Anniah appeared in a golden jewel-toned taffeta gown with an elegant silhouette. The ruched and ruffled bodice was topped with a face-framing asymmetrical collar that sat just off her shoulders. The bodice itself featured an insert of lace that ended in a pointed V at the waist and was hand-beaded with pearls. A choker of pearls with a diamond clasp worn in the front completed this entry.

Again the announcer spoke. "Now we have Cleopatra, queen of the Nile."

Lillian wore a satin gown in a deep plum color that was offset down the left side with a triple band of rhinestones. The off-the-shoulder creation had a single band of rhinestones ending at the wrist of each long sleeve. Her eye makeup perfectly replicated the Egyptian look, and her flawless neck was surrounded by three strands of magnificent rhinestones connected in the center by a huge rhinestone snake. Kat had never seen her look more stunning or more confident.

"And now for Wolf International's grand finale gown, 'Castles in the Air.'" The tuxedoed emcee stood aside as a backdrop lowered to the stage. A hush fell over the audience when the backdrop unfolded to reveal a beautiful turreted castle. A drawbridge came down. In its opening stood Silka. Rebecca gasped and covered her mouth. All eyes locked on the model, who stood motionless until she got a nod from Kat.

As Silka stepped forward, a wispy fog appeared at her feet, just enough to make her seem to be walking on a cloud. Draped over her lithe body was a Greek-style white crystal-pleated diaphanous gown. Shot through with threads of silver, gold, and bronze, it served as an overlay for a bronze satin sheath. A crown of rhinestones stood out against her upswept jet-black hair, and a wide belt of rhinestones cinched the ensemble at the waist. She sparkled with each swish of her hips. This was not the dress of a queen, but one of a goddess, and Silka played the part to the hilt. The audience stood and burst into applause that continued as Silka floated down the runway and back.

Tears streamed down Rebecca's cheeks. Kat beamed from the vantage point of their front-row seats.

"Katarina, I should never have doubted you. I knew this gown was luscious, but the way you and Silka built the suspense by waiting . . . well, it was just . . . just—"

"Ladies and gentlemen, please take your seats." The announcer waited while the audience continued to applaud. "Take your seats, *please*. It's time to announce the winner this year's Fashion show." Again he paused. Silence settled over the large room. "The Grand Prize winner is . . ."

"Oh, for goodness sake, get on with it," Rebecca fumed in a low whisper.

" . . . Wolf International Fashions."

Kat stood and pulled Rebecca to her feet. "I'm not accepting this alone. Let's go, Rebecca."

The audience roared its approval as arm in arm they stepped onto the stage to accept their trophy. Flashes of light from a hundred cameras nearly blinded them, but from the corner of her eye, Kat caught a glimpse of a blond headed man with a handsome face. And then he was gone.

* * * * *

Kat and Rebecca sat in the large chairs on either side of Kat's fireplace.

"I'm too tired to think." Kat yawned.

"Then I'll think for both of us." Rebecca pulled an envelope from her evening bag and handed it to Kat.

She opened it and read the contents. Her eyes glistened with tears. "Are you sure you want to do this?"

"More than ever. I've told you before that you don't know your worth. You're one of the few good things that came out of my marriage to Lincoln Wolf. Surprisingly, Lillian Rae is another. Now the two of you can take this company all the way to the moon and back if that's your pleasure. Me? I'm going to be enjoying life in the French countryside. You now officially own forty-nine percent of Wolf International, and we both leave Paris as winners."

"This is an incredibly generous gift, Rebecca. I don't know what to say."

"'Thank you' will do nicely." She gave Kat a serious look, and then they both broke out laughing.

"But you will keep up with what's going on, won't you"

"Do I need to refresh your memory about the definition of 'retirement'."

"But I want you to have a voice in—"

"No. You have the reins now. Hold on to them. Once I move to the country, you won't hear from me unless it's a social call."

"Oh, Rebecca, whatever will I do without your supervision."

"Sweetie, if I thought you needed supervision, I would not have put you in control of the company. Now let's get some sleep. You're heading back to the States, and I'm about to become a lady of leisure."

CHAPTER THIRTY

Willow Walk was where Kat wanted to be, but the day after the show she found herself immersed in arrangements to have everything packed for shipment back to New York. She wanted to feel grass under her feet, hear the sound of Willow Creek in her ears, and have her loving husband by her side. Willow Walk was an ocean away.

Paris had been a wonderful, exhilarating experience, and it was a gorgeous city. But it didn't even begin to compare with the most beautiful place in the world—her home in West Virginia.

I'm ready to go home where I belong. I want to be with my family, make love with my husband, and forget that I ever let my heart be tempted by . . .

As though conjured up from her thoughts, Mason stood before her, a bouquet of red roses in his hand. Suddenly aware that everyone in the room had stopped packing and was watching them, she wanted to crawl under the nearest large piece of furniture.

"Congratulations on your win, Katarina." He handed her the flowers.

"It wasn't my win. It belongs to everyone here." She gestured toward all the workers in the room. She watched a sad expression pass across his face. "The roses are beautiful. Thank you so much for bringing them." She buried her nose in the blooms to take in their sweet scent.

"Do you have a few moments to take a short walk along the Seine? I know you're busy, but—"

"I think that's a delightful idea." She grabbed her coat and headed out the door, away from the curious stares of the Wolf staff.

He put his hand on the small of her back as they walked outside. She moved ahead, just out of reach."

"Forgive me, Katarina, I know you told me you love your husband, but I cannot simply push a button and turn off my feelings for you."

The sun was sliding below the horizon just as it had the night she drove to Maison LeBlanc for dinner.

"Mason, you've done nothing that requires forgiveness. I'm the one who should be asking for your forgiveness. I had no right to allow you to think we could be more than friends. You filled a huge void in my life with your attention, your kindness, your concern for my welfare as well as that of Rebecca. You are indeed a special man. And for an inexcusable moment, I allowed you to sweep me off my feet."

He took her hand and drew her to sit on a bench next to him. "I know what you're telling me, Katarina. It's not what I want to hear, but your happiness is important to me. The prize you won last night pales in comparison to the treasure you are to your husband. I hope he knows that now."

Kat gazed off into space. She blinked so he wouldn't see the tears that were forming. "Thank you for expressing such kind thoughts about me, even if I don't deserve them. If things were different—"

He raised his hand to stop her. "I think I know what you're going to say. Strangely, I don't think I want to hear it."

"She let go of his hand and stood. "I'll be leaving day after tomorrow." After studying him for a long moment, she wondered if he had heard her. He just sat there, his gaze glued to her face.

"The moon is rising over your shoulder, Katarina. I want to remember you this way—your beauty framed by the moonlight." He stood and placed his hands on her arms. "I've made things difficult by falling in love with you, haven't I?"

The pained expression on his face tugged at her heart. "We share some extraordinary memories, and for that I'll never be sorry. Nobody can take that from us."

"I feel like a broken-hearted lover in a fairytale with an unhappy ending. I wanted to be your prince, but you already have one. I let myself believe that I could be your lover, but I respect you too much to draw you into such a relationship because that's not the kind of person you are. Oh, Katarina, you're not to blame for what happened between us—only for what *didn't* happen. And for that we shall both be eternally grateful."

His words brought a torrent of tears to spill over her lashes. He dried them with his thumbs and turned her face up to his. "Your tears serve only to make you more lovely because they show me your heart."

The wind blew in a soft whisper through the trees, and the moon cast its pale light over them. Without warning, he pulled her into his arms. Their mouths met—a gentle brushing of his lips on hers, but she knew that almost-kiss would leave a trace upon her heart forever.

"I'll never forget you, Katarina." He dropped his arms to his sides. "Come on. Let me walk you back."

She nodded and smiled. He put his arm around her shoulder, but this time she felt no guilt. They would be parting as friends.

At the door he gave her a kiss to the cheek and a loving smile. *"Au revoir, Madame Kahill."*

"Take care of yourself, Dr. LeBlanc."

She watched him turn and walk away. He didn't once turn to look back at her. She knew because her gaze followed him until he disappeared from sight.

CHAPTER THIRTY-ONE

In the darkness just before dawn when most people are asleep, Kat sat at the airport and watched travelers scurry about like bees in a hive. She looked at the clock. Its hands seemed to be crawling at a snail's pace toward her five o'clock departure time. Her plane wasn't late; she was early. No point in hanging around the apartment when she couldn't sleep. In fact, she hadn't slept at all.

Rebecca was staying in Paris another day to make sure Wolf and its employees had everything crated and on its way to New York. *Now they're my employees, too. I still can't believe that half of Wolf International belongs to me . . . and I'll be running the show. I wonder what Dawson will think about that?*

It was hard saying goodbye to Rebecca. We've been through a lot together. I know she's retiring, but I plan to keep her informed about what's going on with the company—whether she wants to know or not. Besides, I want to know how she's doing with her garden and her life.

I need to bring Deb and Bonny up to speed on everything. Won't they be surprised? For years they kept after me to follow through with my expansion, and suddenly we've burst onto the world scene in one night. They've both worked so hard to keep Fashions by Kat going . . . but first things first. I want to spend time with my family . . . with my husband. I can't wait to hold them all in my arms again. It's so good to be going home to Willow Walk.

"Ladies and gentlemen, this is the first call for flight 8011 from Paris to Charleston, stopping in Washington D.C. First class passengers, please begin loading at gate fourteen."

She stood up and grabbed her carry-on bag. Rebecca had insisted on buying her a first-class ticket. "Winners need to travel in style," she had said. At the time she'd objected. Now it made sense. Catching up on her sleep during the long trip would be much more comfortable in first class. She settled into her assigned seat and looked out the window. *I'm coming home, Daw. I'm leaving the city of love and coming home to the love of my life—you.*

"Please fasten your seatbelts."

Shaking her head, she locked in the restraining device. *I must have dozed.* The big plane soared into the sky, tunneling through billowy clouds that looked like huge fluffs of cotton candy. She smiled as thoughts of "Castles in the Air" flitted through her mind. *What an exciting night. It was even better than the first time I won for Wolf, the one Lincoln had claimed to have a hand in. That man hadn't possessed even an ounce of humility. Rebecca, on the other hand—what an extraordinary woman, and a generous one, too. Paris has been an incredible experience, one I'll always remember, but not one I want to repeat. Mason made it wonderful, exciting, scary—and he made me realize what really matters—my family. I hope he finds someone who will love him for the exceptional man that he is.*

She leaned her head back and closed her eyes. Dawson had called just before she left for the airport. His loving words still echoed through her mind. *"We'll all be there to meet you. I can't wait to have you back where you belong. My arms feel so empty without you. I love you, Kat. Come home to me quickly."*

In the few months I've been gone, Joey seems to have grown several inches. He even sounds older. And Carla . . . she's been a lifesaver. Without her, I never could have gone to Paris. She's the first one since Grandma Emma to keep Granddad in line. Sometimes I wonder if they have something going, but then I don't think he would ever look at another woman. Grandma Emma was his whole life. And then there's Deb and Bonny—I owe them so much. I hope Deb and Bill finally figure out that they're perfect for each other and do something about it. That's one wedding dress I can't wait to design.

Her brow furrowed. *I never would have pictured Bonny with Clancy, but Deb says they're an item now. It's a good thing Bonny loves kids—he has more than enough for both of them. He's a good man. I can't imagine how we could have kept the ski lodge running without him for all those months when Dawson wasn't able to do anything.*

She opened her eyes, reached for a pillow, and reclined the seat. Finding a comfortable position, she let her thoughts drift again as she fell asleep. *I wonder what's happening with Cabe. He was a good boy. Has he changed that much since he grew up? Or is there another explanation for what he's done? Granddad seems determined to drum him out of the family, but that doesn't make sense. And it doesn't make sense to say he's just like his father. He never knew his father. He's not sick like his father was. Nothing in his behavior suggests the kind of personality change Dawson experienced. I think there's more to this situation than we know. I think . . .*

The voice of the Captain woke her. She put her seatback upright and looked out the window at the Washington skyline.

She'd been gone just over two weeks, but it felt like two years. She grabbed her bag from the overhead compartment and exited the plane.

Where is he? A lump rose in her throat. *Has he forgotten me?* She scanned the crowd in the reception area.

Then she saw him. Straight. Tall. No sign of his crutches. Her gaze circled him. She raised her sunglasses and squinted to see more clearly. Was that Granddad sitting a few yards away, holding onto Joey? Her heart pounded so hard she was afraid it would burst. She looked back at the man. Their gazes locked. He started toward her, a slight sway in his gait—the only obvious indication of his accident. His blond hair had not darkened with age, and that charming dimple had become more pronounced. He stopped when he reached her, still staring into her eyes. Blue eyes and gray—they both held tears.

"Welcome home, my love." He tipped her chin up and bent to kiss her lips with a smoldering passion that held the promise of more to come.

They turned to see Joey running toward them at breakneck speed. She knelt to receive the hugs her little boy threw around her neck.

"Mama, Mama, take me with you the next time you go to Paris."

She turned to look at Dawson. He took her hand and pulled her and his son into his arms.

"If Mama goes to Paris again, Son, we'll *both* go with her. But right now, let's go home."

"Mmmm, it smells good in here." Kat took a deep breath as she stepped into the kitchen from the wide back porch.

"Miz Carla an' me, we made a apple pie for you, Mama."

They sat around the kitchen table and ate pie a la mode while Kat shared photos of the fashion show.

"Oh, I like this one." Carla pointed to the Cleopatra design. "I'm just not sure it would look as good on me as it does on the model."

"Now don't be too hard on yourself." Granddad gave her a sly grin. "I think it's a real pretty little number."

"I like this one with the smoke." Joey pointed to "Castles in the Air."

"The whole show's on a DVD in my suitcase. Tomorrow evening, I'll show it to anybody who wants to see it. How's that sound?"

"Can Molly Anna come too? She likes purty clothes 'cause she's a girl."

"Molly Anna can be the guest of honor. Do you think she'd like that?"

Joey nodded and gave her a big smile.

Carla cleared the dishes while the family retired to the drawing room. Kat cuddled up in a chair by the fireplace and watched the two men talk about the lodge and plans for the future. Joey sat on the floor, playing with a replica of the Eiffel tower she'd brought to him. She wasn't really listening to anyone . . . just letting the warmth of their presence wrap itself around her.

Joey had been so quiet that she hadn't noticed when he'd crawled under the table and fallen asleep. She stood up and reached down to get him. Dawson was suddenly at her side.

"I can take him up," she whispered.

"I'll do it. He's gotten too heavy for you to carry up the stairs. I'll put him to bed and be right back down."

She watched him gently lift their son and carry him out of the room. "We have our old Dawson back, don't we, Granddad," she said when he had gone.

"When he finally started gettin' better, he came back to his old self by leaps and bounds. Probably all the physical therapy helped. And of course the surgery put the finishin' touches on makin' him well again. I'll tell you, Kitten, I was mighty worried for a while there. I thought for sure we'd lost our boy."

She stood up and stretched. "If it's okay, I think I'll go to bed. I'm still trying to get used to the time difference between Paris and Wheeling. I'll bring you up to date tomorrow on some exciting news about Wolf International and Rebecca. Good night, Granddad."

"Good night, Kitten. It sure is nice havin' you home."

She kissed him on the cheek and grinned. "I think it's nice having me home, too."

Dawson returned just as she was leaving. She raised an eyebrow at him and gave her head a little jerk toward the staircase.

"Granddad, it's late and I'm bushed," he said. "You should get some sleep, too."

Jedediah grinned and waved his hand. "Yeah, I know what you two are up to. I think it's time I'll be headin' to bed myself. Now don't you forget the granddaughter I want to be a little namesake for my Emma."

* * * * *

The master bedroom opened onto a wide balcony. A light breeze floated through the open French doors and rustled through the sheer tiebacks.

Kat stood next to her husband. "Daw, can you ever forgive me for the things I said to you before I left for Paris?"

"I deserved every word of it. I was being a world-class jerk, totally self-absorbed, caring only for the man in the mirror."

"Man in the mirror?"

"Funny thing, though, he didn't like me. He and I pretty much agreed to disagree—until I figured out he was right. I'll tell you about him sometime."

"Does this have anything to do with that new mirror hanging on the wall?"

He raised his eyebrows and laughed.

"I guess we have lots of things to talk about now that I'm home . . . and you're home."

"Are you sure you're going to have time for talk? At the airport you mentioned something about continuing to work for Wolf."

"I can't believe it—Rebecca *gave* me almost half the company. She tried to give it *all* to me, but I agreed to take only forty-nine percent. If she wants to be a silent partner, so be it. However, I could never in good conscience accept the business that's been in her family for generations as a gift. Also, I get to keep Fashions by Kat, which she's urging me to promote under the Wolf umbrella."

He let out a low whistle. "Wow! You're sitting on top of the world, aren't you?"

"The only world I want to sit on top of is *your* world, Daw." She wrapped her arms around his waist and snuggled close to him."

"How are you going to manage? I doubt your new employees will want to move to Wheeling, and certainly your clients won't be impressed if you're located here."

"I've considered that. I'll be setting up an office at Willow Walk that's linked to the Wolf network. Their computer system is quite sophisticated, and someone's coming here next week to install what I need. Lillian Rae will be the physical presence in New York, and I'll be available from here for conferencing—even visually if necessary. Then I'll have a laptop that will keep me tied to Wolf by a cyberspace umbilical cord wherever I go. Lots of big changes for a country girl, huh?" She chuckled. "On those rare occasions when I must make a personal appearance, I'll fly to the city for a day or two. Most of the time, that won't be an issue, and I'd love you to come with me."

He pulled back and looked at her. "This is a little mind-boggling."

"I know, Honey, but the Wolf staff is wonderful. You have no idea how capable they are. Without them, we could never have pulled off the show, much less won it. Deb and Bonny don't need me to oversee things at the boutique; they've been managing the place for years. And I will still be designing the lines for Fashions by Kat."

"Won't that be a conflict of interest?"

"No. We're opening a new boutique in New York late this summer and expanding to Chicago, Dallas, Denver, and the West Coast within the next three years. The girls will be thrilled by that, I'm sure. And we'll be carrying the Wolf lines as well as our own. Our clientele is different, as are our styles. Rebecca and I have discussed this at length. It'll work, you'll see." She hesitated. "Let's talk about all this tomorrow."

He grinned.

"I'm going to take a quick shower. I won't be long."

He gave her backside a quick pat as she walked away. She walked through the bathroom door, then turned and looked at him. Smiling, she dropped her blouse on the floor and closed the door behind her.

Stepping from the shower, she dried with a big fluffy towel, slipped into her black silk gown, and dabbed his favorite perfume behind her ears and on her wrists. *Hmmm. Maybe I should put some here.* One more drop over her heart should do the trick.

Dawson heard the shower come on. The rest of her clothes, he knew, would be lying on the floor next to her blouse. The images produced the effect she no doubt intended. He took a white rose from the vase on her dresser and placed it on her pillow.

My Kat is back and so am I.

She opened the door and sat down at her dressing table. She looked at him in the mirror as he stood at the foot of the bed. He walked over to her, picked up her brush, and ran it through her silken black locks.

"Mmmm. That's nice." It sounded almost as though she were purring.

Turning her around on her stool, he bent down and covered her mouth with his, then led her to the bed. She picked up the rose and sniffed its exotic fragrance before laying it on the bed table. With both hands, she slid the straps of her gown off her shoulders. It dropped to the floor as she fell into his arms. He pulled her close.

"Welcome home, Kat."

* * * * *

The morning sun peeked through the slanted shutters. He stood there, facing the bed and watching her sleep. The sheet covered one leg. Her raven hair splashed across the pillow. The glow on her face told him more than any words she could ever speak. He wanted to touch her, hold her, make love to her again. He resisted. She needed her rest because her life was about to become busier than it had ever been before. A twinge of fear tiptoed through his mind. *Will she really have time for us—for me? I love you, Kat. You're my everything. I can't believe I sent you away. I would've died without you. Believe me, I'll never let you go again.*

He watched as she opened her eyes. A smile played across her face as she reached out to him. "Good morning, Daw."

"Good morning, Kat."

"I have a question."

"So early? You just woke up."

"Who's the man in the mirror?"

"Let's just say he's someone who set me straight."

"Set you straight?"

"Yeah. He told me to get my rear in gear and get my beautiful wife back home before somebody else found out what an irreplaceable treasure she is."

CHAPTER THIRTY-TWO

Jedediah trudged up the stairs and into his room. He grinned at what he knew was behind the attic door on the back wall. "I'm comin, Baby. Yup, I'll be there soon as these worn-out old feet can get me there." It was only mid-afternoon, but he needed to talk with his Emma. Seemed he needed her more and more these days.

He unlocked the door and picked up his journal, then shuffled over to his chair against the wall. No need for artificial light. The sun shone through the south-facing window and, intensified by the glass, heated the space where he sat.

I'll just rest my eyes for a minute before I write what's been happenin' here at Willow Walk. Kat's home now, and I'm thinkin' I'll be gettin' a new grandbaby in a few months. The first one was for me, but the next one's for you, Emma. In fact, I been thinkin' . . .

"I've been waiting for you, Jed." Her busy fingers knitted what looked like a red sweater.

"Aw, Emma Baby, I'm sorry I kept you waitin'. But I'm here now. Remember what you told me once? There are different kinds of vision: some come from seein' and some come from dreamin'. But there's another kind, and that's the kind I see in my mind. My mind still works good, you know. Sometimes it works too good, and I remember too much . . . like about our Cable and that good-for-nothin' son of his. But let's not spoil our visit by talkin' about him. Yes, I know I'm dreamin' now. I been dreamin' a lot lately."

"It's okay Jed, dear. I like it when you dream about me. Then I know you're not thinking about that Weatherbush woman."

"C'mon, Baby, you know I got nothin' goin' with her."

"It's a good thing. She'd get you, but she wouldn't appreciate you like she should. In fact, she'd run you ragged. Now Carla's another matter."

"What are you sayin', Emma?"

"I'm saying I wouldn't object if you and her got together. She's a good-hearted woman, and she takes fine care of little Joey and Molly Anna—when you're not looking, of course. She does a whole lot more than she gets paid for. She's a real giving woman, and she'd take fine care of you, too."

"Now let's not be hasty, Emma. I've got no mind to—"

"I know, Jed. I'm just telling you I'd have no objections if you took a liking to that one."

"Humph."

She gave him a flirty little grin. His heart pounded like it was about to leap out of his chest.

"You know our Kitten's back from Paris."

She nodded.

"She and Sonny nearly wore the carpet out traipsin' up to the bedroom and back. I'm gonna get me that new grandbaby yet. He threw back his head and laughed. "I think they're makin' up for lost time."

"Jed Kahill, you stop prying into those young'uns affairs and stop spying on their comings and goings, you hear me? You'd best shape up now, or I'll be bringing my broom next time." This time she laughed.

"Sorry, Emma Baby. Lost my head there for a minute. I shouldn't be tellin' you these things."

"The problem's not the *telling*, Jed. The problem's the *doing*. Now there's one more thing. Little Joey is Dawson's son, not yours. So you keep your nose out of Dawson's business. Know your place and stay in it."

"You're right about Joey. I just spend so much time with him that he seems more like mine than Sonny's.

"Yes, but he isn't yours, and you remember that."

"He's my only grandson, Emma. I gotta show him I love him."

"He is *not* your only grandson, and you know it."

"That other one don't count."

"Shame on you, Jedediah Kahill. I'll definitely be bringing my broom next time to set you straight on a few things."

"Oh, Emma, you know what a disappointment that boy of ours was. His son's no better than his father."

"I thought you said your mind was still working. Have you already forgotten that Cable had a brain tumor? You saw first-hand how a tumor affected Dawson. Why, none of you could stand to be around him."

"I'll give you that, but the tumor didn't make Cable no skirt chaser. That was a character flaw if ever I saw one."

"Look, you crotchety old man, cut your son some slack. He liked women. So did you."

"Yeah, but I only fooled around with one of them, and you know exactly who that was."

"And I was still pure as a fresh snowfall when we said our I do's."

"That's right. Too bad Cable couldn't have said the same thing about his woman . . . 'scuse me, *women*."

"He's gone, Jed. Our boy died long before his time. Be grateful that he left two sons and that Dawson carries on the family name. And be forgiving of our Cable and his other boy. You don't know how it hurts me to hear you say such hateful things about them. Just remember what an effort Cable made to come home before he died. How he managed to get here in all the pain he was suffering, I'll never know. But he wanted to make things right with you. Is there some reason why you can't accept that."

"Humph."

"You're a stubborn old coot, Jedediah Kahill. Why don't you try remembering how much we loved that boy. Why don't you remember the way he helped you out here at Willow Walk from the time he was big enough to handle a tool and carry a load."

His eyes misted. "I remember, Emma. He was a good little boy, wasn't he?"

"Yes, he was. And he thought the world of his daddy. When he went off to college and you weren't pleased with him any more, he quit coming home. Do you remember that? Do you remember the nights I cried myself to sleep because my only baby never came to see us?"

Tears flowed in a steady stream down his cheeks. "I missed him, too, Emma."

"Did you ever tell him that, Jed? Did you ever *ask* him to come home? If we'd seen him, we might have realized he was sick. He might still be with us, might'nt he? But you didn't ask him, did you, Jed?"

He didn't answer.

"I didn't think so."

"I can't change that now, Emma Baby, no matter how much I want to."

"That's right. But you *can* change the way you're dealing with young Cabe. Don't make the same mistake again, Jed. Please. I don't think I could bear losing another boy."

"But he stole money from the lodge—from Dawson—and for no good reason."

"How do you know it was for no good reason?"

"Because . . . because—"

"Don't 'because' me. You *don't* know, Jed. You're just making assumptions. Now there's no denying that what the boy did was wrong, but you had it in for him the day he walked onto this property. You've not even tried to give him the benefit of the doubt, have you?"

He took a breath and blew it out.

"Give him a chance, Jed. He's a whole lot like our Cable. Find out what *really* happened before you judge him."

"You're right as usual, Emma Baby."

"And since when are you so agreeable? Surely, you're not mellowing with age, Jedediah Kahill."

He sniffed and smiled.

"I love you, old man." She reached over and patted his hand. "Just remember what I said about Cabe."

His eyes fluttered open. His hand lay in his lap on top of the journal, the other one patting it. Tears rolled down his face and dropped off his chin."

He wiped away the tears with his fingers. "I love you, Emma Kahill, more'n anything else in the whole world."

Opening his journal, he began to write.

Dear sweet Emma, love of my life
I miss you so much, my beloved wife,
You set me straight when my thinkin's all wrong,
I wish you was with me where you rightly belong.

CHAPTER THIRTY-THREE

Kat peeked through the bedroom shutters at the breaking dawn. "What a beautiful sky," she said aloud. "That red and orange marbling gives me a great idea for a winter suit. *What's that old saying? Something about a red sky in the morning, sailors take warning?* She grinned. *No worries here. Nobody's sailing today.*

She slipped a white cashmere sweater over her head, slid into a pair of jeans, and walked down the stairs to meet Dawson.

His lips puckered. Out came a soft whistle as she walked toward him.

"Was that little wiggle in your walk for my amusement?" His eyes darkened to the shade of smoke.

"Judging from the smoldering color of your orbs, it worked." She gave him a peck on the cheek and headed for the coat closet. "I'm ready to go whenever you are."

He reached out and pulled her back. "I don't think 'amuse' was the right word. 'Tempt' is a much better fit, I believe." He kissed the corners of her smile and tightened his arms around her.

"Now who's tempting whom, Dawson Kahill?"

"Are you sure we have to leave right now?"

She bit her lip to keep from laughing at his sly grin. "We'd better. Everyone's waiting for us. How about I give you an IOU?" She winked at him.

His rich laugh made her tingle all over. "Alright, but I plan to collect it tonight."

"I'm counting on it." She slipped out of his grasp and shrugged into her coat. "Let's get to the lodge before they decide we're not coming." She looked around. "Where are the kids and Granddad?"

"Joey and Molly Anna are in the kitchen, getting a bag of cookies. Granddad's not coming."

"Why?"

"He says it's supposed to start snowing, but he's never been afraid of the snow before. I think he wants to chase Carla around the kitchen."

They both broke out in laughter.

"What's so funny?" Joey ran in from the kitchen, a large bag of freshly baked chocolate chip cookies in his hand and Molly Anna on his heels.

"Just something Daddy said." She helped them put their coats on. "I see Carla took good care of you two."

"Yeah, and she takes good care of Granddaddy, too."

Kat and Dawson looked at each other and laughed again.

"Did I say something funny this time?" Joey looked from one to the other.

"You sure did. You're just like your Daddy." Kat took his hand and tried not to giggle as they walked out the door.

The road narrowed and changed from pavement to gravel as it climbed and wound around steep curves before opening onto the plateau where the ski lodge nestled among the stately pines.

"Look, Mama!" Joey pointed to the skiers wending their way down the snow-covered slopes. Others rode the lifts back to the top, and some were huddled around huge barrels of burning wood to chat while they warmed their hands and backsides.

The wind whistled around the corner of the lodge as Dawson parked the truck. Large white flakes rode on its currents to find a resting place somewhere down the mountain.

"This new snow is great for the slopes, but the chill factor is another matter. I can feel the cold in my leg. We need to post a warning to make sure our guests are aware of the dangers of hypothermia and frostbite." Dawson opened the door for Kat and the children.

"Brrrrr, Daddy, I'm cold." Joey reached up for Dawson after taking only two steps.

"Okay, Son, Want a ride?"

Kat and Molly watched him scoop Joey up and put him on his shoulders.

"You can be my horse. Come on, Mama, we're gonna race you inside."

Molly Anna took Kat's hand as the walked toward the door. "Boys sure are silly sometimes, aren't they?"

Kat stifled a laugh. "You're exactly right, Molly Anna. Boys can be very silly."

The warmth from the fireplaces greeted them as soon as they opened the heavy doors. She helped the children take off their coats and walked over to the desk.

"Kat!" Polly hollered. "Oh my goodness, Kat, it's about time you got your derriere home." She smiled and ran to hug her.

"How are you, Sweetie?"

"I'm good. Wait till you hear what a great season we're having. And Clancy has been—"

"I believe the guests in 203 have checked out," Clancy interrupted. "Do you know if it's on the cleaning schedule today? We . . . uh . . . have someone checking in for that room this evening."

Polly Dee gave him a big smile and whispered in Kat's ear. "Like I was saying, in the company of Bonny. Hmmm—we all think they're in love."

"You don't say." Kat feigned shock. "I never would have believed it."

"Alright, you two. Enough's enough." Clancy's cheeks outshone his fiery red hair as he stepped out from behind the desk to give Kat a hug. "Aw, me favorite lassie—next to me Molly Anna, that be. Ye made it home just in time to catch all the hot, juicy gossip." His bright green eyes looked like they could dance an Irish jig.

"I can't wait to hear all about your love life, Clancy, but I need a cup of coffee first. I'm still freezing."

"Come sit by the fire, Lassie, while I fetch yer coffee."

Joey and Molly Anna sat at a small table in one corner of the great room. Coloring books and crayons enough to last the day surrounded them. Clearly, Joey was explaining something to her, and, eyes wide, she was hanging on every word. *Just like Dawson and I used to be.*

She glanced up just in time to see someone turn away from the balcony railing and rush into a room. *Must be a novice who took one look at that blowing snow and opted for a nap. Can't blame him.* She shivered.

Clancy brought her a steaming mug of coffee, her husband close behind him. "I was just tellin' Dawson what a fine idea he had, makin' the place here a summer retreat as well as a ski lodge. We have hiking trails, mountain vistas, and great fishin'. The reservations are already comin' in, several of them from folks that came for skiin' and who want to return for the atmosphere and beauty."

"We all got mouths to feed," Dawson said, "and I know you want to bring your boys home as soon as school's over this spring."

"Aye, ye can't imagine how much I miss those ragamuffins. Me oldest is 'most twenty now. Can ye believe that?"

"Do you know how many guests are staying over?" Dawson asked. "It looked like we had a mass exodus coming down the road this morning."

"I'm thinkin' that about half are with us for a few more days, but I'd be checkin' with Darrell if I were ye. Reservations are a wee out of me territory most o' the time."

Dawson ambled toward the desk, then turned back to Kat. "I'll let you and Clancy play catch-up while I check this out. Then I want to show you something. It's a surprise, so don't try to wheedle anything out of Clancy."

"You know I can't stand secrets, Dawson." She gave him a mock frown.

"Live with it, woman. The man's lips are sealed." He walked on to the desk.

"Alright, Clancy. He's out of earshot. What's the surprise."

"Now, lassie, were I to tell ye, he'd be shootin' me at sunrise. And I'll be thankin' ye not to let him think I breathed nary a word to ye about it even though ye tried to make me talk like a parrot. Never let it be said that Clancy O'Malley's a squawker. Now, I was wantin' to tell ye I'm a happy man fer the first time in a long time." He gave her a quizzical look. "Are ye sayin' that me wee Bonny hasna' told ye about me feelin's fer her?"

Kat reached her hand out and laid it over his. "I couldn't resist teasing you a bit, Clancy. Of course, Bonny told me about that . . . and about a lot more, too."

"And what was it that she be tellin' ye, lass?"

"Well, I haven't seen her, but I've talked to her on the phone more than once. From the tone in her voice, I'd guess her feelings for you match the ones you have for her."

Dawson brought the reservation book over and sat down by Clancy. "Looks like you were right. We have several guests coming in tomorrow, and three parties have extended their stays because we had the room. The Stantons in 207; the Grays in 243; and Van Henkle in 201. That name seems to ring a bell for some reason."

"Van Henkle? You said *Van Henkle*?" Kat jumped up. Her coffee splattered out of her cup onto the floor.

"Yeah, why does that sound familiar?" He looked up at her. "You look like you've seen a ghost."

"Well . . . I . . .I . . ." She looked around for a distraction. Joey and Molly were fighting over the cookies. She crossed to the little table and took them both in her arms and closed her eyes. *Oh,God, what's going on? It's got to be him. How many Van Henkles could there be in this world? Why is he here? I should've told Dawson when he came to the boutique.*

She took the children by the hand and walked up to the desk. "Clancy, please take them to play in your suite for a few minutes. We may have a problem here."

He gave her a questioning look. "Molly Anna, ye be goin' to our rooms now, ye hear me, lass." She nodded. "Take Joey with ye now. I'll be right behind ye." The children started toward the hallway. He turned to Kat. "Are ye sure ye won't be needin' me out here?"

"Please go, Clancy, quickly." He hesitated as Dawson walked up beside her.

"What's going on, Kat? Who's Van Henkle?"

"I told you about him one night. I wondered if he might have been the one who vandalized the boutique and chloroformed Bonny."

He nodded. "Go on."

Heat rose in her cheeks. She felt like she was about to faint. "The . . . the night of your accident, he came back. At first I thought he was going to harm me, but in the end he broke down and said he needed help. I gave him the name of a doctor, and when I didn't hear any more from him, I assumed he'd gotten counseling. Oh, Dawson, he's a very disturbed man. I'm afraid he might—"

"Might what?" Rip's voice interrupted her. "Might come after you again? Don't you remember, I told you I'd see you around. I didn't think it'd take this long, but you had to run off to France. Oh, I heard about your big trip and your big prize. You're the talk of Wheeling. You know how it goes: hometown girl makes good. Well, hometown girl, the next headlines you make won't be near as classy."

Rip stood at the base of the stairs, a knife in one hand. In the other, he held Joey by the scruff of the neck. "This time I'm going to take care of you once and for all. I might even take care of your kid."

The few guests in the great room gasped or screamed.

"Shut up!" He nodded toward the far back corner. "Get back there and you won't get hurt. I've got nothin' against you. This is between the lady and me, nobody else . . . except the kid."

With more agility and speed than she believed he could possibly muster, Dawson started toward the stairs. Rip placed the tip of the knife against Joey's throat. Dawson stopped.

"Nobody move or the kid dies."

"Daddy! Mama!"

"Let him go, Rip." Kat tried to force calmness into her voice. She was only partly successful. "It's me you're after. I'll go with you, but let go of my son."

"No." Dawson stepped between her and Rip.

Their gazes locked. *Dawson, I have to get Joey. Let me go, please.* He understood and backed off.

"I'm coming with you, Rip. Let Joey go." Her heart pounded so hard it took her breath away.

He loosened his grip on the boy. "You think I'm crazy, don't you?"

God, please help me say the right things to save my son. "No, Rip, I don't think you're crazy. And I don't think you're a criminal. If I thought that, I would've called the police the night you came to the boutique. I only wanted to help you. You believe me, don't you, Rip?" *That's it. Think about what I'm saying and keep eye contact with me.*

"You're lying, Katarina. I watched you from the balcony. I saw how you are with your husband, how you fit into all . . . all this. Do you expect me to believe you'd leave Willow Walk and everybody here to go with *me?*"

"I believed you when you said you were going to get help for your problems. Now I'm asking you to show me the same courtesy." She clenched her jaw to keep her teeth from chattering.

"Yeah, but I lied."

"That doesn't mean I'm lying."

"And it doesn't mean you're telling me the truth."

She took a tentative step forward. "Come on, Rip, talk to me. You know I care about you. Did you see the doctor I told you about?"

His hollow laugh echoed through the cavernous room. "I saw him a couple of times. He said I was obsessed with you, and that wasn't healthy." A slow, evil grin spread across his face. "It wasn't healthy for him either."

What did he do to the doctor? She tried to remember anything on the news about a doctor being found dead. Nothing came to mind. "It doesn't matter what he said, Rip. What matters is the here and now. Let my son go, and let's get out of here . . . just the two of us. Please." She took two more steps forward.

"Mama!" Joey twisted and turned in an effort to free himself.

"Keep still, you little brat." He swatted at the boy with his free hand.

The knife handle connected with Joey's jaw. He let out a blood-curdling scream. Suddenly, Molly Anna shot out of her hiding place behind a support post and ran straight for Rip.

"Let Joey go, you mean man," she cried out just before her teeth clamped down on Rip's hand. He swore, then dropped the knife and Joey.

In the distance, sirens sounded. They came closer and closer. Dawson, Clancy, and Darrell rushed in to tackle Rip. He picked up the knife and slashed at them.

186

"Stay away or I'll kill them both." Kat and Joey were at Rip's feet. Kat was kneeling at Joey's side, trying to calm him. Rip grabbed her by the hair. "I'm not kidding. One step closer, and they're history."

The sirens grew louder. Kat clung to Joey and looked up at Rip with tears running down her face. "It's over, Rip."

Sirens blared in front of the lodge. Lights flashed.

"It'll never be over for you and me." He ran toward the back entrance of the lodge, Clancy and Dawson in hot pursuit.

"Dawson, no!" Kat screamed.

He seemed not to hear. She knew him almost better than she knew herself. Nothing would stop him from going after the man who'd hurt his wife and son—nothing except Clancy, who pushed him aside.

"This one is *mine!*" the Irishman shouted. "I'll be takin' 'im down." He dashed out the back door after Rip.

The police rushed in the front entrance as Clancy returned. "Dang fool peeled outta here like the Devil himself was on his tail, and he was right!" His flushed cheeks challenged his flaming hair for attention. He got away on his motorcycle, but not before I got a couple o' licks. He was bleedin' pretty good when he roared outta here." He held up his fists. They were covered with blood. "Guess that rogue got me with his knife after all."

Polly Dee rushed up to him and wrapped her scarf around his hand. "It doesn't look too bad, but let's get it cleaned up." I don't know if I should kiss you for being brave enough to go after him or hit you for being dumb enough to do it."

"Can ya be decidin' later, Polly? This is smartin' a wee."

"Everybody in here okay?" A highway patrolman looked like he didn't quite believe what he was seeing. "We got a nine-one-one call from a guest here who said somebody was holding a child at knife point."

"That's what happened." Dawson filled the officer in on the details while two cars, sirens screaming, followed Rip down the twisting road.

"The patrolman's radio interrupted them. "Officers in pursuit of a man on a motorcycle. Heading down the switchback from Willow Walk Lodge toward the highway."

"Keep me posted. I'm still at the lodge. Ten-four."

A moment later the radio crackled again. "Suspect over the edge on Dead Man's Curve. We've called for Search and Rescue."

"Thanks for the update. Ten-four."

Dawson reached for his wife's hand and pulled her to her feet. Then he picked up his whimpering son. Joey wrapped his arms around his father's neck and buried his head in his broad shoulder.

"It really is over now, isn't it, Dawson?" Her voice shook so much that her words were barely audible.

"It's over, my darling, forever." He led her to a chair, and they sat down. Joey wiggled free and ran over to Molly Anna. He threw his arms around her neck and gave her a big kiss on the cheek. "That's 'cause you saved my life."

Molly beamed. "I saved yer life 'cause I love you, and that bad man was hurtin' you."

"You two come with me." Polly Dee took their hands. "You, too, Clancy. We need to do a little first aid here."

Kat watched the four of them head down the hallway, then turned to Dawson. "Who do those kids remind you of?"

"You and me?"

"You've got it. Wouldn't it be funny if—"

"Hold your horses, Kat. Let's not be jumping to any conclusions. They're just in kindergarten. He stood up and looked at the guests who were still huddled in the corner. Others who had been skiing had come in after the patrol cars pulled up and were milling around the room. He walked up to the desk. "May I have your attention, please."

The buzzing quieted as they turned to look at him.

"We want all our guests at Willow Walk Lodge to have a memorable stay with us, but this isn't quite the type of memory we want you to take home with you."

Tittering came from several in the growing group.

"Tonight we'll be ordering in pizzas, salads, sodas, hot chocolate, and coffee for all—on the house. And whoever made that phone call to nine-one-one, thank you. You may well have saved the lives of my wife and son. Please see me before you leave. I want to extend my thanks to you personally."

"What are you going to do, Daw?" Kat had walked up beside him.

"I'm going to give them a free week at any time they choose. And that won't begin to repay them for what they did."

She wrapped her arms around him and held him tight while she said a quiet prayer of thanks. Then she remembered . . .

It had been a red dawn morning.

CHAPTER THIRTY-FOUR

Carla brought a fresh batch of waffles to the buffet table and checked the supply of sausages, bacon, and scrambled eggs. Pots of coffee and hot chocolate sat beside decanters of fresh orange juice on the sideboard.

Everyone except Darrell had gathered for breakfast at Willow Walk. He'd volunteered to man the desk provided Polly Dee brought him man-size helpings of Carla's famous cooking.

Kat grabbed Carla's arm as she headed back toward the kitchen. "Thank you so much for this wonderful feast. I know you didn't plan on such a big group for Sunday morning brunch."

"I'm happy to do it. I'm just grateful that you're all safe and well and able to be here. It could have been a real tragedy yesterday. Besides, Jeddy helped me, so 'tweren't all that hard." She winked at Kat and scurried off. "Gotta check my biscuits."

"You weren't afraid, boy?" Jedediah heaped another helping of sausage and eggs on his plate.

"Uh . . . naw." Joey's eyes widened. "Well, maybe a little bit. The knife was scary. And he hit me with it, but Molly bit him and he let me go."

Jedediah patted the little girl on the head. "You're real brave, Molly Anna. I tell you, I'm right proud of you."

"Let's let it go, Granddad, especially in front of the children," Dawson said in a low tone. They walked away from the table where Joey and Molly were sitting. "Kat and I don't want them dwelling on it."

"You gotta deal, Sonny. He coulda been killed—a lunatic like that. Scares me when I think about it myself. I wondered what all the fuss was when those patrol cars went roarin' up the road yesterday evenin'. Tried callin' the lodge, but nobody answered the phone. I couldn't leave the kids to find out what was happenin', but it's better I didn't know. Don't think this old ticker would've handled that very well." With his free hand, Jedediah tapped his cane on the floor to the beat of "Old Dan Tucker."

"He was a sick man. Kat should've told us, but I understand why she didn't. After the accident, I was hardly approachable. And she truly did think he wouldn't come back."

Deb walked up to them. "I bet he's the one who's been calling the boutique and hanging up when we answered."

"Why *didn't* you tell anybody?" Bonny turned to Kat.

"I believed him when he said he'd get the help we talked about. He sounded so sincere at the time."

"Anyone for more coffee or hot chocolate?" Carla popped back into the dining room. "Lots more in the kitchen."

"I'll take a cup of that coffee if you put some of your good peach brandy in it." Jedediah held out his cup.

"The only peaches you're gonna get today are in the peach cobbler I'm baking for dinner." Kat saw the smile play across his lips as she turned and headed back to the kitchen.

"I'll be takin' mine a la mode," he called after her.

Deb pulled Kat toward the living room. "Can I talk to you for a minute?"

"Is something wrong?"

"Not wrong. Right!" She glanced toward the dining room.

"I don't think anybody can hear us," Kat said.

"Bill asked me to marry him."

"Yes!" Kat squealed, then clapped her hand over her mouth. "When?"

"Last night. We haven't told anybody yet, but I'm about to pop. I had to share the best news of my life with *somebody*. Bonny's too busy making goo-goo eyes at Clancy to see anything else. I could be wearing the Hope Diamond, and she wouldn't notice."

Kat giggled and gave her a big hug. "I'm so happy for you . . . but please tell me you're staying in Wheeling."

"Don't worry, Kat. We're not going anywhere. I told Bill about your holdings in Wolf. He thinks it's great, and he's okay with the idea of my doing some traveling."

"When's the wedding?"

190

"We're talking about June, but that's only six months away. What am I saying? Six months will seem like an eternity before I become Mrs. William Perry. Oh, Kat, doesn't that sound beautiful?"

"Deborah Perry. That does have a certain *ring* to it, doesn't it? No pun intended, of course." She hugged her friend again. "I know this has been on your mind for a while—years even—so what kind of wedding do you think you'd like?"

"Uh . . . um . . . what would you say if I asked that my wedding be here at Willow Walk?"

"I'd say . . . I would be *honored* to have your wedding here. Oh, Deb, what a wonderful idea. Under the willows. It would be beautiful beyond anything you can imagine. And your gown?"

"Well, I know this designer. She's pretty good . . . even picked up a little trophy in Paris recently. I don't know if she'd have time, but . . ."

Kat began to laugh. "If I happen to see your friend, I'll ask her. But I just bet she'd have a fit if you *didn't* want her to design it for you. She probably would even tell you that it would be her gift to you."

"You think so?" Deb was beaming.

"I'm sure of it."

"Now if I can just find my old sketches. You remember them . . . the ones with netting and pearls."

"You wouldn't!"

"Oh, yes, I . . ."

A loud squeal coming from the dining room interrupted them.

"That was Molly Anna," Kat said.

"Let's go see what's wrong."

CHAPTER THIRTY-FIVE

"We're gettin' married! We're gettin' married!" Molly Anna squealed as she ran around the room.

"What?" Kat looked baffled.

"Aren't you a little young?" Deb asked.

Molly stopped in front of them and put her hands on her hips. "Not me, silly. *Daddy* an' me. We're marryin' Bonny. Then we're goin' to Ireland. I have lotsa big brothers there—seven of 'em—and they need a mom, too. O' course, two or three of 'em's all growed up." She put her hands down. "I ain't never had a mom before. I think that's gonna be fun. We can do girl things. Daddies don't know how to do girl things." Suddenly, she turned and looked at Clancy. "Daddy, is it okay that I tell them?" She bowed her head and looked at the floor.

"Aye, little Lassie. 'Tis more than okay that ye be happy enough to be tellin' the whole world about yer new ma."

She looked up and smiled. "Bonny's gonna be my new mommy." Then she grabbed Joey's hand and pulled him along to stand between Bonny and Clancy. "Just like me and Joey are gonna get married."

Joey looked at Molly Anna, then at Dawson, and finally at Kat. "I ain't marryin' nobody, Molly. I'm too little." He ran off to play, Molly Anna on his heels. After a moment of stunned silence, the room erupted in laughter.

Dawson was the first to speak. "Clancy, you old devil, you and Bonny have been holding out on us."

192

"Aye, but we just decided last night. And there was a bit of a ruckus, ya know."

A broad grin spread across Jedediah's face. "It comes as no surprise to me, Clance. I been seein' the way you and that little missy been lookin' at each other."

"There's no way o' gettin' 'round you, Jeddy. Ye seem to be knowin' everythin' before it happens."

"That's right, Clance. My old eyes see lots of things." Jedediah raised his cane and shook it. "Why it was as plain as day—you two smoochin' and huggin' in dark corners and when you thought no one was lookin'."

Bonny twisted her face into a mock frown and shot a glance at Clancy. She poked him in the side, and he grabbed her hands. "She made me promise not to tell anyone till later, but 'tis too late now. The wee lassie made the big announcement fer us." He swept her into his arms, raised her off her feet, and planted a kiss as big as Ireland right on her mouth.

"Clancy O'Malley, we're in public," she scolded when he let her up for air.

"Now, now, me love, we're not in public. We're among friends. Right?" He looked around the room.

"Right!" came the unified reply.

A moment later, Bill stepped up to the table. "Congratulations to you both, Bonny and Clancy. You make a grand-looking couple, and that's the long and the short of it." Everyone looked at six-foot-three-inch Clancy and five-foot-two-inch Bonny and tittered. "Now, as long as we're making announcements . . ." He hesitated and looked at Deb. She walked up to stand beside him. "Looks like we might be having a double ceremony. Debbie has agreed to overlook my many faults and marry me anyway."

Bonny gave her a big hug. "How long have *you* been holding out on us, as Dawson put it?"

Deb looked at her watch and grinned. "Seventeen hours, twenty minutes and . . . fifty-five seconds."

Jedediah tapped his cane on the floor. "Congratulations, you four whippersnappers. I'm an old dog who don't take much to new tricks, but I sure as blazes like this one. A double weddin' calls for double celebratin'. Carla! We're needin' that peach brandy in here."

She appeared in the doorway. "Jedediah Kahill, you're determined to get my peach brandy one way or another." She softened her scowl with a wink. "Peach brandy coming right up."

Clancy stepped up to the table with Bonny at his side. "Jedediah, Dawson, Kat, ye took a chance on a lonely Irishman ye hardly knew, and ye've made me feel like one of yer own. Fer that, me and the wee lassie are beholden to ye. An' now ye've added to that fine friendship by bringing a special lady into me presence." Bonny blushed as he wrapped a big arm around her. "So I'm wishin' ye always walls for the wind, a roof for the rain, and good spirits beside the fire. Laughter t' cheer ye, those ye love near ye, and all that yer heart may desire. I have my heart's desire in me wee Bonny. An' now—"

The sound of the doorbell interrupted him.

"Are we expecting anybody?" Dawson asked.

"Not that I know of," Kat answered. "Maybe someone looking for the lodge got lost."

"I'll get it!" Jedediah shouted over the celebrating. Dawson, Kat, and Polly Dee followed him into the entry hall.

He opened the door. Polly clamped her hand over her mouth. Jedediah dropped his cane. "Jehosaphat! As I live and breathe . . . what are *you* doin' here, boy?"

Dawson walked to the door. "Hello, Cabe."

Cabe extended his hand. Dawson took it.

"I didn't know if I'd . . . we'd be welcome here, but I'd like to come in and talk to you if you'll allow it."

"Dadblamed nerve you've got, boy, comin' here without lettin' anybody know." The young woman with Cabe reached down and picked up his cane. He took it from her. "And just who might you be?"

Ignoring Granddad's gruff tone, Dawson stepped aside. "Come in, Cabe."

Polly rushed up and gave him a hug. He clung to her for a long moment. "Where's Dad?"

She stepped back. "He's at the lodge. Should I call him?"

"Later, Mom." He reached for the hand of the young woman standing behind him and pulled her to his side. "Mom, Dawson, Kat . . . Granddad, I'd like you to meet Conchita, my wife."

Polly Dee gasped.

Kat stepped forward and held out her hand. "Welcome to the family, Conchita. Come in, please." The young woman glanced at Cabe. When he nodded, she stepped forward.

Thank you, Kat. Cabe mouthed the words, then drew Dawson into the drawing room.

"Big brother, I'm so sorry for taking the money. I had to get back to Mexico. Conchita was having big problems at home. She worked to help support her family, but her dad took *all* her money from her as soon as she got paid—bought booze with it. When he drinks—which is often—he gets mean. He's been beating her for years, but I didn't know it. She finally told me when I called one day and she was crying so hard she couldn't talk. She finally calmed down enough to tell me what had happened, and I told her to leave. She had nowhere to go.

"Mom and Darrell didn't know her, so I didn't think they'd understand. I did the only thing I could think of at that moment. It was wrong, but it's done—I can't change that now. I'm asking for your forgiveness." He took an envelope from his pocket and handed it to Dawson. "There's five hundred here. It's not much, but it's a start. I'll make payments on the rest with interest as soon as I find work."

"Don't you think you'll be needing this. Trust me, two *cannot* live as cheaply as one."

"I've got a little more, but I need to find us a place to stay. She's pregnant. I'm gonna be a papa."

Now what? He's my brother. He's trying to make good his mistake. He and his wife have a baby on the way. I've got to help him. "I appreciate the explanation, Cabe. Maybe I would have done the same thing in your situation—I can't say. This answers a lot of questions . . . but it brings up some others."

"Like what?"

"We'll talk about them later. Meantime, let's join the family. Your wife will probably be more comfortable if you're with her." He clapped his brother on the back. "Hey, she's quite a looker."

"Yeah, she's something, Dawson. She can be sweet as sugar, but don't cross her or she'll be spitting vinegar at you."

They were laughing when they returned to the dining room.

"Ah, 'tis the light of a leprechaun that musta shown ye the way home." Clancy grabbed Cabe in a big bear hug. "Welcome back, me boy. I'll be goin' to the lodge now so yer fodder can get 'imself down here to see ya. Wanna come with me, Bonny?"

She nodded.

"Come on, you two, get something to eat." Kat led them to the buffet. "Carla's outdone herself this morning."

Conchita looked at the food and then at Cabe. "I think I'll just have a biscuit."

He nodded and filled his plate.

Jedediah sat in a chair in the corner and leaned on his cane. He never took his eyes off Cabe and that woman he said was his wife. *Dear God in heaven, help me to understand this grandson of mine. I don't like him much because I didn't like his dad much, not after he growed up. And this boy's got a bad turn to him just like Cable. But my Emma tells me I'm wrong, and I'm thinkin' you'd tell me the same thing. I know I should be forgivin' and give him another chance. I'll try my best, but I'm gonna be needin' your help on this one. Meantime, I'll be keepin' my eye on the cash register. Amen.*

Darrell's eyes stung with tears as he stood in the door to the dining room. His throat closed. Taking a deep breath to open it, he let it out a little at a time. *Why did he come back? Is he out of money? Is he in trouble with the law? Who's this girl he married?* No matter. He wanted to hold him in his arms the way he did when Cabe skinned his knee.

"Hello, Son." Darrell choked. "Welcome home."

Cabe put his plate on the table and wrapped his arms around his stepfather. "I missed you, Dad."

Polly swayed in her chair. Every nerve in her body vibrated like a guitar string just before it breaks. The sight of her son eased the torment of endless days and nights of worry. But he was all grown up now. And he had a wife. *How am I going to deal with another woman in his life. For all these years, I've been the only one. What if she doesn't like me? What if I don't like her? What if she isn't good to him?* She stood up and walked toward him. So much she wanted to say, but the words wouldn't come. For several moments she held him close. She stepped back and laid her hand on his face, the face that looked more and more like Cable Kahill. "You look wonderful, Son. Married life must agree with you. I thank God you're home . . . you're *both* home safe."

"Why don't the four of you go into the drawing room and visit." Kat put an arm around Cabe and Polly Dee. She looked at Cabe's still full plate. "Take your breakfast with you. Can't let it get cold now." She ushered them into the guest drawing room.

Cabe gave Polly and Darrell a nervous grin. *How strange that I still want their approval, maybe even more now that I ever did. Funny . . . I never figured on coming back here when I left with the money. But Conchita needs a family . . . I need a family. Our baby needs a family. I'm going to have to work real hard to show them I'm not a thief. Going to help Conchita wasn't wrong, but taking the money was. I should have told them . . .*

He shifted his gaze to the young woman at his side. She wore no makeup on her round face, and her straight black hair was tied back by a lavender ribbon. She watched them from startled eyes that looked like a frightened doe caught in the headlights of a vehicle.

"Your wife is lovely, Son."

He knew that the small smile on Conchita's lips had come from his mother's compliment. A blush tinted her flawless bronze cheeks.

"Forgive me—*perdóneme. Esto es mi mamá y mi papá.*"

Conchita bowed her head and lowered her eyes. *Mucho gusto.*

"Do you speak English?"

"Yes, but my English is not so good as my Spanish."

"How old are you, Conchita?

"*Tengo dieciocho anos.*"

"Eighteen, oh my goodness." She looked at her son.

"I didn't know what to do, Mom. Her dad was beating her and taking all the money she earned. When we came here from Mexico, she was too young to marry without parental consent and was still in school. That was over a year ago. Her dad made her go to work right after we left."

"Where's her mother?"

"She died when Conchita was nine."

"Does she have brothers and sisters?"

"No."

"When did you get married?"

"Two weeks after I went back. I wanted her with me so I could protect her, but I couldn't do that in good conscience unless she was my wife. I took all the necessary paperwork with me, but it was no problem because I was born in Mexico."

"Is she legal here?"

"Yes. She was born in Texas. Her family moved to Mexico when she was three. She has her birth certificate with her in case any questions come up."

"You can ask the questions to me," Conchita said. "I practice my English with Cabe for . . . *tres meses* . . . uh . . . three months before we come. Before that, I study it *en mi escuela* . . . in my school."

"I'm so sorry. I didn't realize how well you speak English."

"*Esta bien.* Did Cabe tell you about our *bebe?*" She patted the little protrusion in her belly.

"No, he didn't." Polly smiled and reached over and laid her hand over Conchita's. "We have much to celebrated today, don't we? Welcome to our family, little one."

Dawson, Kat, and Jedediah stepped into the room. Dawson and Kat sat on the couch opposite the others. Granddad remained standing. He leaned on his cane.

"We're having a grandbaby." Polly Dee beamed.

"Figures." Granddad glared at Cabe.

"We're thinking of naming her Emma Dee if it's a girl." Cabe returned Jedediah's steady gaze.

"I'll thank you not to use your great-grandmother's good name."

"Granddad!" Dawson jumped to his feet.

Conchita stared at the old man. Big tears tumbled down her cheeks.

Jedediah turned to Dawson. "Just like his old man. Makin' babies whenever and wherever without benefit of the marriage license."

"That's enough, Granddad." Kat stood beside Dawson.

"Dad was married to my mother." Dawson's voice took on an edge.

"After the fact, not before it."

"Mom was already pregnant with me when she met Cable, remember, Granddad?" Kat frowned.

"Guess that meant he could see if he liked the milk before he bought the cow and didn't have to worry none about the consequences."

Kat glowered at him. "How dare you talk that way about Mama Suzanne?"

"It ain't Suzanne I'm faultin' here."

"Conchita and I got married *before* she got pregnant, Granddad." Cabe struggled not to sound angry.

"Humph."

Polly Dee walked over to stand in front of the old man. "Why can't you welcome my son home? He is your grandson, after all."

"The boy done wrong, Polly. He's got a lot of makin' up to do before he can even think about gettin' back in my good graces."

"Dawson's forgiven him, so why can't you? Stop being stubborn and open your heart." She turned around and went back to sit between Conchita and Cabe.

Jed forced himself to look at Conchita, but he'd cast nary a glance at Cabe. *Pretty young thing. Just a child though. The boy wasn't just a thief. He was a cradle robber, too. Well, the family can think what they want and do what they want. They're treatin' him like he's the prodigal son comin' home to eat the fatted calf. I'm not buyin' any piece of this one.* His stomach churned. *Musta been something I ate again. Look at them silly people. Rallyin' around the thief of Willow Walk when they oughta be havin' pity for this poor girl he's led astray. Here she is pregnant, and he comes struttin' in here proud as a peacock, like he's done somethin' honorable. Yep, he's just like his father. Emma Baby, you and me gotta have a talk. I can't seem to get the hang of this forgivin' stuff. Seems to me there's got to be a reason to forgive, and for the life of me I can't find one.*

198

He looked at everybody except Cabe. *Emma Dee, huh? Over my dead body that'll happen. Why the nerve of that girl to think I'd approve of her namin' that boy's baby after my own Emma. What's her name? Cheeta? More like alley cat, if you ask me.*

"Won't you come and join us?" Kat was standing in front of him.

"I don't think so, Kitten. I'm not handlin' none of this very well."

She patted his arm and gave him a sad look before she went back to sit down with the family.

A fine kettle of fish this is. Here I am head of the family, and I can't even sit down with them no more. And now there's another young'un on the way that's gonna smear the Kahill name. Besides, what do they think I am around here, a built-in babysitter. Not for this one. Nope, no way.

He turned around and walked out of the room.

Cabe watched his grandfather walk away. *How do I make it right with him. I knew he wasn't going to be easy, but I had no idea how much he disliked my father. I must be a lot like him. Maybe when all the money's paid back . . . I wish I could do everything over again. I'd still have gone to get Conchita, but I would've found some other way to finance my trip. Maybe I should've asked Dawson. He's kind of a cool guy. If I gotta have a big brother, he's a good one to have. Boy, I sure made a mess of things here. Mom and Dad raised me to be a God-fearing man, but guess I forgot that when I stuck my fingers in the till.* He looked around. *I'm a Kahill, and this is my family. I'm going to earn my grandfather's respect or die trying.*

CHAPTER THIRTY-SIX

"Carla, what do I smell?" Jedediah hollered as he took his seat at the head of the dining-room table. "I thought dinner was ready."

She bustled out of the kitchen, carrying an enormous tray of garlic bread. "It's spaghetti and meatballs, and you know darn good and well what I've been cooking because you helped me peel the onions and garlic."

He was not a man who blushed, but he felt the color rise to his cheeks. "Dadburned woman," he muttered under his breath.

Everybody laughed.

"Why, you sly fox," Dawson teased. "What've you got planned for dessert, Granddad?"

"I ain't got nothin' planned for dessert. In fact, I ain't even hungry no more."

"Now don't you get ornery, Jedediah Kahill." Carla put a plate of spaghetti and meatballs in front of him. "You are, too, hungry, because I wouldn't let you do any tasting while we were . . . I was cooking."

Everybody was watching him.

"What're y'all starin' at?" he growled.

"We're just wondering why you're not eating when you helped cook it. Did you put something in the meatballs we should know about besides onions and garlic?" Dawson gave Granddad a serious look.

Everyone laughed except Dawson and Jedediah.

"Some folks at this table are gettin' a mite short on respectin' their elders. There's nothin' wrong with the food. Now eat up and quit makin' fun of me, Sonny." He stuck his fork in the pasta, twirled it against his spoon, and popped it in his mouth. He chewed it long and slow, savoring the piquant flavors imparted by the delicate herbs that had simmered all day in Carla's homemade sauce. "Mmmmm. *Almost* as good as what my Emma made." Jed looked straight at Carla. *Take that, you old biddy. That'll teach you to put me on the spot.*

Carla stuck her tongue out at him and retreated to the kitchen.

Everybody dug in. For the moment, teasing gave way to enjoying good food.

"One more thing," Jedediah said after he cleaned his plate, "I'm expecting a fruit cobbler this Sunday. I'd best be gettin' it, or some women folk I know are gonna be in deep, deep trouble." He tapped his cane on the floor, then hung it over the chair arm.

"Granddad, it's not nice to talk about girls that way." Joey scowled at him.

Jedediah cleared his throat. "You're right, boy. As head of this family, I need to be settin' the right example of respect if I'm expectin' it to be showed to me."

"Well, ain'tcha gonna say you're sorry, Granddad?" Molly Anna chimed in.

"Molly, don't say 'ain't.' It's bad English." Joey shook a finger at her.

"Granddad says 'ain't.'"

"We make a 'ception for him 'cause . . . 'cause he's the boss here."

Molly Anna hung her head. "I'm sorry."

"Okay, you two, that's enough squabblin'." He looked around the table. "Y'all might take a lesson from these young'uns. You've heard folks say 'out of the mouths of babes,' I think. Well, out of the mouths of these babes right here at this table, you've been taught somethin' about respect. See that you remember it."

Kat's eyes twinkled. "What's on the menu for tomorrow night? You and Carla got something else cooking? I'm asking respectfully, of course."

The repressed giggles were lost in Dawson's unrestrained guffaw. At that moment, Carla came in from the kitchen.

"Anybody want more spaghetti?" She didn't wait for a reply. "Jedediah Kahill, you know exactly what's on the menu tomorrow night. You ordered it yourself. Let me see . . . it's baked ham covered with pineapple, cloves, cherries, and a brown sugar glaze. Right? What else was it you wanted? Candied yams topped with marshmallows, wasn't it? And a corn casserole swimming in butter, mashed potatoes, dressing, and gravy. Did I leave anything out?"

"Yeah. You forgot the crow you're makin' me eat." His scowl dissolved in laughter when everyone tittered at his joke. "Why don't you join us, Carla? Dawson, get her a chair. She does all the cookin' and cleanin' here at Willow Walk, and she's like one of the family now."

"I . . . I don't think—"

"That's the trouble with some women folk . . . they don't think. Now plop your backside down here with us, and Dawson will be fixin' you a plate. You'll be doin' that right now, won't you, Sonny?"

"You win, Granddad. You're still on top of your game." Dawson put a chair for Carla next to Jedediah and then placed a full plate of pasta and sauce, generously sprinkled with fresh parmesan cheese, in front of her.

The old man nodded his approval. "You're darn tootin' I am, Sonny, and don't *none* of you forget it."

Joey looked around at everybody. "Us Kahills sure do have a big family. We done run outta chairs."

"A big family is a real blessing, Joey. Especially when they all get along." Polly Dee's gaze fell squarely on Jedediah.

For a long moment, nobody spoke. Then Carla and Conchita rose at the same time.

"Somebody ordered cobbler for dessert tonight, and it isn't even Sunday," Carla said as they headed for the kitchen.

"I hope Granddad likes the one I made. I fix it especially for him." Conchita said. "Is that good English, Carla? "I try to make it right."

Jedediah watched them go. *I wonder what kind of slop she's gonna serve us. She's just a kid. Ain't lived long enough to cultivate the art of cookin' the way Carla does . . . or my Emma did. Oh, well, I'll be polite and take a bite. Then I'll beg off because I'm full. I mustn't take out my feelin's about Cabe on that child. She's tryin' to help and tryin' to fit in. It ain't easy to live up to bein' a Kahill, but she's givin' it a good effort. Too bad that worthless husband of hers ain't doin' the same.*

Carla held the door open as Conchita entered, carrying the largest pan of peach cobbler he had ever seen. Perched on her small shoulder and supported by her hands, it looked like it would topple to the floor at any moment. Cabe jumped up and took it from her. *Humph. At least the boy's got enough sense to help her.* He grinned to himself. Was it really the biggest cobbler . . . or did it just look that way because Conchita was so small? He looked her up and down. The child couldn't be over five feet tall. *I'll run ten laps around Willow Walk if she weighs more'n ninety pounds.*

"There, Granddad. ¿*Es satisfecho usted*? Are you . . . satisfied?" A wide smile lit up her lovely face as Cabe set it in front of Jedediah.

He couldn't help but like the girl. There was something about her . . . *I wish I knew what it is, but I do know we've got a special young lady here.* He looked at her and smiled. "I guess I'll have to let you know after I've tasted it."

No one said a word or took a serving until Jedediah had put a forkful in his mouth. Giving no indication of his thoughts, he took a drink of water and turned to Conchita. "Well, little one, I think you've made a grave mistake here." Disappointment tainted her expression, but her gaze never left Granddad's face. "Now listen close while I tell you what you done wrong. This is far and away the best cobbler I ever tasted. Even beats out Grandma Emma's, and that's goin' some. So the very first Sunday that passes without you makin' one of your cobblers is the Sunday that you'll have to reckon with me. You understand, girl?"

"I understand perfect . . . ly, Granddad." She reached down and took his plate, then gave him a big smile. "Now that you've had yours, the rest of us can share what's left of the cobbler."

"Just a cotton pickin' minute here, Missy. That was only a test. I ain't had my dessert yet, so I'll be thankin' you to put that plate right back down where you got it."

"I don't got no 'sert eider," Molly Anna said.

"I didn't get none neider, Granddaddy. I want some of Cheeta's cobbler." Joey frowned.

"Mind your manners now." Jedediah waggled a finger at them. "And you best be callin' her *Aunt* Cheeta."

"Yes, sir," both children said in unison.

Jedediah looked up just as a smile found its way to Cabe's lips. *Don't be gettin' any ideas, boy. My takin' to your wife ain't got nothin' to do with how I feel about you. Ain't nothin' changed . . . except maybe now I got some respect for your choice in women.*

Joey and Molly Anna stuffed their mouths with forkfuls of the warm dessert between exchanged comments and giggles. *What will they do without each other when Clancy and Bonny go to Ireland? Why, those two have been as inseparable as Dawson and Kat when they were children. And what if the newlyweds decide to settle in Ireland permanently? What am I talking about? The O'Malleys belong right here with us. One big, happy family, that's what we are. Clancy's got long-term work at the lodge, and Bonny surely ain't goin' nowhere now that Kitten's got big expansion plans and a hefty interest in Wolf. Nope, I'm not gonna be borrowin' trouble.*

I got a lot to be thankful for. Even Cabe's here. I know he done wrong, but maybe I ought to cut him just a little slack. On the other hand . . .

He stood up. "I think we need to give thanks for all we've been given." He bowed his head and folded his hands. "Thank you, Heavenly Father, for the meal we just shared as a family. We're grateful to have Cabe and Cheeta with us." He opened one eye and saw Cabe smiling at him. He cleared his throat and closed his eye. "Ummm, we look forward to their new little one joinin' us soon, and we're mighty grateful for all of them. Please help us to be forgivin' as you are in forgivin' us. Amen."

He tried not to look at Cabe, but the draw was too strong. Must have been running both ways because his grandson was still looking at him.

"Thank you, Granddad," Dawson said. "That was very nice."

"*Now* can I have more cobbler, please?" Joey held up his empty plate.

"You betcha." Jedediah scooped another spoonful of the dessert for the boy. "Anybody else?" Empty plates came at him from every direction. "Well, Cheeta, it looks like your cobbler's a big hit with the Kahills. I suspect everybody'll be looking forward to Sunday dinners from now on." He caught a piercing glance from Carla and cleared his throat. "Not that we weren't before, of course."

Dawson stood and looked over the group sitting around the table. He clinked his fork against the cut glass goblet that held his water. At the light tinkling sound, all eyes turned toward him.

"Granddad started something here with his fine prayer, and I think we need to take it to the next level." He glanced at Kat. She was smiling at him. "At this table we have an incredible family, some members by blood and some by heart. But all are treasured equally." He turned to his brother. "Cabe, Kat and I—along with the rest of the family, I'm sure—want you to know how glad we are to have you and your lovely wife with us. There's been an empty spot in the Kahill clan since you left, and having that spot full again is a true blessing to all of us. We hope that you will make your permanent home in Wheeling, which leads me to another topic." He hesitated, cast a quick glance at Jedediah, then continued. "I've been working on plans to add some cabins higher up on the mountain for guests who've expressed a desire for something a little more secluded and private. The blue prints are finished and approved, and I've hired a contractor. Construction will begin next week. Are you interested in hiring on with the crew?"

"Humph. At least that'll keep him honest." Like the flick of a whip, Jedediah's sharp tongue lashed out at Cabe.

"*¿Mande?*" Conchita's quiet little voice took on a commanding edge. "What did you say, *Señor* Kahill? I think you need to know something.

Cabe tells me how he got money to come to Mexico to help me, and we talk about the way he can fix this bad mistake. He talks to his brother at once when he returns and pays back some of the money already. So why do you say such a cruel thing? *No soy estúpida, y mi esposo no es estúpido.* But you, Señor Kahill, are a stupid man." Hushed gasps circulated around the table as she stood up and started toward Jedediah. Cabe grabbed her arm, but she yanked it away. "I know this is your . . . *casa*, and I will leave because you will no longer welcome me, but first I will tell you that your prayer means nothing when this is how you speak. What kind of God listens to a man who says one thing and acts . . . *contrario?* You have a lot to learn about how to forgive, Señor. *Me esposo . . . .* my husband . . . came to make peace with all of you and to pay for his mistake. But your actions say that is not what you want. Now I go. *Y yo no cocinaré para usted otra vez.* No more cobbler." She started out of the room.

"Hold on there, little wild cat. I'm mighty sorry if I offended you." *This one has fire. She'll make a fine Kahill woman.*

"I am not the one you need to say 'sorry' to, Señor." She walked back to stand behind Cabe. "I only speak what your grandson is feeling about how you treat him. He is too kind to say the words, but I am like you, Señor. I say what is in my heart. My Cabe tells me how you do not want him from the first time he comes to your Willow Walk. He says a funny thing I do not understand in Spanish—you look down your nose at him. But now I see you and I understand. You are wrong to say a nice prayer for all your family and then say lies about my husband. You are a . . . I do not know the English word . . . *un hipócrito.*"

Silence hung over the room. Finally, Cabe spoke.

"I worked hard in Mexico, Granddad, and two wonderful things happened there. Conchita agreed to marry me, and she helped me to see how much I was hurting my family by staying away and not making amends for what I did. Oh, I intended to pay back the money someday, but she showed me why I need to make that my first priority. I know you probably don't believe me, but I'm prepared to show you my sincerity if you'll give me the chance."

He looked straight at Jedediah, but the old man kept his gaze on the floor. Tears filled Cabe's eyes as he turned to his wife. Arm in arm, they started out of the room.

Dawson looked at Jedediah, who hadn't budged. He glanced at Kat and nodded. She opened her mouth to speak, but Jedediah stood up and raised his cane in the air.

"Where in blazes do you think you're goin'? Get back here and hear me out."

They stopped but didn't turn around.

Jedediah softened his voice. "Please don't go."

They walked back and stood in front of him.

"You got a good woman, boy. And she's right. I been way too hard on you. I'm sorry. You didn't have to come back, but you did. I've known for a while that I been actin' like a dang fool by bein' so dead set against likin' you, but you're so much like your daddy—now don't go takin' offense because your father had a lot of good in him. I just don't say that much. You see, he hurt your Grandma Emma and me by doin' the things he did. We didn't know he was sick, and I was too dang stubborn then, too, because I pushed him away instead of helpin' him. If I'd done different, he might be here with us today because we'd have seen that somethin' was mighty wrong with him. So maybe the reason I'm havin' trouble forgivin' you is because I can't forgive myself. And when I look at you, I see him and I'm reminded that I did things all wrong back then." Tears cascaded down his cheeks. "It's hard, boy. I want to love you, but I'm afraid. Can you forgive this stupid old man?"

Cabe wrapped his arms around his grandfather, and they cried together.

Conchita wiped her eyes and looked around the table. Everyone was crying. "*Gracias, mi familia preciosa. I love you.*" She stretched her arms abound Cabe's and Granddad's waist. "*Ay, mis hombres son maravillosos.*"

Jedediah smiled through his tears. "Now I know why I seen somethin' real special in that woman of yours, boy. She's just like your Grandma Emma—a little spitfire with a big heart. You take good care of her now, or we'll be at odds again, you hear?"

CHAPTER THIRTY-SEVEN

The chill of winter disappeared with the chill that had hung over Jedediah and Cabe. For the first time in a long time, the newness of the season matched the renewal at Willow Walk.

Spring weddings that had seemed far distant from the snow covered slopes grew close with the advent of green grass and spring blossoms.

"Oh, Kat, this is divine beyond my wildest dreams!" Deb turned first one way and then another in front of the tri-fold mirror.

"You look like a princess." Kat made a minor adjustment on the back of the dress.

"Princess, nothing. I'm a queen." Her eyes glistened.

"It has just the look of romance I wanted to create for you. You've loved Bill for so long, and finally you'll be walking down the aisle . . . well, as close to an aisle as we can get at Willow Walk."

Deb couldn't take her eyes off the gorgeous strapless gown. Crafted of ivory silk, the top of its scalloped bodice was enhanced with tiny beads sewn on in the shape of delicate flowers. The unique design traveled down the front and ended at the waistline. The voluminous skirt, created with bustles of silk caught up with appliqués of the same beading, ended in a short chapel train. Dramatic and elegant, it perfectly suited Deb's personality. A matching veil of illusion lace edged with the beading, was held in place by a headband of pale yellow rosebuds. She would carry a bouquet of pale yellow roses, white lilies of the valley, and English ivy.

"Kat, you've made me happier than I've ever been, and not just by designing the perfect gown for me. I . . . Bill and I want to thank you again for offering to have the weddings at Willow Walk. How romantic it will be to say our vows under the willows while wearing the absolutely most perfect dress in the world!"

"It's just the beginning, Deb. You two are made for each other, and your happiness should grow with every day and every year. Just remember to value your relationship and keep it fresh . . . just like the flowers you'll be wearing and carrying. Live every day as though it is your last. Remember to say I love you often, and never go to bed angry at each other. Your husband will be the most important person in your life, so keep that in mind. Even when you have children—who demand a lot of time, by the way—make sure he knows he still has first place in your heart. Be his treasure, and he will treasure you always."

Deb gave her a long look. "Thank you, Kat. I'll remember your precious advice because I know it came from your heart . . . and because I see in you and Dawson that it works—and the next time you cover the mirrors in the dressing rooms with brown paper so I can't see myself, I'm going to personally rip it off."

"And spoil my fun of enjoying your first reaction when you see yourself? Don't even think about it." Kat grinned. "Now we've got lots of work to do. And let's hope the weather cooperates when the big day rolls around."

"You two aren't making plans without me, are you?" Bonny emerged from the dressing room in her wedding gown and stopped short. "Deb, you're . . . exquisite. I've never seen you look so beautiful."

Deb's mouth dropped open. Even Kat was breathless. Finally, she found her tongue.

"Bonny, oh my. You are beyond stunning."

Deb stepped down from the platform so Bonnie could see herself. Bonnie took a gigantic breath and couldn't seem to let it out.

"Stop it, Bon. Breathe!" Deb ordered. "You're not going to faint on us, are you?"

"I don't think so. It's just that . . . standing here in this gown, I . . . don't know what to say."

"Why don't you just tell me whether you like it or not." Kat waited for an answer.

"Do you have to ask me that to know how I feel in this dress? Kat, I saw the sketch, but I had no idea it would turn out to be so spectacular." Her eyes shone with unshed tears.

"Don't you dare cry! We have to make sure it fits properly. Now turn around and let us take a closer look."

Bonny turned slowly, her gaze still glued to the bride in the mirror. The fitted A-line gown had a sweetheart neckline and demure cap sleeves. Soft Chantilly lace, beaded with Austrian crystals, covered the plunging *peau de soie* bodice. The skirt was gathered with yards of soft tulle. She had chosen not to have a veil. Instead, she would wear sprigs of baby's breath held in place with green rhinestone combs that had been a gift from Clancy. She would carry a nosegay of delicate pink roses bound together by green satin ribbons.

¡*"Ay caramba"*! Conchita let out a soft whistle. *"Tu estás muy bella.* You are very beautiful."

She came often to the boutique to chat with them and to practice her English, she said. Kat looked at her glowing eyes. *I think there's more to it than that. She lost her mother when she was young. Her father drinks. She has no siblings. I think she is enjoying having a family that loves her.* An idea popped into her head.

"Cheeta, what kind of wedding did you and Cabe have in Mexico?"

"Casarse por el civil. We have a civil marriage. My dress is not fancy, but I have my Cabe. And we are legal man and wife. We never live in sin."

"Would you like to have a ceremony at Willow Walk so that your new family can be there to celebrate with you? We'll help you pick out something special to wear."

"Oh, Kat, you would do that for me?" Her black eyes gleamed. Then she frowned and looked down at her growing belly. "Already I am big with *mi bebe.*"

"We can disguise that," Kat assured her. "Remember, dress design is my job."

Conchita turned to look at Deb and Bonny. *"Si,* and your work *es magnífico."*

"What a wonderful idea, Kat!" Bonny smiled, still admiring her image in the mirror.

"Yes, Cheeta, let's have another wedding," Deb agreed.

Bonny stepped down from the platform. "We'll go change and help you find just the right dress. And Kat, we'll take the covers off the mirrors."

"Not quite yet. Let's get Conchita outfitted first. *Then* we'll take them off."

"Sorry I didn't think of this sooner," Kat said while the girls were changing. "We could've had a triple wedding. But everything's already ordered, and the invitations have been mailed."

"Está bien. It is okay. I am . . . *muy felíz* . . . very happy that you think of this *celebración especial* for *mi* Cabe and me."

Kat blinked back the tears. *The things we take for granted are so special to her. She's not just teaching Granddad, but she's teaching all of us to be humble and appreciative. I thought I was that way before, but Conchita is showing me how to be so much more than I am.* What's your favorite color?"

"*Amarillo* . . . no . . . yellow and *azul* . . . blue and *rojo* . . . red. *Me gusta todos colores.* I like all the colors. In Mexico, we use many colors."

"I get the idea." Kat rubbed her forehead. "Why don't you go into the fitting room, and we'll bring you some things to try on. We'll find something we can alter if we need to fit your . . . state of motherhood-to-be. Oh . . . and please leave the paper on the mirrors. We want you to see yourself first in the one out here." *Oh my, it will be a challenge to find something in the colors you like and keep you from looking like a Rhode Island Red hen with a pooch.* Still it was her wedding. *But all those colors? Red is not the color a bride should wear.*

It took most of the afternoon to find the right dress that could be fitted to her bulging tummy, but Kat couldn't help but notice her natural grace as she tried on gown after gown. *After she has this baby, maybe she would like to model for us. She'd be perfect for our new line of petite wear.*

"Conchita, you're gorgeous," Deb said when the young woman stepped out of the dressing room.

"It's perfect." Bonny walked around her and then nodded her approval.

"You look absolutely lovely," Kat agreed.

"I am not so sure about the color." Conchita was frowning.

Kat took her hand and led her to the mirror. "Take a look and see what you think."

The floor length dress in a soft blue shade of silk chiffon flowed from the empire waist to the floor. It complimented her caramel-colored skin and hid the baby bump from all but the most discerning eyes. The fluid lines of the skirt would still look gorgeous after the baby was born.

Conchita smiled as Kat lifted the sides of her hair and pulled them back with pearl combs. "I think we can find the perfect flowers for you to carry in Grandma Emma's greenhouse at Willow Walk. You really are so much like her, and I know she would want you to carry her flowers."

"*Gracias, mi hermana.*" Kat's breath caught in her throat. She didn't know much Spanish, but she understood that Conchita had just called her sister. The young woman took one last look in the mirror and gave them all big hugs. "I think Cabe will fall in love with me *otra vez* . . . again . . . when he sees me. Never do I have a dress so . . . *bonito* . . . *pretty. Gracias, gracias, gracias.*"

"I think we all deserve a break. Let's go to the kitchen for lemonade." Kat led the way.

"I can't wait to meet Bill's Uncle Romeo," Deb said after they had made themselves comfortable around the table. "In fact, I can't wait to see Italy. You know Bill's half Italian on his mother's side."

"I didn't know that," Kat said.

"What a romantic place for our honeymoon. I'm so excited. Believe me, if it weren't for Bill's job and the boutique, we'd be going for longer than a week."

"Hmmmm . . . I suppose Ireland has a lot of surprises waiting for me, too." The wistful look on Bonny's face drew a grin from Conchita. "Of course seven of those things are *not* surprises. I hope Clancy's boys like me. The older ones, especially, will have a lot of memories of their mother."

"What's not to like, Bon? Besides, you'll make a wonderful stepmother. You've always wanted to see Ireland. What better way to do it than with the man you love?" Deb reminded her.

"Yes, but I'm a little worried about coming home with four sons. That's five with Molly Anna, and then Clancy and I want at least one of our own."

"Talk about a ready-made family! But Clancy has seven boys."

"He does, but he thinks three of them will stay in Ireland. The oldest is twenty, and he'll be getting married while we're there. The second one has been accepted at a college in Dublin, and the third wants to finish high school there."

Kat turned to Conchita. "Where did you and Cabe go on your honeymoon?"

"Ay, I think you know. We honeymoon at *americano* ski lodge."

They all laughed.

"One more fitting, girls, and that should do it. We'll get together and check last minute details. Now I've got to go. I have some things to take care of with Dawson."

"Boy, Kat, you two sure have a lot of *things* to take care of lately," Bonny winked at Deb and Conchita."

"Yeah, Kat, every time we turn around, you guys are *taking care of things*. You must have gotten terribly behind when you were in Paris."

"Ay, caramba!" Conchita spun the words off her tongue. She looked straight at Bonny and Deb. "You have more *things to take care of* than you know—soon. I already *take care of things*, you can see." She looked down at her bulging abdomen and nodded.

Laughter filled the room again.

"You ladies think whatever you like, but I'll be working on the fall line of fashions for Wolf, featuring—guess what?" Kat raised an eyebrow. "Wedding attire. And then I have a new line planned for Fashions by Kat."

"That sounds wonderful." Deb nodded her approval. "Are you going to be using our finery?"

"You'd better believe it. After seeing your reactions to the gowns, how could I not include them?"

"So many good things are happening. I know Rebecca will be pleased. How's she doing?" Bonny was washing the lemonade glasses.

"Great. Country living seems to agree with her. She's enjoying her new garden, and as soon as Mason—Dr. LeBlanc—gives her the okay, she plans to ride her uncle's magnificent stallion. And she's keeping busy with Wolf paperwork, despite her stated intentions not to do so. I told her I needed her help . . . and it keeps her in the 'know' as well as helping me. Right now I have all I can handle."

"Do you plan a trip to Paris in the near future?" Deb asked.

Kat didn't answer.

"Deb to Kat. Deb to Kat. Are you coming back to Wheeling anytime soon? Or have you already relocated in the city of love?"

Kat shook her head and stared at Deb. "No . . . no! Just thinking of Rebecca and how we almost lost her. I doubt I'll be making any trips to Paris, but if I do, Dawson will be traveling with me."

CHAPTER THIRTY-EIGHT

Conchita didn't in any way resemble a Rhode Island Red as she came down the stairs. Radiant in the gorgeous blue gown, she exuded a glow that couldn't all be attributed to the new life growing in her belly. Her joy that Cabe's family had provided this wonderful day couldn't be hidden, and they sat in the guest drawing room, awaiting her appearance.

Looking very dapper in his dark grey suit and light blue silk necktie, Jedediah stood at the bottom of the stairs, staring up at her. Never had he seen a lovelier bride. He still couldn't believe she'd asked him to give her away, not after all the hateful things he'd said about Cabe. *Oh, Emma, I wish you could be here to see this. We never had a daughter, so I never had the privilege that I'm havin' today. It's the best day of my life—after the day I took you as my bride, of course.*

Conchita placed her hand through his arm, and they walked slowly into the drawing room because he had insisted on not using his cane. Cabe waited for them in front of the fireplace. The outside temperature was too warm to have a real fire, so Kat had removed the grate and placed two dozen large, light blue candles in the firebox in the shape of a heart. The tiny flames created just the right ambiance. On the mantle, a large bouquet that matched the flowers she carried rose out of an antique cut glass vase.

Eyes wide as he watched his bride approach, Cabe reached out his hand to take Conchita's. Jedediah hesitated to let her go.

"Granddad?" Cabe looked at the old man.

"Just make sure you're good to her, or you'll be dealin' with me," he said in a stage whisper. "She's a fine young woman."

"I've known that since I first met her," Cabe whispered back.

With a nod of his head, Jedediah placed Cheeta's hand in Cabe's and took a seat next to Dawson.

Carla's wedding feast was a banquet to remember. The two-tiered wedding cake covered in marzipan flowers to match the bouquet of red roses, daisies, yellow daffodils, and blue hyacinths that Kat had fashioned for Conchita drew awed gasps from everyone.

Conchita gave Kat a huge hug. "*Muchas gracias* for all you did to make our day special. You make my flowers in many colors just like I want. The dress, the bouquet, the candles in the fireplace, all the food Carla prepares—it is all so wonderful. For the first time, my Cabe says he feels like he really is part of this Kahill family."

"You're so very welcome, Cheeta. It has been our pleasure to give you the wedding you deserve. I think you were right about Cabe falling in love with you again. I watched him as you said your vows. He never stopped looking at you. Believe me, he had all the earmarks of a man totally captivated by his woman."

Kat couldn't wait to go upstairs to help her change for their short honeymoon. She'd laid a beautiful red crepe dress on the bed. In an envelope next to the vase was a reservation confirmation at one of Charleston's finest hotels.

She caught a glimpse of Cabe and Granddad in the kitchen when she went for more napkins. Eavesdropping was not her style, but she couldn't help hearing some of their exchange.

"Now, boy, you be careful drivin' all that way. You got a wife and a little one to watch out for now. I want y'all to come home safe."

"I promise to take it easy, Granddad."

"Yeah, that's what all young people say because they think nothin' bad will ever happen to them. But it does. So just mind my words and watch out for them other drivers."

"Yes, sir. I'll be careful."

Granddad patted him on the back, then pulled an envelope out of his pocket. "Just one more thing. Here, I got a present for your weddin'. Now don't spend it all in one place, and buy somethin' nice for that pretty little wife of yours and take her to dinner at one of them fancy restaurants." He placed the envelope in Cabe's hand.

"I don't know what to say, Granddad. You didn't have to give us a gift, but . . . thank you. And thank you for giving Conchita away. In her heart she has much pain because her father doesn't show her any love. He began drinking after his wife died, and now he doesn't even answer the phone when his only daughter calls him. It meant a great deal to her—to both of us—for you to honor her this way." He reached out to give his grandfather a hug, then pulled back.

"Well, go on, boy. I may be old, but I still know how to hug." Jedediah wrapped his arms around his grandson and then watched Cabe leave the room. *Won't he be surprised when he opens that envelope and finds five hundred dollars? I wonder if he'll know it's my way of telling him everything's okay between us? He's a bright boy—a lot like his dad and his granddad. He'll figure it out . . . I took your advice, Emma. I hope you think I did good. You don't need to be bringin' the broom with you the next time you come.*

All the planning that had gone into the little wedding set the stage for the big one just two weeks away. Kat shook her head. Deb and Bonny were masters of organization at the boutique. But when it came to their weddings, neither of them seemed able to focus on a single detail. *If we're going to pull this off, I'm going to have to do it myself.* She checked her list. The caterers had altered the menu twice when the girls had yet different thoughts about the food. Finally, she'd told them 'no more.' and finished everything herself. They would just have to be surprised.

The day dawned clear and perfect. Kat had never seen a more beautiful June morning. Willow Walk rose proud and tall above the manicured lawn that had been well watered to highlight the plush deep green carpet. Rhododendrons had burst into bloom in shades of lavender, deep rose, and pale yellow. Irises, daffodils, and lilacs highlighted the garden path that led to the arbor under the willows. The arbor Dawson had constructed for the occasion was covered with ivy. Large pots of pink, blue, and white lilacs lay on either side, as well as on the steps of the house.

The girls spent the night at Willow Walk to minimize the rush in the morning. With generous glasses of orange juice in hand, Kat, Deb, and Bonny sat on the porch and stared at the fairytale setting.

"Never in my wildest dreams did I imagine it would be this incredible." Bonny took two sips of her juice and set it on the table. "I can't believe that in just a few hours I'm really going to be married. And a few hours after that, I'll be winging my way to Ireland—literally."

"Believe it . . . believe them both. It's happening. I still think you two should eat something, even if it's light. Don't worry about not fitting into your gowns. That's why I made the back corseted. We can always let it out a few inches at the last minute." Kat laughed at her own joke, and at least the girls smiled. "Come on," she coaxed, "relax. I don't think the makeup will conceal your worry lines if you keep this up."

"I can't eat anything right now, but I might have some toast later." Deb made a face. "My stomach is threatening to revolt over the orange juice."

"Okay, but we don't want anybody fainting during the ceremony. Now run on upstairs. It's almost time for the hair stylist and makeup artist to arrive.

Bonny rose and grabbed Kat's hands. "How can we ever thank you for making this day so special? It's as though we're living in a storybook land, but it's real . . . . and it's ours."

"No thanks necessary. You've more than repaid me by keeping our business running—and very successfully at that—for four years after I had Joey. Now scoot on upstairs so we can make your dream weddings come true."

The guests were seated, and the grooms had taken their places beneath the arbor. A small chamber ensemble played a light symphonic tune, Carla's cue to send flower girl Molly Anna out the door and down the garden path. As the little girl descended the steps, Kat heard the 'ohs' and 'ahs' as the freckled red-head in a simple white eyelet dress belted with a green satin ribbon took slow, precise steps toward the arbor and her daddy. She carried a small white basket filled with pink and yellow rose petals that she sprinkled on the path. Behind her came Joey, dressed in a small gray tuxedo, complete with cummerbund.

Peeking out the door, Carla sighed with relief when they reached the arbor. At the last minute, Joey had refused to put on the cummerbund, tie, and jacket.

"Why I gotta wear this thing. I'm not gettin' married."

"See my pretty new dress?" Molly Anna had said.

"You look purty, but I'm a boy. I don' have to be purty."

"You gotta wear it if yer gonna be in my da's wedding. Please, Joey?"

"Well . . ."

"I'm glad you like my dress, Joey." She turned around with all the grace a five-year-old could muster.

"Yeah, but I like your overalls better. And I don' wanna do this."

He'd finally given in when Deb and Bonny told him how much they wanted him to do it and how important he was to the ceremony. So down the path he went, carrying a little white silk pillow with the rings pinned in place. Not a hint of a smile was on his face, and his pace was not the one he'd practiced. Everyone could see he just wanted to get this over with.

Kat walked behind him as Matron of Honor for both her friends. She wore a gown of fuchsia silk with a keyhole neckline and matching jacket trimmed in crystal beading. Her wide-brimmed white hat of onion skin straw sported silk rosebuds in pink and yellow on the brim. She carried one pink rose and one yellow one to match the bouquets Bonny and Deb held.

The first notes of "Here Comes the Bride" began, and Bonny started her walk down the path. Everyone stood, but she saw no one except Clancy, who took several steps toward her before she reached the arbor.

"What a sight ye be for me eyes, Bonny lass. Ya do me proud."

They stood to one side when Deb began her walk down the path. The beading on her gown caught the rays of the afternoon sun and sparkled almost as much as her eyes as she made her way to Bill.

"Deb, you're the most gorgeous woman I've ever seen," he said in a low, breathless voice.

"You're pretty gorgeous yourself," she whispered back.

After the entire wedding party stood beneath the arbor, Carla slipped into a back row seat to watch the ceremony. She wiped her eyes as the couples exchanged the poignant vows they had written.

For the first time in years, she allowed herself to remember her own wedding and her young husband who had died six months later in a logging accident. It had been her choice not to remarry. Oh, she'd had suitors, several in fact. But her love for her Johnny had been too great. They were the perfect match, and they'd never spoken a cross word to each other. No, nobody could replace Johnny. She didn't *want* anybody to replace him.

The baby they'd planned to have after a year was never conceived, so she became a housekeeper and a nanny to satisfy her love of home and children. Then she tucked her memories away in a far corner of her heart. Why she brought them out today, she wasn't sure. But it was alright. Sometimes, it was good to remember . . .

"It was a lovely wedding, but I still think you should've let me do the cooking." She munched on a plate filled with chicken salad in pastry shells and tiny skewered shrimp and pineapple as she chatted with Kat.

"Not today." Kat wrapped her arm around the shoulder of the woman who'd become one of the family. "Today you don't run back and forth to the kitchen. You enjoy the celebration with the rest of the Kahills. You *are* family, you know."

"Thank you from the bottom of my heart. I've not had a family since I lost my . . . and thank you, too, for this lovely suit." She looked down at the elegant lavender piqué suit with white lace collar.

"It was my pleasure, Carla. I think you've caught the eyes of a few gentlemen here this afternoon."

"Better not let Jedediah hear you say that." She winked at Kat.

Dawson walked up to them. "Mind if I steal my wife? I want her to get something to eat before the food's all gone."

"You can't steal what's already yours." She gave them a warm smile and watched them stroll away, arm in arm.

They remind me of Johnny and me. A tear threatened to spill down her cheek. She wiped it away with her napkin and nibbled on a small shrimp. Yes, it had been an extraordinarily lovely day.

Conchita was sitting next to Cabe, eating her second slice of cake, when she felt it.

"Ouch!"

Cabe swallowed. "You okay, Honey?"

"I think so. Little Emma is kicking real regular for the last hour."

He laid his hand on her belly.

"Oh, there she goes again."

"That doesn't feel like a kick to me." Cabe frowned. "I felt the baby kick lots of time, and it didn't feel like this."

"I think she moves in a new position, so she feels different."

"This cake's really good." He stood up to get his second piece.

She grabbed his arm. "Cabe! Help me."

He sat back down beside her. "What is it, Honey? What do you need me to do?"

"I need to go, Cabe."

"You know where the bathroom is. Do you want me to take you there?"

"Not that kind of go. *¡Ayúdeme! Debo ir al hospital ahora.*"

He swallowed hard. "You need to go to the hospital? Now?"

"*Si, mijo*, now."

"But it's not time. Little Em's not due for another six weeks."

"I do not think she knows that. Ohhhh . . . ouch! *¡Ay, caramba!* The baby is coming. We go—now!"

Kat and Dawson walked past, turned around, and came back.

"Are you okay, Conchita?" Kat asked. "You look like you're . . . in pain."

"*Si, si*, the baby comes now."

"Are you sure?" Kat shot Dawson a concerned glance.

"Ahhhhhhh." She winced. "I am sure."

Cabe stood and turned in a circle. "The baby's coming!" he shouted. "The baby's coming." Everybody turned around to look. He turned back to his wife. "Don't worry, Honey, I have everything under control. You go get the car. I'll get your suitcase. Or do you want to get the suitcase, and I'll get the car?"

Kat reached out and touched his arm. "Cabe, her suitcase has been in the car for a week. We thought she might go early because she's so big."

"Give me the keys," Dawson said. "Better yet, we'll get the suitcase out of your car and Kat can drive you in her van."

"I'll be right back, Sweetheart." Cabe kissed Conchita on the forehead and followed Dawson to get the suitcase and bring up the van."

Kat helped Conchita to her feet. The tap, tap, tap of his cane on the ground announced that Granddad had come to help, too.

"Now where's that boy? He's needed here."

"He's gone with Dawson to get the van."

"Since when does it take two of them to drive the van?"

"Since Cabe had to get Cheeta's suitcase out of their car. Here they come now."

Conchita grabbed Granddad's arm as another pain gripped her. "That's right, girly, you just hold on to me. It'll pass in a minute."

Cabe bounced out of the van and ran up to them. "Hurry, Cheeta, let's go."

She still gripped Granddad's arm. "The pain . . . oh, the pain. When it's over, I come, *mijo*."

"Calm yourself down, boy. Birthin' babies is a natural thing. Folks've been doin' it ever since Adam and Eve."

"My poor baby," Conchita said as Cabe helped her into the van. She patted her tight belly. "Not *this* one. I talk about you, *mijo*. Ohhhhh."

"Better hurry it up, Kitten. I think Little Em's in a big hurry."

Kat gave Dawson a quick kiss. "You and Granddad are in charge. Carla will help you if you need anything. Tell Deb and Bonny I'll call them from the hospital."

"Don't worry, Kat. We can handle things on this end. Granddad and I will be along in a couple of hours . . . or whenever the reception's over, whichever comes first."

She slipped the gearshift into drive and headed slowly down the driveway.

Cabe stared at his wife. "Don't you dare have this baby here. You wait till we get to the hospital. Understand?"

Conchita laughed. "I understand just fine. But I don't think our Emma understands. She wants out."

The short drive seemed to take forever.

"Here we are." Kat pulled up to the emergency entrance. Cabe jumped out and returned with an orderly and a wheelchair in less than a minute. The two of them helped Conchita into the chair, and the orderly whisked her off, Cabe hurrying along behind.

Dawson and Granddad sat in the family waiting room. Jedediah looked around. "Place ain't changed much."

"That's right. You spent a lot of time here the night Joey was born."

"Yep. I figure on this time bein' a much more pleasant experience."

"Is this where you met Clancy?" Dawson put down the magazine he was reading.

"Sure is. The one and only time I saw them seven boys of his. They were scallywags, let me tell you."

A nurse approached. Jedediah gave her a once-over. *At least she don't look like Helga the Hun.*

"Mrs. Kahill is in labor," she announced.

Granddad looked at her. *Tell us somethin' we don't know.*

"Her contractions are two minutes apart, but she's only dilated to four centimeters. It could be a while. It's hard to tell with these first babies. She's pretty large for thirty-four weeks. Are you sure her due date's right?"

"I don't think little Em's got a calendar," Granddad suggested. "But I can tell you she's gonna be a special little girl because she's in a hurry to get here."

The nurse gave him an indulgent smile, then turned to Dawson. "We'll keep you posted."

"Yeah, right," Jedediah mumbled. "Been there, done that."

Cabe stood at the head of the bed while the nurse examined his wife. "We've got a ways to go yet."

Cabe's eyes widened. "You mean it's going to get worse?"

She smiled. "Not worse, Mr. Kahill, more exciting."

"Oh. That doesn't sound so bad."

"Look at the monitor." She pointed to a jagged line running across the screen. "This is the baby's heartbeat. She's doing just fine, by the way. You did say the baby's a girl, didn't you?"

"That's what the ultrasound indicated. It looked pretty definite."

"Cabe, my love, are you sure you want to be here? You do not have much good color in your face."

"I'm fine, Cheeta. I wouldn't miss the birth of our Em for all the money in the world. I'm staying right here at your side for the whole thing."

"Okay, but you cannot faint when the blood comes."

"Blood! Who said anything about blood?"

CHAPTER THIRTY-NINE

"A boy? A boy! What's goin' on here? I thought we was havin' a girl. Where's our Emmie?" Jedediah ranted at the lady who worked in the family waiting area.

"Mr. Kahill, please keep your voice down. I only pass on the information that's been given to me. I'll double-check, but I'm sure I got it right."

"I'll be thankin' you to do that."

Dawson walked up beside him. "Calm down, Granddad. "They have a baby boy. I don't think we can change that."

"Humph. That just goes to show you that all this high-tech, highfalutin machinery stuff don't work. That sonic gram, or whatever they call it, was wrong. It's pretty bad when it can't tell a boy's equipment from a girl's."

"I'm sure there's a logical explanation for this." Dawson said. "I'm also sure the doctor knows the difference between a boy and a girl once the baby's here. You know, I saw the pictures from the sonogram, too, and I wasn't all that sure what I was looking at. And you're right that technology isn't perfect."

"Wow! That was some experience!" Cabe stood in the doorway. He was still pale, but he was grinning.

"What happened to our baby Emma?" Granddad was still scowling.

"Two."

"Two what?"

"Two babies. Nobody knew. Even the sonogram didn't show it."

222

"Twins?" Twins!" Jedediah didn't even try to hold down the volume. "Did we get our baby Emma?"

The family stood around Conchita's bed in the birthing room. The nurse came in to check the new mother.

"Looks like you're celebrating."

"We're wanting to see our babies." Granddad waved his cane in the air. "We did get our baby Emma, right? You do know how to tell the difference between a boy and a girl, don't you?"

The nurse kept a straight face. "We covered that in nursing school, but it was a short course. However, your babies have different plumbing, so I'm pretty sure we have one of each. Now let me examine Conchita. The little ones are in the nursery right now, getting weighed and dressed. And they need to have a couple tests."

"What kind of tests?" Jedediah's voice went up a notch. "They just got here."

"It's standard procedure, sir. We'll have them back here in a few minutes."

"You're sure they're both okay . . ."

"They cried, Granddad, so that's a good sign." Cabe nodded.

"There're quite a few of us here," Kat said. "Why don't Dawson and I go back to the waiting room and let Granddad see the babies first?"

Fifteen minutes later, two nurses came in, each with a bundle in her arms. Granddad was sitting in a chair next to the window. One of them handed the pink bundle to him, and the other nurse gave the blue bundle to Conchita.

Jedediah looked down at the tiny girl in his arms and didn't even try to stop the tears in his eyes from rolling down his cheeks. He peeked under the soft knit cap on her head and saw a head full of black hair. She wiggled in his arms and opened her eyes.

"Hello, little Emma Dee." His voice was barely above a whisper.

She sneezed.

"Our girl's not gettin' sick, is she?"

"Sneezing is normal," one of the nurse's assured him.

He stretched out his forefinger and stroked her hand. She wrapped her tiny fingers around his big gnarled one. He thought his heart would explode with all the feelings that were chasing one another through it.

"Granddad, come over here." Conchita's was smiling.

Cabe took the baby from his arms. Jedediah pushed himself up and walked over to the bed.

"Meet Carson Joseph Kahill."

"You're . . . you're namin' him after *me*?"

"We decided that before we knew we were having a girl," Cabe said.

"Well, I'll be. Don't recall that we've had twins in the family before. This may be a Kahill first." He lifted the edge of the cap on the little head. More black hair. "He's a fine lookin' boy. Right handsome for a newborn, if I do say so. It's the Kahill blood." He looked back at the baby in Cabe's arms. "See what I told you. She's a right pretty thing, too."

"So what do you think, Granddad? Did we make you proud?" The big smile on Cabe's face wrapped itself around his heart.

"You've come a long way, boy. And I'm mighty proud of both of you. But right now, I'm thinkin' I'd better sit down. This is quite a surprise for an old man. Twins!" Leaning heavily on his cane, he eased his way back to the chair by the window and looked out at the cloudless sky. *We did it, Emma Baby. We got our girl. They named the boy after me. Can you believe it after what a stinker I was? Now I got two grandsons and two great-grandsons carryin' my name. Guess that leaves my mark on the world. The Kahill name will go on. That's what I been waitin' for . . . and of course, the little girl you and I always wanted but was never blessed with.*

He closed his eyes. *I thank you, Father, for bringin' our babies here with no complications like we had with little Joey. I appreciate all three little ones who will carry on the Kahill name. They sure were a long time comin' . . . I mean me approachin' a century old. But they were worth the wait, and there may be more in the future. I'm tired now, but one of these days I can finally lie down and go to sleep with my Emma. It's been a long life and sometimes a hard one, but I'm grateful for the many blessin's you sent my way, even when the goin' got tough. And I'm grateful, too, that you helped me see the light about young Cabe. He's not a bad boy, and he's tryin' real hard. He's got four mouths to feed now. I'm gonna suggest we forgive the rest of the debt he owes. Better yet, I think I'll just pay it. That way the books balance. Sonny tells me he's one of the hardest workers up there on those new cabins, and he's paid back more'n half already. I'm thinkin' that covers his mistake. What do you think?*

CHAPTER FORTY
Two months later

"Woe is me." Jedediah leaned on his cane and stared out the kitchen window.

"What's the matter, Jed? You having a bad day?" Carla put a cup of coffee on the table.

"No more'n usual. Here I am, almost as old as Methuselah, and I'm still babysittin' young'uns."

"Those kiddies keep you young, old man."

"Isn't that one of those silly oxymoron things—'keep you *young, old* man'?"

Carla laughed. "You'd better drink that coffee. A little caffeine will do you good."

He sat down at the kitchen table. "You know, Carla, if I'd been a bit younger, I might've done a little sparkin' with you. You're a good woman and a fine addition to this family. We might even have made it official."

She laid her hand on his arm. "That's a real nice compliment, Jed. I'm honored to know that you consider me worthy to be a Kahill. I feel like I've found a permanent home here. Being included as family is one of the greatest joys of my life."

Joey shot through the back door, Molly Anna hot on his heels. He ran behind Granddad's chair.

"She's tryin' to kiss me, Granddad. Tell her to stop it."

Molly Anna stood beside Carla. "I'm just tryin' to show ya I'm glad to see ya. I was in Ireland a long time, but my brothers and me came home last night."

"I saw them brothers. They're big. What's their names?"

"There's Darren and Conner and Dylan, but they all stayed in Ireland. Darren got married while we was there, and I got to be a flower girl again."

"I'm glad I wasn't there. So who's your brothers that's here?"

"Oh, yeah. There's Patrick. He's fourteen. Liam is twelve. Ian's ten and Sean's eight. We gotta get a bigger place to live. Our li'l 'partment at the lodge ain't . . . isn't big enough for so many people." She turned to Granddad. "I heard you got twins here. Can I see 'em?"

"Carson and Little Emma are with their mother at the boutique."

"Why are they there, Granddad? They're too little to work."

"That's a dumb question, Molly Anna."

Jedediah patted Joey's head. "Now, boy, there's no such thing as a dumb question, 'specially when you're young and just learnin' about life. Now, Molly, the babies are with their mama because she's workin' with Kat now."

"How come?"

Joey raised his eyebrows and shook his head.

"Your new mommy was in Ireland, and Deb needed help."

"Where's Aunt Kat?"

"She works here part of the time because she has another company to run in New York."

"This isn't New York. How does she do that."

"With a computer."

"Girls sure do ask a lot of questions," Joey grumped.

"I told you, Son, that's how they learn things."

"I'm glad I already know things. I don't have to ask all those questions."

"Jed, you're looking a little weary. Why don't you let me fix these youngsters a bite of lunch and you go take a nap?"

"I'm thinkin' I'll take you up on that, Carla. I thank you."

He pushed himself up with his cane and headed for the stairs. By the time he reached the top, he had to lean against the wall to catch his breath. The walk to his bedroom seemed to be getting longer all the time, but today it was extra long. He shut the door behind him and went straight to the attic. Shuffling across the large room, he slumped into his chair. *I'm so tired . . . so tired . . . so . . .*

"Are you here, Emma Baby? I can hardly see in this dim light."

"It's not dim, Jed. You're just wearing out. Those kids are keeping you hopping, aren't they? Relax a bit now. I'm right here next to you."

"Have you seen the kids? Joey's growin' like a weed. And those twins, why I've never seen anythin' so sweet. Emma's almost as pretty as you, and Carson—what a name they tacked on him—he's a handsome boy just like his granddad. Of course, his colorin's a lot like his mama's, but he's got the Kahill nose for sure. Then there's Molly Anna. She came home last night from Ireland. Clancy and Bonny brought four of his boys with them, too. Willow Walk's bustin' at the seams, I tell you."

"Yes, Jed, but that beats being lonely, doesn't it? We need family. This old world doesn't seem to put much stock in family any more. So many children grow up never knowing their grandparents and sometimes even their mom or dad. They've got no roots. And too often they don't even learn how to love. Speaking of love, I'm real proud of the way you made up with young Cabe. What did Dawson say about dropping the rest of what the boy owed him?"

"I decided to pay it myself so the accountant could balance the books. Dawson's gonna tell Cabe it's been taken care of the next time he brings in a payment. Oh, Emma, I don't know how long I can keep runnin' this family. I'm feelin' all worn out."

"You're doing just fine, Jed. Remember that Dawson's ready to step into your shoes whenever you need him, so lighten your load a little. Appreciate the children and your grandsons while you can. Little Em and Carson are growing fast, and Joey, well, he'll be playing football before you know it." She laughed that special sassy laugh, the one he loved. "And keep working on making up for lost time with Cabe. He's a good man—the kind of man his daddy would've been if he hadn't gotten sick."

"I'm workin' on it. You were so right about makin' peace with the boy. I been feelin' a whole lot better since I got all that straightened out."

He watched Emma rock while his thoughts turned to his grandson. "I been thinkin', Baby, and I might just set up a trust fund for the twins, maybe one for Cabe and Cheeta, too. Dawson and Kat, they're well fixed financially, and Dawson gets Willow Walk. I've already got a college fund for Joey. Cabe and his family are gonna be strugglin' for a while . . . but I hear Kat's trainin' Cheeta to be a model for some new project she's got goin'. I tell you, I can't keep up with that Kat. She's got more energy than ten people oughtta have."

"Sounds like you're taking care of business, Jed. You always were good at that. I wouldn't be waiting too long to put things in motion for Cabe. You never know what's going to happen tomorrow."

"I'll get busy on it this afternoon after my nap, I promise." He was quiet for a moment. "Did I tell you that Cabe's little wife reminds me a lot of you? She's a tiny thing, but a real beauty. Get her back up, though, and all hell breaks loose. She doesn't care if you're six-foot-ten, she'll tell you what's what and not mince any words doin' it. She'll keep young Cabe in line, that's for sure." He chuckled. "She's put me in my place more'n once."

"Not that you ever needed that, Jed." Emma winked at him.

What's that racket. He opened his eyes and shook his head. There it was again. Somebody was knocking on his bedroom door.

"Hang on to your britches," he hollered. "I'm comin' fast as these old legs'll let me."

"It's Cabe, Granddad. Can we talk for a minute?"

"Come on in." He locked the attic door and shoved the key in his pocket before sinking into his rocker. "Take a seat, boy."

Cabe started to sit in the other chair.

"No, no! Not there." He waved his cane. Cabe jumped back. "On the bed, boy. That's Grandma Emma's chair. Nobody else sits in it, not even me."

Cabe nodded and glanced at his watch. "I had a few minutes after eating lunch and wanted to see how you are."

"Tolerable. That's the best that can be expected at my age."

"You know, Granddad, I have a lot of respect for you and for what you've done in your life. I . . . wish I'd known you a long time ago."

"I wish you had, too, boy. I'd like to have had a hand in guidin' you as you grew to be a man. Of course, Darrell and Polly Dee did a fine job, I just wish . . ."

"Life doesn't always make things easy for us, does it?"

"No, boy, it doesn't. Is somethin' special on your mind today?"

"I just wanted to tell you that . . . I . . . I love you, Granddad."

His eyes misted. He looked at Emma's rocker. He could almost see her there. *Did you hear that, Emma? He loves me. Cable's boy loves me. What's that you say? You want me to tell him I love him, too? I'm gonna be showin' him by takin' care of his financial needs for the rest of his life. You say he needs to hear the words? I know money doesn't replace the lovin'. Okay, okay, you're right as usual.*

"I think you know this, boy, but your granddad loves you, too."

"He does? You do?"

They stood up at the same time. "I love you, Cable Darrell Kahill."

Jedediah started forward. His balance wavered. Cabe grabbed him and held him tight. "Thank you, Granddad. I needed to hear that." He helped his grandfather to the bed. "Why don't you rest a little more? I have to go back to work now. Cheeta and I are coming for dinner tonight, and we'll be bringing Em and Carson. You can have a nice visit with them."

"Thank you, boy. I'll see you later." He watched Cabe walk out, then turned to Emma's rocker. He couldn't envision her there anymore. But she floated through his mind as he drifted back to sleep. Her dress was long and white with eyelet embroidery and a violet lace yoke. She looked as beautiful and young as the day he married her. *I don't remember seein' you in that dress before, Baby. I'm gonna rest a bit now. Can you come back later?*

"You sleep, Jed. I know you're tired. I can't tell you how happy I am at the way you're accepting young Cabe. It's almost like your giving our own boy a second chance. And you're doing it just in time."

His eyes brimmed with tears. "In time for what, Emma?"

CHAPTER FORTY-ONE

Another Sunday meant another of Carla's delicious brunches. The whole extended family gathered in the dining room, filling their plates with some of the best home-cooking in West Virginia.

"Daw, I think we'd better take Granddad for a doctor's visit tomorrow," Kat whispered in his ear. "He's too quiet today. Carla told me he's been taking morning *and* afternoon naps all week, and he hasn't been playing with the kids at all. I'm worried. That's not like him."

Dawson looked over at the old man. He sat in his chair, an untouched plate of blackberry cobbler in front of him. "His appetite isn't up to par either, is it? I'll call in the morning for an appointment."

Kat took her plate and sat down next to Jedediah. "Hey, Granddad, What's wrong with the cobbler." *I can see you slipping away from us. Please don't go yet. We just got the family all back together. We aren't ready for you to leave us.*

"Ah, Kitten, I just don't have much of an appetite today. I think I ate too much of that chicken last night. It's not sittin' right in my stomach. I'm just enjoyin' the family. I can't hardly believe how just a few years ago it was you and Dawson and me. Now we're a whole houseful. I been lookin' at those twins. In no time at all, they'll be runnin' all over Willow Walk. But don't you go worryin' that pretty head of yours none about me." He took her warm hand in his cold one. "You know I love you, Kitten, just like you was my own daughter. Emma and me, we never had a daughter. You took the place of the one we didn't have, and you filled it real good."

"And you know I love you, Granddad. When you're back to your old self, I've got some good news for you. I think it'll make you very happy."

"Then I'll be mighty glad to hear it. I think I'll go sit on the couch for a bit. Where's Joey?"

"Here I am, Granddaddy. Wanna play with Molly and me?"

"I think I'll sit and watch you play today." They followed him into the drawing room. "Now come give me a big hug." As soon as he sat down, they both climbed up beside him."

"Will you tell us a story, Granddaddy?" Joey asked. "One about Grandma Emma and the cows that come home."

"You remember that, Joey boy?" Jedediah squeezed his great-grandson and ruffled his hair. "Let's wait for another day. I'm feelin' a little uder the weather right now. Think I'll go take a short nap. I love you, boy. You, too, Molly Anna." His arm stretched around her in a little hug before reaching for his cane.

He tried to push himself up from the couch, but fell back in his seat. *Doggone cane ain't workin' like it's s'posed to.*

"Need some help, Granddad?" Dawson walked up to him.

"If you don't mind, Sonny." He reached out his hand. "I seem to be a bit unsteady on my feet today. I told Kitten I think I overate last night. The old system doesn't work quite as good as it used to."

"Can I help you get someplace?" Dawson walked him into the entryway.

"I'm just gonna take a little nap. I'll feel better after that, I'm sure."

"Then let me help you up the stairs."

"I think I can manage, Sonny. I got the railin' on one side and my cane on the other."

"I know, but humor me this time." Dawson grinned at him. "I like to feel needed once in a while, you know." He walked Granddad to his room. "Can I turn down your bed for you?"

"No . . . but I do wanna tell you somethin'. You've turned Willow Walk into a grand place, and I'm so proud of the man you've become. I love you."

"And I love you. Now have a good rest. I'll come up to check on you in a little while."

He watched Dawson go, then closed the door behind him and headed for his desk to get the key. He felt steadier on his feet now. Sticking his hand into the slot, he felt all around. The key wasn't there. *Where is it? Did one of those little whippersnappers come up here and get my key to play with?* Then he remembered. It was in his pants pocket.

Picking up his journal as he walked past the old table, he headed straight for his corner. A weakness swept over him. He dropped his cane and grabbed his chest. Beads of sweat popped out on his forehead. He sank into his chair. The pain subsided.

Opening the journal, he pulled the pen out of its spine. Before he could start writing, he nodded. A moment later, a vision of Emma appeared in the chair beside him. Her white hair was wrapped in a bun and tied with a pink ribbon at the base of her neck. She winked at him. Her intoxicating honeysuckle scent filled him with warm memories.

"You get prettier every day."

"You always were a fancy talker, Jed Kahill."

"And you always did wear that sweet perfume to tempt me, Emma Kahill."

The richness of her laugh set his heart aflame. "I wish you could've stayed with me to see Joey and those twins."

"Oh, Jed, I would have loved to rock them to sleep and hear them call me 'grandma.'"

Her clear blue eyes beamed like a beacon, then filled with sorrow.

"What is it, Dear Heart? Emma, tell me what's wrong."

"We're not going to be able to meet like this any more."

He couldn't get his breath. He felt like one of those cows had come home to sit on his chest. "Why not? I can't get along without you, you know that."

"I know, but it's time."

"Time to leave Willow Walk? But I'm not ready. I want to say good-bye to everybody."

"Jed, you've lived long enough to know we don't always get what we want."

"Do I have time to write in my journal?"

"I don't know. But you'd better hurry, or it'll be too late."

The pain shooting down his left arm startled him out of his sleep. He grabbed the pen and began to write.

Dawson, Kat, Joey, Cabe, Cheeta, Carson, and Em, I think my time has come to leave you. Don't you worry none about me now. I've lived a good long life. He wiped the tears out of his eyes so he could see the words. *Dawson, teach the children how to look after Willow Walk and how to love it like I do. Now there's a folder in the left-hand drawer of my desk. Had my lawyer draw up some papers last week to take care of Cabe and Cheeta and their family. You get Willow Walk. It's always been yours, but they're family, too. I want them to get a good monthly income for the rest of their lives to add to the livin' they make. One more thing—Emma would want the cameo in the teak box in the attic to go to her namesake, Emma Dee. I trust you'll see to that. I've gotta go now. I love you all more than you'll ever know. Granddad.*

The pain shot down his arm again, but he had one more thing to do. He gripped the pen and pressed its tip against the paper.

> *"Ol' Jed Kahill led a happy life*
> *With his dear, sweet Emma as his wife.*
> *Now it's time to leave his family*
> *To sleep beneath the willow tree.*

The pen dropped from his hand. He grabbed his chest.

"Emma . . ."

His journal—opened to the words he'd just written—fell to the floor. They spoke of the love he had for his Emma, for his family, and for the love of Willow Walk.